<u>LAnd of Snakes</u>

Families are destroyed, and no one can be trusted.

Nisha Lanae

LAnd of Snakes

A gritty tale by Nisha Lanae

<u>Check out these other titles by this author</u>
Pounding The Pavement
Dice…The Queen of Murder

www.ConcreteRosePublications.com

Concrete Rose Publications, LLC
P.O BOX 16207
Long Beach, Ca 90806

Land of Snakes

*This is a work of fiction. Any reference or
similarities to actual events, real people, living, or
dead, or to real locales are intended to give the
novel a sense of reality. Any similarity to other
names, characters, places, and incidents is entirely
coincidental.*

Nisha Lanae

Dedications

I dedicate this to every mother everywhere who
has lost a child to the streets, prison or a grave.
You can't beat yourself up for the life they choose.
You raised them with core values, morals but
they get to a certain age, where they start to live
life according to how they see fit, and that has
nothing to do with you. So stop caring that
burden, if you know you did your best raising
your children, how they turn out and the
mistakes they make are their own.
To The Women and Men who may come across
this book, if you're out in those streets, or sitting
in that jail cell, call your mother, grandmother,
father, sister or whomever raised you. Let them
know you love them, and that they can't carry the
burden for your mistakes in life.
R.I.P to all those who aren't here with us
anymore no matter if it was police brutality,
black on black etc. murder is murder

Land of Snakes

Acknowledgments

I have to give the upmost to my heavenly father God for bringing me through every storm I have encountered in my life. If it wasn't for prayer and his coverage over my life I would've lost my mind a long time ago.

To My Parent Tara West and Warren Williams (RIP) thank you for life, and even the struggles I was forced to face in my childhood and even in my adult life, they have made me into the women I am today, and the women I'm growing and destined to be.

To my siblings I love y'all each one of you. Dontrell, Travina, Tyrell and Keion. We may not have the best relationships but there isn't anything I wouldn't do to protect all of you. And I can't forgot my poo-poo the chubbiest meanest cutie on earth my niece Kilee Grace.

To my Auntie Gina and Cousin Ronnisha and all my family that supports and motivates me to keep at my dream and career I'm forever thankful for you all.

To my love, friend, shoulder to lean on, my man, my ace ;)- Dominic you work every nerve I have but when I'm feeling down, you uplift me. When I feel like giving up, you remind me why I started. You support my dreams and understand the time it requires for me to succeed, while pushing me when I get off traffic and punishing me lol I love you (I remembered) lol thank you for being so supportive, even when I couldn't see it, and thank you for extending your family to me.

To the many women who have come into my life, leaving me with precious gems about love, life and respect for myself I am truly grateful for you all. Henrietta Binford, Latrice Lewis, Wanda Trotter and the Davis family, Cynthia Clark

Nisha Lanae

NEVER LAST My Readers y'all rock! Y'all don't understand the power y'all have with authors. I can't count how many times within this year I felt like giving this thing up. Then I see a review, or a tag on Instagram and Facebook that made me smile and realize why I do this, it's because I love it, and it's what God has called and blessed me to do. I'm so beyond thankful for the support given to me and my work.

I always show love to my Facebook readers so I have to do it for my Instagram readers. Jessica Jewel, carel_n_ann,urbanfictionreader,chocolatelady88, ms_btaylor, showstopa, adivas_bookstore, beauty_ismyname38, mamibutterfli, got_bookphetish, Jovi_baby1, faithfirst_rel,Kiachew08, shesthisfancyface, misspretty1981 My JoJo and JS promotion for always going hard for me from day one Tiffany Kirkland my day 1 reader and all of the author who have given me advice since I released my first book. If I have forgotten you please charge it to my brain and not my heart. I'm thankful for everyone who has supported me this far it's so damn appreciated. Here is my third baby, it's been a long time coming enjoy!

With Love Nisha Lanae

Don't forget to follow me on social media

Facebook- Nisha Lanae
Instagram: Pendiva_Nisha
Twitter: Pendive_Nisha
Email: Author, NishaLanae@yahoo.com

Land of Snakes

ONE

Micah sat at the craps table in the underground gambling shack, nursing his seventh shot of Hennessey Black, straight. He had been sitting in the same spot for the last three hours. He was up two hundred grand, from the two thousand he walked in with. Instead of cashing out and walking away with ten times the amount he came in with, Micah betted again.

"Your turn sir," The young dealer said sliding the dice Micah's way.

Micah looked around at the five men and the one woman that stood around the table. The look of envy was displayed over their faces praying that he took a lost, since he had cleaned house leaving them with almost nothing. Micah picked up the dice, shaking them in his hand, before dropping them and watching them dance around the table before they came to a standstill. Double snake eyes looked him back in the eyes as the dealer's voice rang in his ears.

"You lose," The dealer said.

Micah took the last of his shot straight to the head throwing his last twenty on the waitress cart, before staggering out of the gambling shack. Micah arrived to his car, barely able to stand. He climbed in and sat there with his thoughts. He was down two hundred grand, and some weak product that the streets didn't want. The fiends had lost faith in him, and were copping from the next local dealer, who got his hands on top of the line product. On top of that he owed fifty thousand to Gator, one of L.A.'s grimiest loan sharks.

"FUCK! FUCK!" Micah yelled banging his hands against the steering wheel. The ringing of his cell phone pulled him together. It was Alysia, an Asian chick he had been fucking off and on for a few months. He knew whenever she called she wanted one thing, some dick. Just thinking about sliding into something wet and gushy made Micah's dick harden. "I'm on my way," Micah said into the phone, cranking his engine and pulling off. He needed a good nut to ease his worried mind. It didn't take long for Micah to arrive at Alysia house; it was only a few minutes from the shack. It was where he met her, she worked there as a waitress.

Micah pulled in front of the triplex and laid on the horn, Alysia pranced sexily to Micah's truck. He didn't pay her any mind. Micah focus was on the blunt he was rolling. Alysia climbed inside the truck, surprised that Micah already had his dick freed from his pants and waiting on her.

"What's good?"

"I'm not up for all the small talk, so let's just handle business," Micah said as he sparked the blunt in his mouth, pushing his seat back making sure to give her just enough room to handle the task at hand.

Alysia smiled as she leaned over and took him into her mouth greedily devouring all of his length. Alysia was a stone cold freak, with a little effort; she had Micah deep in her throat.

Land of Snakes

Weakened in the knees; Micah jerked her head up before he could no longer hold his build up. Micah handed her the gold wrapper. Alysia smiled, ripping the package open she slid it down on Micah's rock hard dick. Mounting on his dick, she winded her hips rocking back and forth. Micah sat back smoking his blunt as he watched Alysia move her pretty tanned ass on his dick. With one hand, he reached over fingering her vagina. The double friction caused Alysia to move faster, as her sugar walls clinched around his dick sucking him in. Micah smiled at the tight grip of her walls sliding around his dick. With all the liquor he had consumed, it didn't take long for him to release his hot semen into the condom. Not getting hers off yet, Alysia continued to bounce her pretty ass on Micah's dick that hardened back up quickly while inside of her. Alysia grinded until her nipples hardened against the thin fabric she wore, her legs jerked, gripping the steering wheel her eyes closed as she experienced her orgasm. Gripping her by her waist, Micah released another nut, more powerful than the first one. "Shit!" He panted not expecting it. "Damn I needed that," Micah exhaled sliding Alysia from his lap and putting the end of the blunt in the astray. Fixing himself back into his pants, Micah looked over at Alysia.

"Thanks, I really needed that. I will get with you later."

"I'm glad I could help" She smiled. "Stop being a stranger," Alysia said getting out the car. Micah didn't wait for her to get inside as he smashed off. He had a long drive in the morning, and needed some rest to even commit to the drive. Along with being so close to his older brother Sin. With all that was taking place in the streets he knew Sin was about to ride him. Especially since Sin was coming back home to the streets that were rightfully his, but it wasn't what he would expect. Micah wasn't fully truthful with his brother on how things had been running lately. The streets were out of hand; Micah knew Sin wouldn't be pleased.

Land of Snakes

TWO

The sounds of Nipsy Hussle new CD, bumped through the speakers, as Micah sped down the 99 freeway, alongside him sat his younger brother Rich. The music filled the car as they sang along wishing the three hour drive to Corcoran State Prison, would end soon. After four years of incarceration, their older brother Sin was finally being released. Sin was a menace, and had been all his life. He was always into something. If it could make him money, Sin was into it. He was 19 and running the streets. Moving fast, his name came across the police radar and eventually led to the door of his safe house being kicked in and raided. Being that he knew they were onto him, he didn't keep much in one spot. After everything was done, and a large portion of evidence went missing Sin was only sentenced to 8 years, with having to serve 85%. After serving close to five years, he was being released on parole.

Micah and Rich pulled into the prison gates and parked in the appointed parking spaces. Micah ran inside the building to let them know the ride for Sin, had arrived and would be waiting outside. It was blazing hot; it was the middle of spring and felt like summer, as the California sun beamed on them.

Micah do you think you can turn on the air conditioner? Please! Its hot ass fish grease in this damn truck." Rich complained wiping a trail of sweat from his face.

"You got some gas money?" Micah questioned.

"No."

"Then shut up. Talking about its hot as fish grease, how you know how hot fish grease is? You don't even cook. Ma' does everything for her little baby." Micah laughed teasing his younger brother.

"Shut up, she does everything for you too."

"I got bitches to do my shit. Something you don't know anything about."

"I get pussy." Rich boasted to his older brother.

"Really? From who?" Micah questioned like he hadn't been hearing the numerous stories about the little girls sweating his brother.

"Don't worry about it; just know I get my share. You keep talking; I might take a few of your chicks. They already say I'm the more handsome brother." Rich laughed.

"They just tell you that because you a baby." Micah chuckled.

After an hour of waiting, a tall buff man stepped out the building, looking like he had been stuffed with paper, resembling a linebacker.

"There go Sin, right there," Rich laughed at how big and swollen his older brother was. Sin stood 6'ft tall, broad shoulders, his skin resembled a hot mocha latte; his beady eyes were dark and always so dangerous looking.

"About fucking time, nigga had us out here baking," Micah said. Micah was the second oldest, and Sin's flunky. He wanted to live up to his brother's rep in the streets so bad. But, he always fell short. As a kid he followed Sin, and his crew around town causing trouble, and trying to fit in.

"Shut up nigga, it's not even noon yet and you already whining," Sin said hopping into the car. Giving the police that watched them as they passed the finger "Fuckin' Pigs!" He shouted.

"Welcome home, you gone come to my game tonight?" Rich asked. Rich was the youngest of the trio, and the only one who actually had something going on for himself. He was 17, an all-star running back for his high school, He was on the dean's list and vice president of his senior class.

"I got some shit to handle, but I will try and make it. I heard you been killing shit out there on the field?" Sin stated, looking at his younger brother. "Where is Ma? Why she didn't come?" Sin asked. It had been two years since the last time he saw his mother. She visited him once, during his bid and told him she couldn't do it, and wouldn't make it a regular habit. He had gotten himself into the mess and would have to face the time for the crimes he committed. Sin, had always been a pain in his mother's side, from the time he knew how to walk and talk.

"She had to work. You know if she didn't have to work she would've been here, but she don't miss no work." Rich said to his brother.

Micah shifted in his seat. "She wants to work, she isn't going to take money from me," Micah said before Sin could get a word out. "I've tried, more than once, she isn't going for it."

"So you are telling me, you out here getting money and your mother still cleaning them white folk's funky ass toilets?" Sin asked.

"She doesn't take the money; she said its drug money. She doesn't want any of it. I have tried many of times," Micah spoke looking at Sin from the corner of his eyes. "Let's see if you can convince her to move."

"How about you kid? Is Micah, looking out for you?" Sin asked looking Rich over.

"Yeah, he lets me rock all his fly ass gear and paid for all of my senior stuff. You still buying me that fly ass white tux for prom right?" Rich questioned.

"Yeah," Micah flatly replied.

"Cool, Imma' be the freshest dude up in that joint." Rich beamed. No matter what people may have said about his brothers, Rich looked up to both of his older brothers, they were the only male figures in his life since they all didn't know their dad.

Their mother Pamela, worked four days at a small law firm as an assistant and six days for an small cleaning business, cleaning high rise buildings. She had been with the companies since the boys were young. They didn't pay much, enough for bills and to put food on the table. She managed it, the best she knew how being a single mother of three boys and one daughter. Growing up, she made sure they always had the essentials they needed.

"Where is Gia?" Sin asked. Gia was the trio's only sister.

Land of Snakes

"I don't know, she don't be home much since she fuckin' with this slob ass nigga," Micah spat angry that his sister chose to date a dude from across the way.

"And you are allowing her to date that nigga?" Sin questioned. He had heard numerous stories about his brother not fully holding shit down like he would've done, or wanted his brother to do.

"What the fuck am I supposed to do, she my fucking older sister," Micah advised already getting annoyed with Sin, and they hadn't even made it to the freeway yet. It wouldn't be easy with Sin being home watching his every move. He wasn't the young teen anymore hanging onto his brothers every word. The streets loved Sin, they only respected Micah because he was Sin's younger brother, and knew what could come if Sin, felt his brother was being disrespected.

"Seems like I have a lot of shit to take care of, since yo' pussy ass can't handle shit. I know what's going on in the streets, remember the streets talk and niggas in prison are listening."

"Whatever," Micah said, switching the music to Rick Ross cranking it up, and ignoring his older brother. As he rapped the words of the song, hoping Sin didn't bitch the whole way home.

The drive back to the city was filled with Rich and Sin catching up. Rich was very young when Sin was locked up, and Pamela refused for him to be took to a prison to visit him. She didn't want it to taint his young mind, that it was a good place. Micah drove in silence, his mind was elsewhere, occupied on how he was going to get his hands on some money, since he took the lost the night before.

"Take me by Kym's house," Sin said as he saw them nearing the 110 freeway.

"Don't have time, Rich has to be at the school and I got some shit to handle," Micah said trying to speed past the exit to Kym's house.

"It's gone take me five fuckin' minutes, take me to Kym house or I'm gone take yo' shit and take myself. The choice is yours." Sin barked. Micah hawked at Sin as he jumped off the freeway's next exit and sped to Kym's, running every light he could.
Kym was Sin's girlfriend. Her and Sin had connected while he was in prison, she had been by his side since they met over two years ago.

"Man don't be in there tryna' get ya' dick wet, I have shit to do."

"Shut up! Damn all you been doing is complaining," Sin said getting out the car. Sin hated the fact that all Micah did was complain. Since he was young, it was all he did when he

Land of Snakes

would follow him and his crew, they would tell
Micah to do something, all he would do is
complain before, during and after he did it. Sin
thought being hard on Micah, giving him tough
love, like his mentor had given him would have
made Micah man up, but all it did was make
Micah bitter.

"That nigga Sin treat you like a bitch," Rich
laughed. He saw Micah smack dudes for less than
that. When it came to Sin, he folded.

"Shut yo' little ass up, before I make you walk
to your game tonight." Micah said out of anger,
his little brother was making fun of him and like
everyone else, taking up for Sin.
Sin staggered to the front door, and banged on it
loudly "Kym, open the damn door, daddy home."
He snickered.
Kym hurried to open the door for Sin, she had
been waiting two years for the day Sin could
come home.

"Hey baby," Kim smiled opening the door.
Within minutes of Sin entering the apartment
loud shouting could be heard all the way out on
the streets.

"This fuckin' hot head," Micah said getting out
of the car and running up the apartment stairs.
Sin had Kym held up against the wall, pounding
her head against it.

"You better have my fuckin' money, when I
come back around this bitch or I'm gon' fuck you
up. Now get this place cleaned and I want steak
and potatoes ready when I get back."

17

"What the fuck man, let her go Sin. Go get in the damn car. You fucking wilding, you got all her neighbors outside looking and shit." Micah shouted seeing Sin's hands gripped around Kym's neck.

"Mind yo' fucking business nigga. This my bitch," Sin roared glancing at Micah then back to Kym. "And be prepared to get ya' back blown the fuck out, a nigga horny as fuck," Sin said releasing her neck letting her body drop to the floor as he turned peering at Micah before walking out. "I want my money Kym," He yelled.

"You okay?" Micah asked helping Kym up from the ground.

"Yeah, why you didn't tell me you were going to bring his ass over here?" Kym asked looking around Micah's body for any sign of Sin. He was getting into the car. "I could have been better prepared for that damn psycho."

"I didn't know, he said the shit last minute. I didn't have time to warn you. Just get what this nigga need, I will handle the rest. I will try and keep him busy and at the house. Get this house cleaned up, I will be back around later. Do you remember what we talked about a few days ago?"

"Yeah."

"I might need that."

"I don't know Micah; he wants it all when he gets back."

"I will figure something out." Micah said taking Kym's chin into his hands and giving her a peck on her lips before jetting back out the door.

Land of Snakes

Micah jumped into the truck and glared at Sin.

"You haven't been out but three fuckin' hours, you tryna go back already? You need to calm your ass down sometimes. She doesn't deserve that shit." Micah cranked the engine and sped off. "You haven't even seen your parole officer yet, and your crazy ass assaulting somebody."

"Kym, not about to call no damn police, she know better," Sin chuckled.

Micah just shook his head at Sin's comment. The older he got, he realized he didn't want to be like his brother. He was a coward, he got a kick out of causing harm to those who he felt feared him. Micah knew he could never be like Sin, because he was better than him, better then he would ever be. *That's why I'm fucking her,* Micah said to himself.

THREE

Pamela, struggled with the bags of groceries up the four flights of stairs to her apartment. She had just gotten off work, and was preparing to cook for the boys. She knew Sin, would like a nice home cooked meal after having to eat that slop they called food inside. Pamela got to her apartment door, when she heard her manger, Mr. Kirby call out her name.

"Pamela, it's the 20th and you still owe two-hundred and fifty dollars on this month's rent." He smiled, eyeing her curvy behind. Even at 55 years old, and giving birth to four children, Pamela still managed a very well tamed shape.

"I will have it this week," Pamela stated trying to walk into her apartment.

"You know you can do that thing I like to spare you an extra week or two," Mr. Kirby said getting close up on Pamela. He knew she couldn't afford it and used it to his advantage, like he did to everyone else.

Pamela hung her head low. She had been living in the tiny three bedroom apartment since she arrived in the states eighteen years prior. The managers changed over the time, but Pamela stayed. Pamela was of Jamaican decent, she up and moved to give her children a better life then the blood shed that surrounded her in her hometown of Kingston. Even with working two jobs, she struggled to make ends meet.

Six months ago, Mr. Kirby raised the rent. Pamela couldn't afford it, and had been struggling to stay afloat. Every month, he offered her the same

20

Land of Snakes

bargain. A trip in between her legs for extra time, or be thrown out on the streets. In the beginning she protested, she wasn't the least bit interested in the old man. When he showed up with a three day notice, to pay or get out, and let her know she could still take him up on his offer. Pamela felt torn; she had no family in California. With too much pride to seek money from her children, Pamela took Kirby offer, she hated herself for it.
 Pamela bit her pride once again, pushing the door open; she sat the bags down on the counter. "Come inside," She said in a low whisper. Tears threaten to fall from her eyes. She never felt so low in her life. But she wouldn't let him see her cry, and get joy out of it even more. Mr. Kirby grinned, stepping into the apartment, closing the door behind him. Pamela made her way into her room, Mr. Kirby following close behind her. His boner sticking out of the flooding khaki pants he had on. Pamela slid out her shoes, pulling down her stockings and panties. She laid on the edge of the bed, hiking up her shirt, her eyes focused on the ceiling praying God would make it end quick and easy.

Mr. Kirby quickly pulled down his pants, letting his wrinkled penis sprang out. Without putting on a condom, he entered Pamela and plunged away.

Pamela laid there, tears in her eyes, she felt worthless, that she had to resort to this. She hated herself for it. But, she couldn't stomach not having a roof over her children's head.

Mr. Kirby paid Pamela no mind. "Ahh, ooohh..." He grunted, plunging inside of her, beads of sweat dripping from his face. Pamela hoped he hurried before the boys got home, she knew if they walked in with Kirby on-top of their mother, they would kill him where he stood. Pamela wasn't the one for violence, so she never spoke one word to her children, because death would be the only result in their eyes.

"Aaaahhh, uggghhh..." Mr. Kirby grunted with one final plunge, before he pulled out, releasing his load onto her legs and sheets. "Damn that was good, just like the last time," Mr. Kirby grinned, pulling up his pants. "If you threw it back and acted like you liked it, you could get more time." He spat patting her on her leg, before walking out the room. With tears in her eyes, Pamela got up removing the sheets from her bed, and showered. She scrubbed and scrubbed, as a river of tears cascaded down her face. Pamela sat down, as the shower ran down on her, bringing her knees to her chest, she rocked and cried. She had escaped her cheating abusive husband, only to let a man have his way with her for more time to pay the rent.

****

Micah drove in silence; his mind was all over the place. He hadn't realized he was speeding and had run through two red lights, and a stop sign nearing colliding with another car.

Land of Snakes

"Nigga' what the fuck is wrong with you? Running red lights and shit, you almost hit that fucking car. I'm not tryna' go back to jail," Sin yelled.

Micah looked at Sin, then back to traffic, without saying a word. Micah swooped in front of their apartment, throwing the car into park and hopped out.

"What the fuck wrong with this nigga'?" Sin questioned, getting out the car.

"I don't know, he be on some weird stuff sometimes. Plus I don't think he like how you be punking him," Rich said rushing up the stairs behind his older brothers.

As the trio walked down, the long hallway to their mother's apartment, they spotted Kirby coming from that direction. He was glistened with sweat and a wide grin on his face. Mr. Kirby was so busy grinning from the sweet loving he just received from Pamela to see her son's headed his way.

"What's good Kirby?" Sin said first, noticing Mr. Kirby walking from his mother's apartment direction. Micah quickly caught on. It wasn't the first time he had saw Kirby headed from his mother's direction, and now he was curious as to why.

"What you doing by my mom's crib?" Micah questioned, as they neared him.

"If it isn't the Jones brothers," Mr. Kirby said nervously.

"That's not what he asked, what were you doing in my mother's apartment is what he asked?" Rich chimed. Out of all the boys he was the most over protective over his mother, he was truly a mama's boy. He adored the ground she walked on; she could do no harm in his eyes.

"If you gentleman care to know, I was telling your mother, she has five days to pay the rest of the rent. If it's not paid, she is out! You all are out here getting money, but can't help your mother. Fuckin' losers," Mr. Kirby huffed, trying to walk pass *"I like she can't afford to pay,"* Kirby thought to himself letting out a loud chuckle.

Micah knew he couldn't stand there and do nothing. When he saw the look on Sin's face, he knew he had to do something "Not too fast. So how much does my mother owe on the rent?" Micah questioned ice grilling Kirby, making him extremely nervous.

"Four hundred and fifty dollars," He stated greedily fumbling with his words.

Micah rumbled in his pockets coming out with a few bills that he managed to scrape up from some chick. "Well this should do," Micah said throwing a few of the bills into Mr. Kirby's face. The money fell to the ground. Mr. Kirby quickly bent over, scraping up the twenties, fifties and hundred dollar bills.

"Stay the fuck away from my Ma's crib nigga' or Imma' fuck yo' old ass up," Sin said brushing past Kirby hard, almost causing him to lose his footing.

"From now on, come to me and only me about the rent," Micah added as he and his brothers walked off.

Land of Snakes

"Ma," Rich called out as they entered the apartment. The bags of groceries still sat on the counter. Rich searched the house, looking for his mother, when he heard the shower on. "Ma in the shower," he said entering the living room where Micah and Sin stood.

"Okay, well hurry up and get your stuff, so I can drop you off," Micah told Rich, his eyes glued to his cell phone. He was trying to come up with the money he owed Gator. He hoped Kym would still be able to give him the fifty thousand, she had offered to give him just last week.
Rich headed towards the room he shared with his brother's, to grab his gym bag. He tried to stall time to see his mother before he left; Micah was acting weird since Sin had got home. Usually it was all fun and games between them, especially with him playing in the big game; he had been waiting all year long to play.
It didn't take Pamela long to shower once she heard the boy's talking. She didn't know how she was going to deal with Sin being home. Since he was little, he had always caused some kind of trouble, she hoped he was ready to live right, and not the life of mayhem and dealing drugs.
Clad in a lounging dress, Pamela headed into the living room, where she heard her children's voice.

"Hey," Pamela said, trying to sound as cheerful as possible as she entered the room.

"Hey Ma, what time you coming to my game?" Rich asked.

25

"I will be there before it starts, and yes I will bring you some food and Gatorade, the green one," Pamela smiled, already knowing what he was going to ask next.

"Thanks Ma," Rich smiled, grabbing the lunch she had already prepared for him. "I'm ready Micah," he yelled.

"Boy stop that yelling," Pamela said, using a newspaper, lightly smacking Rich upside his head.

"Hey Ma," Micah said entering the room. "Oh, and don't worry about that issue with Kirby, I took care of that," Micah said his eye's still glued down to his phone.

"Wh...What?" Pamela asked, nearly choking on her own spit, at the mention of Mr. Kirby's name. "What did he tell you?" She questioned. Pamela prayed Kirby didn't say a word about what just took place.

"Nothing, but you were behind on the rent. Why?" Micah questioned, looking at his mother strange.

"Nothing," Pamela assured. Trying to calm herself down, and catch her breath. She knew if he had said anything anyway he would've been dead. "I don't need your money Micah I will give you the money on Friday," Pamela stated, putting the groceries away.

"Ma' chill. Why you didn't tell me you were behind on your rent?" Micah questioned. "You know I would've helped you."

Land of Snakes

"She shouldn't have to tell you shit," Sin spat walking past Micah. Choosing to not respond Micah just glared at Sin.

"Don't start that, I don't want to hear it," Pamela stated, looking from Sin to Micah.

"Hey Ma, How are you doing?" Sin asked giving his mother a hug.

"I'm fine baby. How are you?"

"I'm good." Sin spoke looking at his mother.

"Rich you ready?" Micah questioned. He wasn't in the mood to be so close to Sin with everything he had going on.

"I been ready," Rich replied. Grabbing his bag and lunch and headed for the door. "Later Ma," Rich and Micah said in union, as they headed for the door.

Sin waited until his brother headed for the door he turned headed to his room he shared with his brothers. Flipping the twin size bed over, stomping on the floor tile three times, the tile popped up. A wad of cash with a Mac11, .45 and 9mill. Sin grabbed the 9mill and money and stuffed it into his waist band, and pockets. Flipping the bed back over leaving back out the room. Sin made his way back to the living room, took a seat on the couch picking up the phone, he dialed a number. "I'm at my mom's" Sin said into the phone before hanging up.

Pamela was in the kitchen, putting the dinner on when Sin walked back into the room. She could hear him on the phone talking. "Sintrell, have a seat," Pamela said hearing him near the front door. She poured two cups of her homemade lemonade and sat them on the kitchen table.

"I have somewhere to be Ma, I will get with you as soon as I get back," Sin said continuing to walk towards the door.

"Have a seat," Pamela said sternly.
Sin turned, looking at his mother. He knew the look very well, and wasn't about to try and challenge her.

"What's good Ma?" He questioned, taking the seat.
Pamela joined him, sliding the glass of lemonade in front of him. "What are your plans for your life Sintrell?" She asked, studying her child's face. Sin was a very attractive man, standing 6'0 ft. tall, mocha chocolate skin tone and dark eyes. His deep Jamaican roots were evident. Pamela stared at Sin for a moment; he looked like his father, a man she despised with every ounce of her being.

"What Ma? Why you just staring at me like that?" Sin asked, looking back at his mother.

"I hope this was your last trip to that place. What are your plans since your home?" She questioned, taking a sip of the lemonade.

"I'm not trying to go back to that place," Sin said and that was a guarantee, he rather they killed him then to lock him back up like a caged animal. Prison wouldn't be a revolving door for him like juvenile hall was.

"What are you going to do differently, to insure that?" Pamela questioned.

Land of Snakes

Sin sat and pondered over his mother's questions. He couldn't tell her what he really was thinking. "I'm not sure Ma," Sin admitted.

"Selling drugs isn't it. You will find yourself back in there. You have so much potential Sintrell; you just have to apply yourself. Find you a nice job, and a nice girl," Pamela said, she had high hopes for Sintrell, even though, she knew he would let her down. He wasn't nothing more than a drug dealer, like his father, it was in his blood. Pamela hated it, she uprooted from Jamaica for him to not be around that life and become what everyone around her growing up was, yet he turned out to be that very same thing and it saddened her.

"Ma, I can't make any promises. I can only do what I know and what I am good at," Sin spoke staring his mother in the eyes. He could never lie to his mother, in her face. She would know it was a lie anyway, even if he tried.

"Sometimes you have to apply new aspects to your life to find out what you're good at. I really hoped you never turned out like him, yet you have," Pamela said low on a brick of tears.

"Like who? My fuckin' daddy?" Sin yelled, he hated when his mother referenced him to a man he didn't know, and couldn't recall seeing in his 24 years of life, let alone doing anything for his mother and siblings. The images of his father were tainted with bad memories, he wanted to forever forget.

"You better watch your mouth in my house, Sintrell Jones," Pamela stated sternly.

"Ma, I don't know that man. Don't care about that man and will never. I don't care if his ass is dead in a ditch. I watched you struggle for years raising Gia, Rich, Micah and me, without any help from a man. Since a man can't help you around here, I will Ma," Sin spat.

"I don't want that damn blood money! I don't want money you make from ruining people's lives. You want to help me, find your ass a job," Pamela yelled jumping up from her seat. All her life she had to watch people lives change for the worst because of drugs and everything that came with them, she refused to live off money that was earned from drugs.

"You struggling Ma, those little jobs aren't working. You don't like what I do, that's okay. But, I will not sit and watch you struggle no more. Next time Kirby need something; tell him to get at me, or.... Never mind. I gotta' go Ma, see you later," Sin said standing up, giving his mother a kiss on the cheek. "I love you and I promise you will be taken care of." Sin said before turning to walk out the door.

Pamela wiped the tears from her face, grabbed her bible and said a special prayer for her son. She knew not only would he need it, but she would need it as well. He would continue to live life the way he knew, dangerous.

Land of Snakes

FOUR

Micah dropped Rich off at his high school for a meeting before the final game.   "See you later kid," Micah said as Rich got out the car.

"See you later," Rich said grabbing his bag and hopping out the truck. "Micah," he called out before closing the door.

"What's good?"

"Don't think because Sin is back home, that things will change. I love both of y'all."

"I love you too, now go ahead your friends are waiting for you."

Micah watched Rich meet up with his friends before pulling off headed towards the boogie joint. Micah tried to follow in Sin footsteps with selling drugs, but it wasn't for him. He just wanted to show Sin, that he could do anything he could do. Micah didn't want to give up because he still wanted to prove to Sin, he could do it.
The boogie joint was a local spot the old heads hung at. It was run by Gator, an old hustler from around the way. He was a major player back in the day. He ran with the original crips in the 70's. He was one of the few still left; he opened the boogie joint in the late 90's in the area he grew up in. The spot was known for running numbers. Gator was old, but still was heavy in the game; he just ran different type of business. Gator was loaded and had become the hoods loan shark.

Micah pulled around the back and entered through the side door. "What's good Tommy? Where Gator at?" Micah asked, giving the old head some dap.

"He back there in the back yougin', I heard that crazy nigga Sin walked out them gates today," Tommy said while playing a game of chess with another old head, by the name of Shine.

"Yeah, he home," Micah replied, walking off. He wasn't in the mood to talk about Sin. Micah walked towards the back. Gator took no shit from anyone. Micah was sweating, he owed Gator fifty thousand dollars, and he didn't have it. One of the traps he ran got busted last week, making him take a loss of a few grand. Kym had saved him with some of Sin's money; he had stashed away for when he came home so that he was able to stay afloat. But Micah had gambled with the money and lost a big portion of it. Micah cooked up a few batches mixing it in with the left over product. Only thing was, it was weak and the fiends didn't care for it.

"Micah, I hope you're here with my money," Gator stated.

"I got some of it Gator, give me until next week and I will have the rest," Micah stated.

"So you came in here wasting my fuckin' time yet, again?" Gator questioned.

"It's not like that Gator," Micah stated.

"Let me tell you what I can do for your dumb ass," Gator said, rising from his seat. Gator was pushing three hundred some odd pounds standing at 6' foot 'five, he was built solid. He walked with a limp from being shot several times years ago. He always strolled with his custom cane. Capone and Bishop stood on guard, they were his muscle. "I have bets on the game tonight, if your brother team wins, I lose sixty grand, but if he loses I gain eighty grand. So if you can get your little brother to throw this game I will give you an extra three weeks to get me my paper," Gator stated, clinching his cane. "Because, from what I hear you pushing some weak product on the streets and that Turk is scooping up all the fiends on the block." Gator said peering at Micah.

"Football is Rich's life, he not gone throw no game. Especially not this one, he has been waiting all year to play in this game," Micah stated. Ignoring the jab Gator threw his way.

"The season is already over, everybody already knows UCLA gave him a full ride. This game just some extra shit the school system putting on. Hell, this season I made thousands off Rich's ass, one game not gone hurt him."

"Rich still isn't about to throw no game. He has a rep to keep, he been killing shit on the field, he is not going to do it." Micah pleaded.

"Then you have until twelve to have my money, or it's yo' life," Gator glared before brushing pass Micah. "Oh, and tell Sin welcome home and to get at me. The streets been missing real stand-up dudes like him."

Micah stalled and thought things over before rushing out the boogie joint, he didn't know what he was going to do; he knew Rich wasn't going to throw the game away.

"You heard him," Bishop said as he and Capone stood guard waiting for Micah to exit Gator's office.

Micah glared at Capone and Bishop. "I'm leaving," Micah spoke walking out the office. Jumping in his truck he sped back to the school in search of Rich. Football season was over, but for the last three years the schools system would pick the best players of the season from different schools to play against each other. It was the most competitive game of the year because the best played against the best. Even the college players, coaches and scouts came out for the game. Micah found Rich on the field talking to a crowd of people and a sports reporter. He didn't know how he would be able to form his lips to ask his little brother to throw a game like this away. All the years of playing football since peewee, all the hard work, late nights and practices led up to this moment. Getting a chance to play against players, that was just as good as him. Since they came up with the idea for the game, Rich couldn't wait to play in it. The game was only for seniors and it was finally Rich's turn.

"Rich?" Micah called out.

Rich saw his brother standing on the hill shouting his name. Quickly Rich jogged his way.

"What's up man, what you doing up here so early?" Rich questioned looking around for Sin and his mother.

"I was still in the area and needed to rap to you about something," Micah stated, staring at his young brother. He hated he had to ask him this, but it was the only way to spare him time to pay Gator, or he was dead.

Land of Snakes

"What's good?" Rich questioned noticing the perplexed look on his older brother face.

"I'm in some shit. I need you to fall back tonight and not show out on the field," Micah stated looking at Rich.

"What?" Rich frowned. "You want me to throw my game away because you into some shit. You got me fucked up, this is my life. I don't wanna' be no drug dealer, like you and Sin," Rich sneered, looking at his brother. "I'm the only one who hasn't let mama down, and I plan to keep it that way. I will make mama proud of me, for raising me alone and not following behind you and Sin."

"This is my life too," Micah stated. Worry and fear laced in his voice. "He said he would kill me, I don't want to die," Micah stated.

"And this is mine. You shouldn't have gotten in bed with Gator. Yeah I know you owe him a lot of money. I'm not about to throw away my game, to save your ass. You know how long I've been ready to play in this game, and how much it means to me. It's your mess, you fix it," Rich stated, looking at his brother in a different way. "I just pray you fix it and not break Ma' heart, by having to bury you."

"You right kid, it's my mess. I gotta fix it," Micah stated. He didn't have a clue on how he would fix it. "You mind keeping this between you and I kid?" Micah asked.

"Yeah, I will see you later," Rich stated jogging back over to the crowd of his friends.
Micah rushed back to his truck and peeled off, heading to Kym's house, he needed that money

from her, even if he couldn't pay Gator all of the money, some would have to work. He couldn't let Sin catch wind of what was going on he would never let it down how bitch made he was.

****

Sin sat at the bottom of the staircase waiting for a car to pull up. Once Sin saw the car pull up he stepped on the block, it felt good to be back home. Even though so much had changed. It was better than being locked in a cell twenty-three hours a day.

"Welcome home Sinister," Wako raspy voice yelled from the car. He was one of Sin's older homies that had looked out for him while he was on the inside.

"Shit it feels good to be back home. The block, seeing my mom's and younger siblings, seems like shit has changed a little bit and I never thought I would come home and my nigga, not be here," Sin spoke. When Sin, caught his case, his partner in crime and best friend Case beat the case against him. Two years ago, they found him slumped in his apartment. They still hadn't found his killers, even after the exchange of gun fire with several gangs in Los Angeles. The lost hit Sin hard. He and Case had been friends since the sandbox.

"Nigga it has, you was gone damn near five years, a whole lot has changed. I know that shit with Case, still fuck me up too. We still don't know who offed him, you got at Micah about what I told you? If we still tryna' run the concrete jungle, it's a must he fall back. I got mad love for you, but nigga, it's been a full-time job keeping niggas from offing yo' brother. These youngin' ruthless, and not giving a fuck who you are. They knocking niggas left and right," Wako said.

"I haven't, but it will happen as soon as this nigga get back here. He went to drop Rich at the school for his little game tonight. I will get at him, and get with you tonight. Set up that meet though, let's get back to this paper," Sin slapped hands with Wako. "And let these niggas know my brother is off limits or I'm coming blasting, and that's on Crip. Nobody will be off limits."

"I got it, this should do," Wako said handing him a small baggie filled with already bagged packs.

"Good looking out cuh', see you later." Sin spoke looking down the street he noticed it was a few dudes hanging on the block he didn't recognize. Once Wako drove off, he decided to see who the new faces were.

"Who are you youngin'?" Sin questioned walking up to a dude, who stood on the block, serving a fiend. Two dudes stood around him.

"Nigga who the fuck are you?" The young dude spat looking Sin up and down, reaching for his strap, tucked in his pants. "You must want to die rushing up on me?"

"Is that the Sinister?" A voice called out from behind Sin, just as he was reaching for his own strap to show the youngster who he was and his life was just expendable as his. Sin could hear feet approaching him fast. Sin had a lot of homies but more enemies. Sin turned gun in hand.

"Who that?" Sin asked, ready to let off on anyone he didn't recognize. Despite it being almost five years since he had been gone. He still had many enemies that didn't want to see him come home, or even breathe the same air they did.

"Cuh' it's me, Turk." The man said getting closer to Sin.

"What's good Cuh', you know this little nigga?" Sin asked turning towards the young dude, who now had his gun in Sin's side, ready to plant a bullet inside of him.

"Put that shit away, he good people. This Sin, most called him Sinister. I told you about him." Turk told the young dude. The one, who put me on, and looked out for me when I didn't have shit," Turk told the young dude. "This my little worker, Badass." Turk chuckled. "The nigga name describes him to the tee."

"The nigga need to know who the fuck I am, I ran these blocks before you even knew how to spell your name," Sin spat, pissed the little dude had a gun pointed at him. Even more mad at himself for allowing him to be able to. That was a golden rule. Never turn when a man has or possibly could have a gun. Shit like that could cost you, your life. "Word from the wise, never pull a gun, if you not prepared to pull the trigger. That's the quickest way to get yo' ass popped." Sin stated, stuffing his gun back into his pocket.

Land of Snakes

"Look like you was the nigga about to get popped." The young dude spat, walking off to serve a fiend.

"The nigga a little hot head, just like you use to be," Turk chuckled, "Let me rap to you though, I'm glad your home. The streets been missing you, your brother don't have it in him Sin. You know I've always looked up to you, when nobody was tryna' fuck with me. When I was out there stealing and shit." Turk stated, as they walked into the neighborhood drug house he operated.

"What you mean my brother don't have it in him, I taught that nigga most of everything I know, which is the same shit, you know." Sin said getting offended Turk was speaking ill of his brother. He knew what the streets were saying about Micah, but he didn't care. It was a known fact, Turk didn't care for Micah. He felt he should have been the one given the blessing too. He worked hard under Sin and Case, before Sin got locked up. When Case got killed word from inside put Micah in position to run things, and Turk felt it wasn't right. Slowly he worked hard and sat up shop on the block, despite Micah not wanting him too. Once Sin, gave the okay Micah had to be okay with it. Sin and Micah may have had their differences, but they were brothers and Sin, didn't tolerate someone speaking ill of his brother or family period.

"I'm not knocking Micah, but he not built to slang yay. He owes a lot of people. Everybody been giving him passes cause the streets know that's your brother, but nigga's getting tired of that. I don't know how true it is, but niggas' saying he in business with that old head Gator. And you know how that can go. Niggas already talking about offing him, and you too if you don't like it. That's just the word on the street." Turk said.

"That's the word huh?" Sin asked. He didn't know what Micah was up to, but he was going to figure it out. "Well I'm back; so let these niggas know, bring everything to me. I will handle my brother, and if niggas want to dead my brother, tellem' make sure they moms have her money right, cause I'm goin' dead each and every one of them motherfuckas'. If my mom has to burry a child, so will theirs. I'm not worried about a nigga getting at me; I'm still Sin the menace. Let them know that's words from the Sinister." Sin said walking out the trap. He had to get his money from Kym, so he could get the ball rolling when Wako gave him the green light.

Sin walked down the street, his mind was trying to figure out why Micah was in business with Gator. He knew his brother had been skipping over shit when he was telling him about business. Micah kept insisting that business was doing well. Wako had always kept him informed about what was going on in the streets; he just didn't know this shit was out of hand like it was. Sin stopped and gave a crowd of fiends some freebies. "You want some more of that, holla' at me," Sin said approaching his mother's building, seeing his sister exit a candy apple red Benz. The windows were too dark for him to see inside, but

Land of Snakes

he already knew. It was a dude from the other side, from a rival gang, the Pirus, out in Compton.

"Gia," Sin called out, walking closer to where she was, as she neared the curb.

"Welcome home brother!" Gia yelled, jumping into Sin's arms. Sin and Gia were only 11 months apart. And the closet of the all the siblings being they were the close in age. The car reversed, rolling the passenger window down.

"Gia!" A deep voice yelled from the car.

"What?" She yelled towards the car.

"Bring yo' ass here bitch!" The voice spat. Sin pulled out his strap; he didn't tolerate anyone disrespecting his mother or sister. "Gia you better tell yo' little friend to get some fucking respect or get his cap pilled disrespecting you. Especially bringing his slob ass on my block." Sin yelled loudly making sure he could hear as he approached the car.

"Sin... Sin... I got it, go upstairs. I will meet you in the house," Gia pleaded. She knew her brother, and she knew Kenny, her boyfriend wasn't built to go against Sin in anyway. Sin backed away from the car, but didn't go upstairs. His trigger finger was itching; he was ready to body a nigga. He didn't like the dude already, because he knew he was from the other side, a fuckin' slob. It was crip on his end, all day. He could hear Gia's voice yelling, which she didn't do often and it pissed him off even more. Sin waited a few more minutes all he kept hearing was his sister yelling. Sin walked up on

41

the car, almost pulling Gia out the car. "Get out the car Gia, and go upstairs NOW!" He demanded.

"Blood, get yo' hands off my bitch," The dude spat, never moving out his seat.

"Shut yo' slob ass up. Nigga I know about you, fucking mark," Sin said hawking the dude, who didn't say anything. He knew who Sin was, and wasn't trying to beef with him, especially since he wasn't packing heat.

"Gia, take yo' ass in the house," Sin said lightly shoving Gia towards the apartment. Gia tried to linger, she didn't want her brother to kill Kenny. He had just come home; she didn't want to see him catch another case. Gia, knew if she stood there, Sin, wouldn't kill him, not in front of her.

Approaching the window, Sin still held his gun in his hand. Sin looked Kenny, in his eyes. "Don't bring yo' ass around here again, what was going on between you and my sister, is over. I see you in my hood again, Cuh, You dead. That's a promise; you're not wanted in these parts. " Sin spat backing away from the car, never taking his eyes off of Kenny. He hawked Sin, but didn't speak a word, as he sped off the street.

Sin turned and faced Gia. He knew she was scared that he might kill the dude, which is why she wouldn't go inside. "Why you fuckin' with that lame ass nigga? The nigga didn't even bang shit back," Sin laughed.

Gia just looked at her brother. "You still a damn bully. Imma' be an old hag, with a cat, dealing with you," Gia laughed.

Land of Snakes

"No you want be, just find a real nigga, that yo' big brother approve of," Sin smiled, as they climbed the stairs to their mothers apartment.

FIVE

Micah parked his truck a few blocks from Kym's house, just in case Sin showed up. He didn't want him to see his truck parked outside. Micah jogged back towards Kym's apartment, constantly looking over his shoulder, he didn't know if Gator had someone trailing him. Micah slipped his key into the lock, and let himself in. He found Kym, stretched out on the bed, with nothing on.

"Kym... Kym." Micah yelled shaking her. "Get up, I need that money," He shook her, until she was fully woken up.

"What? She asked groggily, rubbing her eyes. The house was clean spotless, something he didn't see too often. Kym didn't work, and was extremely lazy and was a major pack rat. All she cared about was looking good, and staying laced in the latest fashion, and hitting the club to show off.

"What? You were expecting that nigga Sin? I see you got up and cleaned up. I always have to ask you more than once to do it," Micah was jealous and it lingered around his words. He knew Kym, was supposed to be Sin's girl, but along the way he feel in love with her. Sin treated her like she wasn't shit, and she had been down for him for a while.

"Nah, I was waiting for you baby," Kym smiled.

"Yeah whatever but check this shit out, I need that money tonight, or that nigga Gator gone be peeling my cap back," Micah stated, taking a seat on the bed next to Kym.

Land of Snakes

"I gotta' wait for my mom's to get home," Kym stated, caressing Micah's leg.

"What time will that be, I gotta have the shit by twelve?" Micah stressed.

"She should be home, before that," Kym stated, using her tongue, to run small circles around Micah's neck.

"Chill, I got a lot of shit on my mind," Micah spoke annoyed, jerking away from Kym. He wasn't in the mood for sex. He was trying to find a way to handle Gator, before Gator and Sin bumped into each other.

"Well excuse the fuck outta' me. I was trying to make you feel better. I said I will get you the money. I have to pick my mother up from the airport; she will call me when she finds out her arrival time. I will get the money then. You need to worry about how we gone get this shit over your brother head. What am I supposed to tell him when he come asking for his shit? He knows how much it's supposed to be." Kym said lying back on the bed, spreading her thick legs open.

"Tell him you spent it, or used it to help a family member out."

"Okay, I will do that, now stop stressing on it, I got you. Have I ever let you down?" Kym questioned.

"Nah," Micah replied.

"Alright then, so chill. Now bring that sexy ass over here, I haven't seen you all week," Kym said seductively, her fingers caressing her small perky boobs. Slowly she let her fingers trace the frame of her plump pussy. Letting two fingers slid inside. Soft moans escaped her lips as her fingers penetrated her walls.

Micah stood at the foot of the bed watching her please herself. He was a fiend, he loved pussy and Kym had a fat tight one. He watched her please herself. Micah pulled Kym to the edge of the bed, wanting to feel the insides of her warm pussy. Spreading her legs apart, he let his tongue do the work. Micah grinned, licking Kym's juices from his lips. Kym gripped him by his pants, pulling him closer to her. Slowly she unbuckled his pants, until she pulled his semi-erect penis from his boxer briefs. Kym licked her lips, before sucking the head of his penis into her mouth. Micah's penis instantly grew with the first touch of her watery mouth. He stood at the foot of the bed rocking back in forth in pure bliss, as Kym gave him the sloppiest head known to man.

"Come give me that dick," Kym moaned.

Micah gladly removed his pants, and slid into her plump wetness. He exhaled, at the warmth, and tight fit around his thickness. Gently he gripped her legs, as he thrust inside, slowly picking up his pace, with every deep thrust inside.

"Yeessss.. Fuck this pussy....right there ... fuuuck." Kym moaned as Micah plunged inside of her rapidly hitting the bottom of her pussy, just like she liked. "YYYYYYEEEESSSS!" She exhaled in sheer pleasure.

Lightly winded, Micah laid on the bed. "Get on top," He said grabbing Kym's petite frame. Kym straddled him, her lips locking with his, as she

Land of Snakes

slid down on him. Making sure she was all in, Kym slowly winded her hips. Micah held her guiding her up and down his dick.

The two went at it for another fifteen minutes, before they both erupted in bliss.

"I needed that shit, damn." Micah exhaled heading towards the bathroom to wash up.

"I know. Don't I always know when you need it the most?" Kym yelled from the room.

"You do," Micah said coming back into the room. "Hit me when you get that Kym, no fuckin' around,"

"I got you baby, as soon as I pick my mother up from the airport I will call," Kym said from the bed, with a slight grin on her face as she watched Micah get dressed.

"Cool, I will see you then."

"Alright," Micah said exiting the apartment as quickly as he entered.

****

Gia and Sin entered the house; Pamela was standing over the stove putting the final touches on dinner.

"Is that curry goat I smell?" Sin asked sniffing loudly.

"It sure is, with yellow rice, and cabbage," Pamela said turning to face Sin.

"Hey Ma," Gia said by passing her mother, going into the kitchen to get something to drink.

47

"Guess who decided to find where they lived", Pamela laughed "Gia are you coming to your brothers' game tonight? You know it would be really nice for all his siblings to be at his game," Pamela stated hoping they all came to support Rich.

"Whatever Ma, I do be at home sometimes. I'm going to show support. Rich out there serving them niggas', I'm proud of my little bro," Gia beamed. She knew she let her mother down, she was the only girl. Pamela had high hopes Gia would go to college and make something of herself. She never applied to any universities, and never stepped a foot into any community colleges. She wanted street royalty. Gia thought she was too pretty to work. She wanted to shop, party and look cute. She wanted to stay at home, take care of her man, while he supported her. Since she could remember, Sin, spoiled her with anything she wanted. She wanted a man who could do what her brother did. Pamela hated it. She didn't raise her to want to be with a drug dealer. Or a drug dealer's wife, it was much more to it than Gia knew about. Pamela knew if Sin couldn't do anything else, He could get to Gia. She valued her brother's opinion, and knew with him around, a man would have to be approved by him before dating Gia.

"I can wait to see him. Everybody been telling me Rich good on the field," Sin added. "People in prison was even talking about Rich and reading about."

Land of Snakes

"Gia, please leave Kenny at home," Pamela asked, looking from Gia to Sin, then back to Gia. Hoping she was getting the signal, she didn't want any drama.

"I get it Ma," Gia laughed. "Let's say, Sin may have scared Kenny off, permanently" She laughed.

"I hope you didn't hurt that boy Sintrell."

"I didn't hurt him Ma; I didn't even put my hands on the coward. He is a punk," Sin laughed, thinking how fast Kenny speed off the street.

"Good. I'm sorry Gia, but I didn't like Kenny. Why do you have to date those low-life drug dealers anyway? You are a very pretty and a smart girl. Those types either end up in prison or dead. I don't want that for you. I already have to worry about whatever women your brothers bring home." Pamela stated.

"I know Ma, Kenny knew that, too. And can we please not get into this right now."

"Get into what? I'm just asking a question. Its fine you don't have to answer. Are you two hungry?"

"Yeah," Gia and Sin said in union.
Pamela turned back into the kitchen to make all of them a plate.

"I don't know why she trippin' two of her sons are drug dealers," Gia whispered.

"Shut-up, she can hear you," Sin replied looking at his mother making the plates.

"No, she can't."

"I can, hear you two," Pamela said never turning around.

"I told you," Sin laughed. Pamela may have not seen everything, but she didn't miss a beat.

"Where is Micah? Pamela asked sitting their food down on the table.

"I don't know Ma'," Sin said.

"You didn't have to fix our plates. We not little kids anymore ma' we should be making your dinner and bringing you a plate." Gia spoke looking down at the hearty plate her mother sat in front of her.

"Gia, just eat child so when Micah is ready we can go see your brother." Pamela said, grabbing her plate. Just as she took a seat Micah walked through the door.

"Hey son, are you hungry, I made curry goat, yellow rice and cabbage?"

"Nah Ma, I'm good. What's good Gia?" Micah said embracing his sister in a hug.

"Hey big head. Where you coming from?"

"Doing a little business," Micah replied retreating to his room.

"Your brother is a weirdo," Sin laughed looking at Gia.

"He's your brother too," Gia replied.

"Cut it out. He is my child and both of y'all brothers. You know how your brother gets Sintrell, he wants to be just like you and do everything you do."

"He needs to be just like himself, Like Micah. Because there is only one Sintrell, I can't be duplicated. And, there is no carbon copy of me." Sin said with a smile.

Land of Snakes

"Oh boy hush your mouth. You gotta' stop being so hard on him."

"Ma', Micah is a grown man. You still baby us, but I'm not about to baby Micah. I give him a dose of reality. He is grown, wants to act grown, until you bring him grown man problems. Then he starts acting like a little boy.

"You kids are something else," Pamela said shaking her head finishing up the food on her plate.

SIX

Sin finished his food. Waited to see what Micah was doing. When he heard him, go into the bathroom and turn the shower on. Sin quickly slipped into the room and searched the room until he found Micah's keys.

"Gia tell Micah I got his car. I will be back in an hour," Sin told Gia as he passed her in the living room before heading out of the door.

Sin jumped into Micah's truck, adjusted the seat to fit for him and smashed off. He was full, and in desperate need of climbing into something warm and wet. It had been way too long, and he was determined not to go another night stroking on his dick. Baring the sounds of Nipsey Hussle, he headed towards Kym's crib. He knew Micah, would be pissed when he realized that he had took his car.

****

Micah stepped out the shower, towel draped around his waist, he made his way into his room to dress for the rest of the night. Plopping down on the twin bed, which belonged to Sin, he noticed it had been tampered with. Micah stood to fix the bed, when he noticed the floor board was slight moved. He hadn't ever seen that. The bed didn't get much use; Since Micah was always at one of his chick's house or Kym's. And Rich didn't like sleeping it in.

The apartment wasn't plush, but Pamela made sure they kept it up to par. Micah tried to slide the broad over thinking it was broke and someone had kicked it over. But, when it didn't bulge, he became curious. "What the fuck?" Micah said to himself, lifting the title, still it didn't move. Micah pounded on it twice and it popped open. Oh shit," He said, a smile creep upon his face, seeing the wad of cash, drugs and guns inside. Micah emptied the small safe Sin had install many years ago. Stuffing everything in a small knapsack, Micah dressed, and was ready to leave, when he couldn't find his car keys. Making his way into the kitchen, checking the counters for his keys.

"Looking for something Micah?" Pamela questioned.

"Yeah, my keys. I thought I took them into the back with me, but I can't find them," Micah said scanning the kitchen.

"Check the bathroom and the room. You didn't even go into the kitchen," Pamela said. Micah headed back into the bathroom, and still couldn't find his keys. Walking back into the living room, he finally noticed Sin wasn't there.

"Where Sin at?" He questioned his mother.

"I don't know. He went out the door. He didn't tell me where he was going. Ask your sister," Pamela said, focusing her attention back into the book in front of her. Pamela loved reading. Urban drama and romance were her favorite. She had just gotten the next book in a series she loved, and couldn't wait for. She had met the author a few weeks ago, while she was hosting a book signing. The book was filled of juicy plots and twist, that had Pamela all in.

"Gia You saw my keys? Where Sin go?" Micah questioned. Gia was all into the television. She was trying to get caught up on her favorite reality show.

"Sin took your car, he said he will be back in an hour," Gia replied never looking up from the television.

"What?" Micah yelled. "How this nigga just gone take my fucking car without asking?" Micah roared Sin was trying to play him like a real bitch, and he didn't like it one bit.

"Boy why you doing all of that hollering in this house. This isn't the streets?" Pamela was startled by Micah's loud outburst.

"Sin took my car and didn't even ask me. He don't have no damn driver license, he just got out of fucking prison," Micah sneered out of sheer frustration.

"This is not the street." Pamela reiterated. "And I am not your friend. Watch your mouth in my presence. You're not about to act foolish or be disrespectful to me, in my household with that cursing. Now your brother is wrong for taking your car without your permission and I will tell him when he gets back. Until then take a seat and calm your nerves, or take that loud talking and use of those foul words outside to the streets," Pamela stated peering at Micah.

"I'm sorry ma', I'm just upset."

"And you have the right to be, but I don't want to hear that hopping and hollering."

Land of Snakes

"Imma' chill outside for a minute if you need me," Micah said walking out the door. As soon as Micah step foot out the building, the fiends swarmed around him, in search of Sin.

"Where Sin at? I need a fix," A fiend said.

"Yeah, of that shit he gave us earlier." Another added.

Micah was pissed Sin jumped on the block and started slanging work, without letting him know. Micah knew he had hand out the work he had just found.

"What my brother tell you?" Micah questioned. He knew a fiend would tell you anything you wanted to hear, for a hit.

"He gave us some freebies, and told us he was the nigga to see about that good shit," The fiend spoke fumbling with his words. "So where is that nigga at? Because I need some more of that shit,"

"Oh really? He that nigga? Well let me inform you. My brother works for me. So get at me for all your needs. I will make sure I hook you up," Micah told the fiends before giving them a hefty amount of packs for free. Micah knew he would have to stay ahead of Sin, because he was coming back for what was his, and was doing it hard, and moving sneaky. "Snake ass nigga, didn't even come to me and tell me what the deal was." Micah said out loud to himself. He knew Sin, and the rest of the hood wanted him to redeem the streets, but he wasn't ready. Micah wanted Sin to come work under him, even if it was just for a little while.

****

Sin parked the truck in front of Kym's building hawking the dudes, which stood out front. It was known who Sin was, what type of man he was and where he was from. Kym lived in the neighborhood controlled by the Bloods. Sin walked slowly daring any of them to say something to him. Sin got to Kym's door, and banged on the flimsy screen door hard.

"Kym. Kym," He called out. "Answer the fucking door."

Kym had fallen back to sleep once Micah left.

"Here I come damn," Kym yelled, grabbing her robe to cover her nude body. Kym peaked through the tiny hole, and saw Sin standing there. "About time," Kym smiled, opening her robe, before opening the door. "What took you so long? You left hours ago?" Kym questioned, as if she really cared.

"I had some shit to take care of," Sin said by-passing her and scanning the apartment. "Did you get what I asked you?" Sin questioned, taking a seat on the couch.

While Sin was locked up, he was introduced to Kym, from another inmate that shared a cell with him. The two hit it off, instantly. Kym was a down chick, and help him smuggle drugs and cell phones into the prison. Needing to stay afloat doing his bid, he confided in Kym and told her where his stash was, and had her running things for him. She had always remained loyal, showed up to every visit weekly. Sin never cared if she took a little extra for herself, she was his woman and someone he trusted, she always handled his business in a timely manner.

"Nah, it's at my mothers, and she isn't home," Kym said, standing behind the couch massaging his shoulders.

"Why the fuck is my money at your mothers?" Sin roared jumping up from his seat on the couch and peered at her.

"Where else was I supposed to hide it, here? These niggas' know I fuck with you, if they even thought I had that kind of money in here, they would rush my spot," Kym spat

"Yeah okay, so let's go get it."

"My mother went out town to visit her boyfriend, she won't be back until later," Kym stated.

"Why yo' dumb ass didn't say that shit earlier then?" Sin asked, jumping into her face. I could've done some other shit.

"I just fucking found out, and who the fuck you calling dumb, fucking jail bird?" Kym roared. Sin was known to flip out; when things didn't go the way he wanted them. But Kym wasn't the one to back down.

Sin grabbed Kym throwing her body against the wall. "Bitch! Watch that fucking mouth of yours before I stick my foot up your ass," Sin sneered, gripping her face, in his hands. "Now what fucking time are you picking up your mother?"

"At ten," Kym said through clinched teeth.

"Good," Sin said letting her go. "Now bring yo' dumb ass over here and give me some pussy," Sin spat, dropping his pants and taking a seat on the couch.

"I have to use the rest room first," Kym said walking hastily to the bathroom.

"Well hurry the fuck up, I gotta' take punk ass Micah his car back before he have a bitch fit," Sin said taking the pre-rolled blunt from his pocket, that was left inside of Micah's car.

It was times like this, when Sin treated her like a random bitch, he fucked with that made Kym not care that she had been creeping with Micah. Kym rambled through the cabinet in search of the china shrink she had. It was a small tube of cream formulated to tighten the vagina. She found the tube, quickly cleaned herself with a summers eve's feminine wipe, before applying the cream to her vagina. Flushing the toilet, Kym washed her hands. She waited a moment, to make sure the cream had kicked in and couldn't be noticed.

As far as Sin knew, Kym hadn't stepped out on him since they met. It was somewhat true. She dabbled a little. It wasn't up until a year ago, when Micah came to pick something up for Sin. Kym took a liking to Micah. He was the opposite to his older brother. He was gentle, treated her with respect and was able to give her what she needed at the moment, a warm body to lay next to at night. Kym and Micah had been sexing each other ever since. Neither regretted one moment of it.

Sin sat on the couch, blunt in his mouth, as he stroked his penis, which grew with every stroke as he watched the new upcoming porn star Sky Goddess on the plasma television.

"So you just come to my house, and buy porn on my TV? Didn't even ask me, then have the nerve to be jacking' yo' shit off too?" Kym asked. She was delighted he was getting himself pumped. She needed it to be quick and easy. She was still satisfied from Micah.

"You are always running that big smart ass mouth of yours. How about you stick my dick in it, or shut the fuck up. I've been getting myself off for a good while now, I'm use to it. Remember who I am, getting pussy hasn't ever been hard for me. So if you can't handle it, another bitch can," Sin spat knowing the mention of him fucking another bitch would send Kym over and make her do what he wanted.

Kym dropped to her knees in front of Sin. "I can do better," She smiled. Removing his hand, and devouring all of his eight inches into her mouth.

"Oooohh...shiiiit.." Sin moaned, gripping a fist full of Kym's weave. Bringing himself to the edge of the couch, Sin forcefully fed Kym all of himself roughly. It had been so long since he had gotten his dick sucked like that, Sin let loose quickly. Kym wasted no time, sucking him back into her mouth until he was rock hard again. Kym gripped his balls tightly.

"Shiiit," Sin whiled at the unexpected rush of pain.

"Keep saying you gon' fuck another bitch. You won't have a dick for her to suck, keep fucking with me Sin," Kym smiled loving having the control at that very moment.

"Let my fucking balls go, that shit hurt."

"Take the shit back, and I'll let go."

"I take the shit back. Damn!"

"Good," Kym smile taking his balls into her mouth, and sucking on them hard, and intense.

"Bend that ass over," Sin said, pulling her body up from the floor.

Kym gripped the back of the couch, arching the small of her back, spreading her legs open, throwing her plump ass into the air.

"That's what I'm talking about," Sin grinned, smacking her ass, watching it giggle. Pulling her hips back, he jammed his harden dick inside.

"Whhhoooaa....shiiittt," Kym grunted, almost flipping over the couch, from the pain. The china shrink was in full effect, had her feeling like it was her first time again.

"Don't run from me now, bring that ass back," Sin grinned, pulling her back. Jamming his dick back into her pussy, that ran like a streaming river.

Finally working all of him into her. Sin gave her slow and steady death strokes. Gripping her by the hair, he speed up, as she backed her ass up harder on him.

Land of Snakes

"Oh you ready to be fucked huh?" Sin asked. Sparing her no mercy as her repeated plunged his dick into her. Inserting his thumb into her anal, repeatedly finger fucking her ass.

Kym wasn't expecting it, but she loved the rush she felt from the double penetration. With every deep plunge, Kym backed her ass up on him even harder.

Kym sucked Sin's dick into her walls. Clinching her muscles with every deep stroke he gave her. Those many nights spent training with the kegels. It allowed her to flex her muscles around Sin's dick.

"Ahh, shitt...fuck!" Sin moaned the death grip Kym had around his dick, he couldn't bear, and it felt too good. With a fist full of her weave in one hand, and his other clasped around her neck Sin plunged harder and faster. "Fuuucccckk......" He grunted his legs becoming stiff, as he slowly jerked, releasing his nut inside of her. Spent, he collapsed next to her, out of breath. Sin didn't care if Kym had gotten her rocks off, as long as he did. Sin was a selfish lover, only looking to please himself.

"Shit," Kym stated flopping down on the couch, she was sore, felt like him had ripped her inside open.

"Where are the towels at?" Sin questioned.

"In the hall closet, next to the restroom," Kim replied, lying back with her eyes closed.

Sin proceeded to the restroom. As soon as Kym heard the water from the sink run, she dug into Sin's pockets. Flipping through the wad of cash,

she peeled off ten crispy hundred dollars,
stuffing them into the side of the couch, and put
his money back into his pockets. Kym laid back
down, like she was before he left the room.
Sin rushed back into the room and began to get
dress, without paying much attention to Kym.
Who sat just watching him carefully. He was sexy
as hell, but crazy and controlling.

"I'm about to get out of here." Sin said
leaning over the couch gripping Kym's face
forcing his tongue inside her mouth. "Make sure
you hit me, as soon as your mom calls you," Sin
said fully dressed and preparing to leave.

"I got you," Kym said watching him walk out
the door, before jumping up to lock the door
behind him.

Land of Snakes

SEVEN

Micah paced around the apartment waiting for Sin to return with his car. It had been two hours, and with every minute he grew angrier with his brother.

"Micah have a seat, you making me nervous. With all that pacing," Pamela stated. "Your brother isn't going to mess up that precious car of yours."

"Ma' that's not the point, he shouldn't took my car, without asking me," Micah roared. "I have things to do."

The front door opened. In walked Sin with mischief in his eyes, a wide grin plastered on his face. The way Micah paced the floor he knew he was vexed. Anytime Micah was angry he paced.

"Sintrell give your brother his keys," Pamela stated, looking over the rims of her eye glasses. Looking at the mischief that lay in Sin's eyes. She knew he was just messing with Micah.

Micah snatched the keys from Sin's hand. "Don't touch my shit again," He spat.

"Or you gone do what? Huh?" Sin challenged, knowing Micah didn't want to go up against him.

"Like I said. Don't fucking touch my shit again, Nigga!" Micah barked walking off.

"Micah! Sintrell!" Pamela yelled sternly. "Now I have told the two of you about that loud curing in my house. I'm not about to say it again. What time will you be back? You still taking me to Richard's game aren't you?" Pamela

63

questioned seeing Micah with a bag headed for the door.

"Yeah Ma', I just gotta run an errand, I could've had out the way two hours ago," Micah said throwing subliminal messages around.

Sin chuckled. Hawking his younger brother. He could read between the lines. "Yeah, whatever nigga. You so worried about that car. Where is Ma' car? How you out in them streets, and Ma' is still on the bus? Huh? Nigga riddle me that shit." Sin braked.

"I've been holding this shit down since you left, don't fucking questioned me. Who made sure your books was stacks, packages, cell phone and anything else you needed, I did that shit nigga," Micah spat jumping into Sin's face. "I know your sitting on money, so, if you don't like what I am doing. Let me see you do better." Micah stated.

Sin smiled, loving the inner tiger inside of his brother, especially with what the streets had to say about him. "I guess you aren't as soft as the streets think," Sin chuckled.

"Fuck you, and what them streets gotta' say,"

"If you two don't quit it, I don't want anything from you Micah. That's blood money y'all playing with, I don't want no parts in it," Pamela stated, standing in between her sons so they wouldn't go to blows. "Micah now go where you have too, and we will be ready when you get back. Sintrell go have a seat."

Land of Snakes

"Ma, it's cool. I'm back, the streets know. I'm gone handle shit around here. You will have a car in a month, anyone you want," Sin spoke. His eyes never leaving Micah's gaze.

"Yeah, I will love to see that, nobody fucking with you. You just got out. News flash YOU'RE HOT!" Micah said with a smile. "I'll show you who in charge Big Brother."

"I don't want anything from you either Sintrell, with that blood money. If you want to something for me, get a job before them streets kill you, two. And I don't know what's this between you two," Pamela pointed at each of them, still standing in between both of them who towered over her. "But, y'all better get it together. You are brothers. Because, if you two keep using that foul language in this house, I'm going to go upside both of y'all heads."

"I will be back in a few," Micah rushed out the door. He didn't know what Sin would use to re-up, and touch the streets. He had his stash from the room, and planned to take everything he could from Kym, any and everything she was holding for Sin. "That will teach his bitch ass," Sin plopped down on the couch he didn't know what his brother meant by that, and didn't care. He had spoken to his old connect, who was going to plug him in, on some coke and heroin, to get him back into the game.

"Ma, wake me, when your son comes back to get us," Sin said walking toward the room to take a nap.

"Okay," Pamela said.

Gia sat on the couch just watching the drama unfold between her brothers. She thought it was cute and funny how they challenge each other.

"Your son's are crazy."

"Tell me about it," Pamela said getting her some water. She would sure need her blood pressure medicine dealing with Micah and Sin together.

****

Micah speed over to Kym's apartment. He knew that's where Sin had just come from. He couldn't leave the money he had taken from Sin, at the house. With the stunt Sin pulled earlier, his truck was out the question. Leaving his truck on the back streets, he entered the building, from the alley.

"Kym...Kym!" Micah yelled, scanning the house. Kym wasn't home. Micah through the bag down taking a seat on the couch, pulling his cell phone out, he dialed her number. Micah looked around he could hear Kym's phone running. Going into her room, he found it sitting on her vanity mirror.

"Damn," Micah said to himself, looking down at his watch, it was almost seven, and he knew he had to get back home to take his mother to Rich's game.
Micah hid the bag in Kym's closet, and was about to leave when she came through the door.

"Hey Babe, how long you been here?" Kym asked nervously.

Land of Snakes

"I just got here, I had to drop something off, that I couldn't leave at my Ma's house," Micah said taking her into his arms, planting a tender kiss on her thin lips. Micah glazed into her eyes he had truly fallen head over hills for her. He knew as long as Sin was around, she would never fully be his, and he wanted her all to himself. He couldn't image Sin getting her sweetness that was reserved for him. Out of the dozen of chicks he messed with, he really couldn't see himself with anyone, but Kym. She was perfect for him, and the fact she wasn't even his, toyed with him.

"What's wrong?" Kym asked, noticing the strange look in Micah's face.

"Nothing, I was just admiring your beauty. I left a bag in your closet. Imma' get it when I come back to pick that money up from you," Micah stated, kissing her lips again, this time his tongue traveled inside her mouth, slowly stroking hers.

"What time will you mom be back? I hope before midnight?"

"Yeah, she said her plane arrive at ten."

"Well hit me, once you pick her up."

"Okay. Later," Kym said watching him leave. From the patio glass door. She could see Micah getting into his truck. Something with him was off, and she knew it. When she saw him pull off, Kym ran to her closet to see what was inside.

Micah pulled in front of his mother's building, laid on the horn signaling for them to come down stairs. On his way home, he had called Gia, to let them know he was in route.

"Can you please not play that loud gangsta rap Micah, it makes my head hurt," Pamela said as she climbed into the front seat.

"What you want to listen to? We can listen to anything but that gospel."

"What's wrong with gospel? It's good for the soul. Just play the radio."

"She wants to listen to the wave," Gia chimed. Micah turned to the station, before pulling off. The ride was silent. Besides the light humming from Pamela. Micah's, mind was on getting Gator off of his back, and Sin out the way. He studied his brother from the rearview mirror. He wasn't shocked, that Sin, was watching him too.

Land of Snakes

EIGHT

It was half time, and Rich's team was up. Rich was the illest on the field. He was the teams all-star Quarterback, and showed out every game. Rich played his heart out, the other teams Quarterback always competed with him, Rich wanted to show him, he was the better player, and let the whole community see.

"I'm about to get something to drink, anyone want something?" Micah asked prepared to head for the concession stand.

"No, I'm good son," Pamela said her eyes scanning the field for Rich.

"I do," Gia said. "Bring me some nacho's big head, extra chesses, please."

Micah passed never mentioning or caring to see if Sin wanted something. Micah stood in line, waiting for his turn to place his order when he saw Bishop Gator's henchmen lurking around the area.

"Fuck," He said to himself lowering his head, trying to stay out of his eye view. He knew Gator's men would be out lurking looking for him at the game. The way Rich, and his team was playing, he knew Gator was taking a loss for the night.

Micah finally made it to the front of the line, getting him some knick knacks, and Gia nachos. He could feel eyes watching him, to nervous to look up. He rushed back towards the bleaches were his family were sitting. Half way back to his seat, he saw him. Gator stood, with a wicked grin on his face. "You must have my money, Micah?

69

The way Rich out there playing on the field," Gator said sternly.

"I'm gone have your money Gator," Micah said, glancing at Gator and his two henchmen.

"You better. Meet me at The Joint, at midnight. Not a minute late. Oh and since I had to wait so fucking long throw in an extra 10%, for my inconvenient."

"What? An extra ten percent, really?" Micah winded. He was barely getting what he owed, let alone having extras.

"I don't think I have a speech problem, so you heard me right. An extra ten percent and I want it tonight, no excuses."

"Alright," Micah said. He could see Sin approaching them from a distance. Sin had watched the whole ordeal go down.

"If it isn't the legend. One of the greatest to ever do it," Sin joked approaching the gentleman.

"You got that shit right, OG all day long now. Welcome home little nigga. Come holla' at me, the streets been missing real niggas' like you,"Gator said never looking at Sin, but at Micah the whole time.

"I just might do that, OG," Sin said.

"I will get with you later Gator," Micah said preparing to walk off, before any more words were exchanged.

"Midnight Micah, not a minute later," Gator said as him and his men walked off, leaving Micah and Sin standing there.

"What business you have with Gator?" Sin questioned, hoping Micah would tell him. He

Land of Snakes

knew for his brother to be in business with Gator, he had to be into some heavy trouble, or bull shit.

"Don't worry about it, I got my shit handed. I don't need your help," Micah spat, walking off, leaving Sin standing there. He knew Sin, could get Gator to hold off, but his pride wouldn't allow him to reach out to ask Sin, for help.

The game was in its fourth quarter, and Rich's team was blowing the other team out. Micah nervously watched his watch, it was a little after 9 o'clock and he hadn't heard from Kym yet. Micah sent Kym a text asking if she had spoken with her mother. She hit him right back, letting him know her mother's flight would arrive at the Long Beach airport 10 o'clock and she would call him once she was on the freeway headed back to her house. Content with that, he focused on his little brother running his last yard, and scoring the last touch down before the time ran out.

"That's my baby!" Pamela cheered like a proud mother

"That's my little brother," Gia, Micah and Sin chimed cheering Rich on.
Rich danced his way to the end of the field sending the whole crowd into laughter.

"I'm so proud of my baby boy," Pamela smiled on the verge of shedding tears of joy.

"Don't start crying mama," Gia laughed.

"Oh hush Gia,"
The team was rushed into the locker room, as the crowd cleared the bleachers spilling into the

parking area, waiting for the winning team to emerge.

Micah stood next to his truck. Nervously his eyes shifted around the swap of people in passing as they waited for the teams to be released from the locker room. It was ten minutes til'10pm, Micah hadn't heard any update from Kym. From the corner of his eye, Micah could see Gator, two women and his henchman approaching.

"Is that Pamela Jones?" Gator said licking his lips at Pamela curvy frame.

Pamela who had been talking to Gia turned to see the face of the voice that was approaching from behind her. "Tisk!" She mumbled instantly getting annoyed with Gator. Gator had been trying to get with Pamela for years, each time she declined. Gator wasn't her type. He was a scum.

"You still look good. Better than half of these women half your age. When you gone let me take you out? A nice night out on the town," Gator said. Reaching for Pamela's hand to plant a kiss on it. Pamela jerked her hand back flaring her nose up.

"You're not enough man for me. So chance of that will never happen. So do me a favor, and stop trying," Pamela spat. *"This man a damn fool,"* Pamela thought to herself glaring at Gator, and the women around him.

Gator chuckled. "But Kirby is?" He asked with a smirk on his face. His eyes drifting to Sin, Micah and Gia, before they laid back on Pamela. Gator was also in Kirby's pocket. Kirby knew Gator had a thing for Pamela, so he made it his duty to tell him every chance he got, that he was hitting that.

"Get the hell outta' my fucking face," Pamela spoke her face frustrated with embarrassment. "You better get away from me and I do mean fast as hell, before they have to call the damn police on me," Pamela shouted.

"Hol' up OG, What are you talking about?" Sin asked. The look on his mother face and use of words she didn't use often told him she was bothered by Gator comment referring to Kirby, and Gator in general.

"Ask your mother," Gator said. Preparing to walk off. But, stopped and turned. "Micah.... Midnight. Not a minute late. Have a good night Pamela," Gator smiled a mischievous grin creep on his face, that didn't sit well with Sin.

"OG, I respect you. But, I respect and love my mother more. You make her feel uncomfortable, and that shit don't sit well with me. So as a man, I'm asking that you don't speak to my mother again, like ever again. You see her, just turn your head. " Sin said

"Aww, it's nothing youngster. I just think she fine. But, if it makes you feel some way, I'll respect that, and won't speak to her. Well at least coming from you." Gator laughed as the old school caddie pulled up, he got in and it drifted off into the distance.

"Micah what is he talking about midnight? What kind of business do you have with that devil?" Pamela questioned. She knew whatever

business her son had with Gator, it wasn't good.
Nothing about it was good.

"What is Gator talking about ma'? Are you
fucking old ass Kirby?" Micah questioned. He
hadn't seen his mother use that many curse
words in one sentence, since she went off on his
middle school principal.

Pamela approached Micah so close, he could feel
the fire steaming from her body. She was furious.
Before she could think, she raised her hand, and
landed it across Micah's face slapping fire from
him. "Don't you ever in your life. Speak or use
that manner to talk to me. You maybe this big
time drug dealer in these damn streets, and these
people fear you, I don't. I am your mother, and
you will respect me. I'm not one of your damn
friends or whore you sleep with," Pamela snared.
Micah gripped his face. He was in shock that his
mother had slapped him.

"Ma' you still haven't answered the
questioned. Are you sleeping with Kirby?" Sin
asked hoping it wasn't true. The way she
smacked Micah. Sin, could tell his mother was
on a rampage, and he didn't want any parts of it.
Even though a murderous fire was burning inside
of him, Sin knew it was more to the story. Gator's
slick comment, and what he witness earlier in
the hall. Sin knew it was more. As much as he
wanted to wild out, and force his mother to tell
him what was wrong, he couldn't because like
him, there was a fire burning inside of Pamela,
and Sin wasn't a fool, he knew his mother wasn't
nothing to play with.

Land of Snakes

"No," Pamela yelled a stream of tears rolling down her beautiful mocha skin. She was embarrassed; she couldn't tell her children that Kirby had been bribing her into sleeping with him for months. She knew Sin would kill him. The look in his eyes, and the stories she heard told her so, and she couldn't deal with his blood on her hands. Or the fact, it could send her son back to prison, and this time for life.

"Then are why you crying ma'? Gia chimed, just like her brothers she wanted to know the truth, because her mother's actions were out of her norm. Gia embraced her mother into her arms. "It's going to be okay."

"Just let it go. This is Rich's day," Pamela stated wiping the tears from her face, as she watched her baby make his way towards them she didn't want Rich to worry. "There goes my baby. You were doing your thing on that field tonight," Pamela beamed giving Rich a big hug. "I'm so proud of you."

"Y'all saw me. I was smashing those fools. They weren't ready, at all. I've been waiting to play in this game all year long, and my team won, just like I knew we would. Take that Patrick, its Rich the Champ," Rich chanted.

"You a beast out there on the field little Bro', keep that shit up, for real I'm proud of you shorty," Sin said sliding two crispy hundreds into Rich's hand.

"Let's get out of here, before we get stuck into the madness of traffic." Pamela said making her way to the passenger's side of Micah's truck.

"Ma, can I go with some friends to celebrate?" Rich asked.

"Where and with who?" Pamela questioned.

"We all going, it's like ten of us. We going to the bowling alley, off Manchester," Rich stated, his eyes practically begging his mother. Pamela didn't allow Rich, to go many places without her. He was her baby, she wanted to protect him.

"Why can't you just celebrate with your family?" She questioned, she was scared for her youngest child. The streets of Los Angeles were crazy, and they had already taken ahold of three of her children. Rich had too much going for himself. She didn't want the streets sticking their teeth into her baby.

"Ma, let him go with his friends. Rich is 17years old. He doesn't want to always be under his mother," Sin laughed.
Pamela peered at Sin. Then back at Rich. His eyes pleaded with her. She wanted to say no, so bad.

"Please Ma; I will be home by 1 o'clock I promise. Micah can even pick me up," Rich stated looking at his brother for reinsurance.

"Ma, leim go have fun with his friends," Micah stated.

"Yeah Ma, Rich isn't a baby anymore," Gia added.

"Y'all shut up; He will always be my baby. You can go Richard, but you better have yourself in the house by 1o'clock in the morning and no later. And you three," Pamela stated pointing at her three oldest. "You three better see to it, that my baby gets home safe and sound. By one or it's y'all asses. Now let's get out of here,"

"Thanks Ma," Rich beamed as they all climbed into Micah truck.

"What's up with all of this cursing?" Micah questioned as they waited in the long line to get out of the parking lot.

"Yeah, you haven't cursed that much in a long time." Gia added.

"I'm grown. I can speak how I chose. Y'all just watch your mouths around me."

"But, we grown," Sin laughed.

"Sintrell don't make me reach behind me and touch you."

Sin just laughed trying to lighten the mood. He could tell his mother was still slightly bothered about what just happened and it made him even more furious. He couldn't wait to get back to the apartment.

They rode in silence as they dropped Rich off at the bowling alley where his friends were waiting.

"Thanks ma" Rich said as he jumped out the car.

"Be safe Richard and make sure you out here at twelve forty-five. You need to be in the house by 1 o'clock." Pamela reminded glaring at Micah.

"Go have fun and I will pick you up at twelve forty-five." Micah said with a smile as he drove off.

NINE

Micah parked in front of their apartment complex everyone quickly getting out of it. Sin had one thing on his mind. Finding out what was going on between his mother and Kirby and why she burst into tears, something wasn't right, and he was going to figure it out. Sin let his mother go up the stairs first trying to linger in the back.

"So what we gone do?" Gia asked noticing Sin lagging behind.

"You just go upstairs, and keep ma' inside. I got this." Sin spoke.

"Cool. Get to the bottom of this shit Sin. Find out what's going on with ma' and that fat fuck." Gia spoke rushing behind her mother.
Sin hoped Micah caught his drifted to linger behind. But, Micah had other things on his mind, and didn't pay Sin, any mind as he walked slowly behind him, his eyes glued to his cell phone.

"Micah let me wrap to you," Sin stated turning to face his brother.

"What man? I have some things to do," Micah stated a strange look on his face. It was well past ten and he hadn't heard back from Kym, after texting and calling her repeatedly.

"So you have something more important to do then find out why your mother is crying at the mention of some dudes name?" Sin questioned. He didn't get his brother. They weren't alike in any way. "What type of nigga are you? Like for real Micah? In case you missed it. Our mother burst into tears at the mention of some dudes name. She even slapped the shit out yo' black ass, so either this nigga raped our mother, or forcing her to fuck him. Neither of them sits well with me, at fucking all. Do you get my drift?"

"Man what's up, what you tryna' do?" Micah asked with annoyed.

"You deserved that slap ma' gave you. She should've just punched yo' punk ass."

"Whatever Sin, So what you trying to do? Because I'm not about to stand here and go back in forth with you. I have better shit to do then that."

"I'm about to step to that nigga Kirby, at his crib. I don't know what's going on, but I've never seen ma' like that, and I don't ever want to as long as I live," Sin stated.

"Alright, let's go," Micah said walking into the building.

"You strapped?" Sin asked.

"Nah,"

"What kind of hustler are you? You not strap the streets dry? You make me regret giving you my blessings, damn!" Sin said in disgust.

"Sin, I don't have time for this shit. To be going back and forth with you, or dealing with your bullshit. Let's go find out what the fuck is going on with this nigga Kirby. Because I have some other shit, I have to get too," Micah said as he stared at his older brother, he never did anything good enough for Sin. He wanted to scream and tell him after tonight he would have more money and product to flood the streets, and he was strapped, strapped with his shit and was ready to dead him where he stood. "Yeah man whatever," Micah replied following behind Sin.

As they approached Kirby's door, Sin pulled out the 9mm that was stuffed in the waist of his jeans, siding the silencer on. "And you just that nigga that carry guns and silencers around in your pocket? Huh?" Micah smirked. Making a statement rather than asking a question.

"I'm still the same nigga, who hustled day in and out, on these streets. If you would've handled shit the way you claimed you were, I wouldn't have to be this way. I planned to come home and change, do something positive with my life. But, my mother still resides in the tuft where I sold those same drugs, where my rivals, enemies and the police know me and my whole family by name. In a fuckin' tiny ass apartment and working two jobs to support her family. That doesn't sit well with me, I don't know about yo' punk ass," Sin sneered. Using the butt of the gun he tapped on Kirby's door. "I started selling drugs because I was tired of seeing Ma' struggle to take care of us," Sin admitted.

Kirby who was inside pulling on his scribbled penis watching multiply screens of his tenants apartments. Unknowingly to many of the women tenants in the apartment complex, Kirby had hidden camera's installed why they weren't home in their bedrooms and bathrooms. He got off on watching them having sex, showering or simply getting dressed. Kirby heard the knock on the door, but ignored it. He was too close to

Land of Snakes

eruption and his tenant in 4b, was engaging in some steamy girl on girl action, he couldn't miss. He knew it was only one of the tenants complaining about something wrong in their apartment.

The knock came again, this time harder than before. "I'm busy, go away," Kirby yelled as his legs began to stiff.

"Open this fucking door old man," Sin sternly spoke. Using the butt of his gun, Sin banged on the door. Hearing the stern voice, Kirby penis went limp, he had no desire to finish. Shutting off the monitors, Kirby straightened his clothes unknown of the large wet spot on his pants, from his first eruption. He made his way to the door.

"What can I do for you young men?" Kirby asked. Swinging the door open, meeting the barrel of Sin's 9mm. "Whoooaa... wha- what's this about?" Kirby questioned nervously, his hands in the air. "I don't have any money in here."

"What the fuck is yo' old ass in here doing?" Micah questioned noticing the large wet spot on Kirby's pants. Without waiting for him to respond Micah pushed passed to search the apartment.

The shabby apartment was cluttered from wall to wall with all sorts of junk.

"We don't want any money from you." Sin spat.

"Well what can I help you fellas with?" Kirby tried to remain calm but the barrel of the gun aimed at his face had him shaky. He didn't know

81

if they had found the camera hidden in their mother's apartment or had she told them what he had been forcing her to do, either way, Kirby was nervous. He had heard the numerous horror stories about Sin.

"I have a few questions for you. What has been going on between you and my mother? And don't fucking lie. Are you fucking my mother?" Sin questioned, his fingers clasped around the trigger, itching to blow Kirby's head off. If he gave him the wrong answer, or even an answer that didn't sit well with him.

"Ummm...ummm!" Kirby stuttered. He didn't know how to answer the question. He didn't know what they already knew, and didn't want to give them information they didn't have. "No," He paused. "Your mother and I are not sleeping together," Kirby chuckled as if it was merely an outrageous statement. His eyes darted around the room looking for Micah. He was trying not to be nervous but, Sin still had the gun pointed at him.

 Micah let Sin handle Kirby while he ram shacked his apartment looking for any clues or signs of anything odd. There was several dozen DVD's stacked against the wall labeled with dates and initials.

Micah searched the TV stand, and didn't find anything odd. He was about to turn and head into the bedroom when something told him to stop and turn on the television. When they approached the door, he thought he had heard other voices, but no one was in the apartment

Land of Snakes

with him. Micah hit the tiny button on the side of the television. "What was this nigga watching?" Micah said out loud waiting for the television to come on clearly. Multiple scenes popped on the screen. The first screen was Pamela empty room.

"Sin check this shit out, this motherfucka' got a camera in Ma' room," Micah said as he scanned the other five scene's on the screen. A murderous volt spread through Micah's body seeing that Kirby had a camera in his mother's room. Micah darted over to where Kirby stood. "What kind of shit is this, you recording your tenants?" He questioned. Micah didn't wait for Kirby to respond. With a closed fist Micah extended his arm punching Kirby dead in the face. Knocking his pudgy frame to the ground. "You sick ass bastard."
Sin had to smile, seeing Micah have a little heart within himself. "What's this Kirby?" Sin asked circling around Kirby who lay on the floor covering his leaking nose.

"I did it for safety reasons," He whined.

"Safety reasons huh?" Sin smirked. "Bro' run those tapes back. Kirby for your safety my mother's naked body better not be on that screen. Because, that's your life, my friend," Sin sneered his tone had changed. He no longer sounded angry, but deranged. Despite the up's and down's they went through, she was his queen. And he would lay his life on the line, to protect and save her. Her behavior earlier wasn't normal. Pamela didn't cry often, and for her to do so, someone had to feel the raft for her pain.

Micah gripped the remote in his hand playing back the last few hours of recording. He wanted to see what Kirby was doing leaving his mother's apartment. A small feeling in his gut, told him he wasn't prepared to handle his actions if he found Kirby doing something to his mother.

If the eyes were the windows to your soul, Kirby knew his life would be ending. The deranged murderous glare in Sin's eyes told him so. He was infatuated with Pamela. He loved everything about her. He knew the only way to sleep with a woman of Pamela's caliber; he had to bribe her to do so. So when she started to fall behind on the rent, it gave him the perfect opportunity. Daily he watched the recorded footage of him and Pamela sexual encounters. Hoping one day, she would actually enjoy herself with him, without having to be forced to do so. Until then he watched the tapes daily, getting high off being so close to her.

Micah's knees buckled at the sight of Kirby jack hammering on-top of his mother in her room, minutes before they arrived. The absent and tears in his mother eyes, told him she was doing something she didn't want to, and that made him furious.

Micah leaped over to where Kirby still lay on the floor, too scared to move a muscle. Bringing his size elven sneakers down onto Kirby's body. All Micah saw was black; he hated himself for not paying attention to the signs. He knew Sin would blame him for this too, he was so caught up in his life, that his mother had fell behind on her rent,

Land of Snakes

and Kirby used that to silicate sex from his mother. Micah took all of his problems out on Kirby, his problems with Gator, Sin and with being in love with a woman who would never really be his, because like everything else, she was Sin's. For a moment, he pictured it being Sin laying on the floor, and not just Kirby. He took all of his anger out on him.

Sin stood back and watched Micah turn into a maniac. He didn't think his brother had it in him. He had heard a few stories of Micah knocking out a few dudes who got out of line. Sin had just never saw it, Micah always acted so soft around him. Always complaining about any and everything.
Blood covered Kirby's body as Micah continued to stomp his limp body. Sin watched like a proud big brother. Sin didn't know what set Micah off, but he liked it. Sin could hear grunts. Sin looked around to see where the source of the noise was coming from when he remembered the television was still on. Briefly Sin took his eyes off Micah and focused at the screen. Sin's heart dropped when he saw his mother laid on her bed with her legs open and tears in her eyes. Kirby stood in front of her with a wide grin plastered on his face as he zipped up his pants.

"Move Micah!" Sin shouted hatred rose in his heart for Kirby. "Why? Why was my mother crying? You raped my mother?" Sin ran the questions off so fast Kirby didn't have a chance to answer before Sin rapidly brought the gun down on his face.

"Dead this nigga," Micah spoke, his eyes locking with Kirby's who pleaded with him not to end his life. "Fuck you! Don't look like your sorry now; don't try to plead with me. My mother probably was pleading, but you weren't hearing that huh? Fuck you, you fat fuck." Micah spat. Sin regained his composure, firing round after round into Kirby's body. Sin and Micah watched as his body jerked with every round that pierced his body, until Sin was out of bullets and Kirby was riddled with bullet holes. His lifeless body lay with his eyes wide open, with an absent look. A look quite like the one Pamela's wore while he took advantage of her.

"Let's get the fuck outta' here," Micah spoke, making his way towards the door.

"Hol' up," Sin said, walking up to the television using the butt of the gun, he shattered the screen. Sin tried to pull all the wires apart and destroy every DVD around. Sin and Micah exited Kirby's apartment like nothing happened. Micah was covered in blood. Micah quickly removed his shoes as they neared his mother's apartment.

"I'm gone run in here. I need you to distract Ma, so she doesn't see all this blood."

"I got you if she in the living room just keep heading to the back and I will answer all of her questions."

"Cool," Micah said tuning the knob to enter the apartment. Like always Pamela was sitting at the kitchen table. Micah took hasty strides trying to bypass his mother and the billions of questions he knew she would ask the moment she saw him.

"Where did you two go?" Pamela questioned quickly peaking up startled by the crimson stains all over Micah's shirt "Is that blood?" Pamela asked frantic looking at Micah practically running down the hallway.

"He good Ma', it was just a little misunderstanding," Sin said taking a seat on the couch wiping the beads of sweat from his face.

"What do you mean misunderstanding? Who did that?" Pamela questioned looking at Sin for answers.

"I didn't. The nigga still my brother, I wouldn't do nothing to him."

"You better watch your mouth Sintrell," Pamela said going to look for Micah.
Micah could hear his mother's footsteps getting closer to the bathroom. He quickly washed the blood from his hands, and removed his shirt and pants that had blotches of blood on them.

"Micah, are you okay son?" Pamela knocked on the door.

"I'm good Ma', I will be out in a second."

"Okay." Pamela said making her way back to the living room.
As soon as Micah heard his mother walk down the hallway he exited the bathroom and went into his room to change clothes before heading to the living room to answer his mother's questions

"What happen? You had a lot of blood on your shirt? I hope you didn't hurt somebody Micah,"

Pamela questioned looking Micah over for any signs of him being the one hurt.

"Nothing Ma, it was just a little confusion, I'm good," Micah stated as his eyes was glued on the text message he had just received from Kym. "I got something to take care of; I will be back in a few hours."

"Aye, drop me off at Kym house. I gotta' get something from her," Sin asked following behind Micah.

"I don't have time, I'm running late and I'm not going that way," Micah replied quickly. He was trying to hurry and get out the house before Sin, refused to take no for an answer.

"Fuck it, I will call her ass and have her swoop me up," Sin said.

"Cool," Micah said walking out the door. He knew he would already have the money by the time Kym picked Sin up.

Land of Snakes

TEN

Micah made it to Kym's in record timing. He spoke to her moments before he pulled up; she had the money and was on her way to the house. Like always, he parked on the side street and made his way into her building through the back door. Flipping the switch on Micah took a seat on the loveseat, and pulled the already twisted blunt from behind his ear, sparking it and waited for Kym to arrive. By the time he finished the blunt, Micah was high, and growing impatient. "Where the fuck is she at?" Micah said to himself out loud picking the phone up to call her, but received no answer. Micah leaned back on the couch. A knock at the door, startled him. He ignored it, Kym was known to sell a little weed from time to time; he knew they would eventually go away, if he didn't answer. Micah made his way into the kitchen to see what Kym had in the fridge, like always it was empty. The knocking only got louder. "They ass persistent," Micah laughed checking the time. It was a little pass 11 o'clock, and Kym still wasn't there.

"Kym!" Sin yelled as he banged on the door loudly. "Open the fucking door, I see your car outside," Sin sneered.

"How the fuck he get here so damn fast." Micah thought to himself. Until he realized, he had been waiting well over thirty minutes. Ducking off into the room he called Kym again, but, still no answer. He tried her three more times, and still there was no answer. Sin was still banging on the door, Micah knew at any moment he was going to take the door off the hinges and barge his way in. Micah opened Kym's closet to retrieve the bag he put in there earlier. Micah almost shitted bricks, he closed the closet door then opened it again, hoping his eyes were playing tricks on him. The closet was empty, not even a hanger left on the hook.

"Fuck!" Micah yelled as he paced the floor, almost in tears. His phone began to vibrate in his pocket. It was Kym. "Where in the fuck are you at? This nigga Sin beating on your damn door like he the fucking police, and all your shit is gone?" Micah didn't care if Sin heard him, he needed that money.

"I can't do this shit anymore Micah. I'm out," Kym said into the phone.

"What the fuck you mean you can't do this? Do what? Where the fuck is the money Kym? I told you I needed that money," Micah roared into the phone.

"I'm keeping the money Micah. Charge it to the game. You weren't loyal to your brother and you my darling just got JACKED!" Kym laughed into the phone before hanging up in Micah's face. Kym sat next to her girl Shira, as their flight prepared for take-off to their next destination, Atlanta. Sin didn't know, but all along Kym was only after his stash. It was known that Sin was young wild and paid. When he got sentenced, she made it her duty to link up with him, like so many other men in her past. She devoted time, loyalty and dedication to them, and eventually she got full access to all their loot.

Land of Snakes

Micah was only collateral damage, for her. He
was making a little money, and broke her off
nicely. He always brought back more money, than
she let him hold, from Sin's stash. Plus, he knew
how to lay the pipe, but he was soft, too soft for
her. He didn't see any of the signs she threw
around. For Kym and her crew money was their
only love, and where their loyalty lied. Men just
supplied the cash and dick.

Micah felt sick, he had gotten played and now his
life was on the line. Pulling himself together, he
exited the same way he came. Sin must have left,
because the banging at the door had stopped.
Micah got to the back of the apartment and from
a distance he saw Sin's shadow staggering
towards him around the back of the apartment
complex not wanting to be seen, Micah quickly
ducked behind a parked car, until Sin passed and
then made a run to the front entrance. Making
sure the coast was clear, Micah ran to his car. He
only knew two places he could get that kind of
money from. Checking under the seat, to make
sure his gun was there, he sped off.

■■

Rich, and his crew which consisted of other
member of his football team, staggered down the
pathway leading into the bowling alley. They
captivated the attention of every young girl
nearby.

"Rich," Donte called out. "Look at all these honies checking us out." He beamed smiling at the flock of young girls.

"I see them', check out the dark skin one, in the skirt. Baby sexy ass fuck," Rich chuckled his eyes dancing around a slender dark chocolate girl clad in a short pin stripped skirt, and a half tank, that stood in front of the flock of girls.

"Great game Rich," The dark skin girl spoke in a soft tone, with a grin plastered on her face. Rich hadn't seen her around, because if he had, she would have already been his. He was well known with the ladies. Rich stood 5'11 with a well tamed stocky frame, hazel bedroom eyes and a perfect wide smile. Two deep dimples complemented his honey brown sugar skin tone. Even with the two inch scar, on his face Rich was handsome, and every young girls dream boyfriend. Pamela made sure to check the young girls at the door. Rich was to keep his head in the books and focus on football. She refused to let him be another statistic of young athlete, getting a young girl knocked up because she saw him as a meal ticket. He was the only one amongst his siblings to be on the right track, and Pamela was proud, and would make sure he continued the path all the way.

"Thank you gorgeous, what's your name? I haven't seen you around these parts. You must be new around here?" Rich asked. His eyes glazed at her slender waist and small round assets.

"The name is Sydney, and yes I am new around here. I just moved down from Richmond."

Land of Snakes

"Bay area huh?"

"Born and raised, up until now," She beamed.

"Well Welcome to LA Sydney. What are you lovely ladies getting into tonight? Rich questioned noticing the girls who were once standing behind Sydney were now occupying his crew's attention.

"Whatever you have planned," She smiled coming closer to Rich biting her bottom lip that was glazed with shiny mac lip glass.
The sexy glare in her eyes, which danced around him, let Rich know she wanted him, and that was what he intended to give her. With a boyish grin, Rich through his arm around her neck, pulling her close to him, as they made their way through the entrance of the bowling alley.

"Good game Rich! Can't wait to see you on the college field! Keep it up!" Patrons hollered out as Rich and his crew walked through the bowling alley beaming with pride. Rich was the communities football champ and hood celebrity. Not only was he a beast on the field, he was the baby brother of the notorious Sin the menace who many feared. It didn't take long for the fun to begin; the young teens occupied 4 of the 10 lanes. Pizza and drinks flowed commentary of the owner, who was a big fan of Rich and the communities football team. He had also just won a hefty amount on Rich's win tonight.

Sydney sat on Rich's lap, lightly she grinded on his manhood, trying to get a rise out of him. Neither of them was concerned with the game, letting others take their turns, as they were engaged in idle conversation. Rich was digging Sydney, and the way she toyed with his manhood, to the music being played. He grinned listening to her talk, as he ran his hands through her silky thick long mane, as he planted soft kisses on her earlobe. Skillful in the pleasing department, Rich knew most girls' tender spot was located there, and he aimed to please. The way Sydney squirmed with every touch of his lips. Rich smiled. It worked every time. He knew he was getting lucky tonight, she loved it. Sydney had gotten, Rich beyond excited, anticipating a travel between her thighs. When they felt no one was looking Rich and Sydney ventured off to the darken area of the bowling alley, where the arcades were located. At a certain time they closed that section off.

Sydney fumbled with the zipper on Rich's pants, as their tongues lip locked with each other. Freeing his manhood from his briefs Sydney gently stroked his semi-erect penis until he was rock hard. Dropping to her knees, Sydney wasted no time slurping him into the contours of her warm dampen mouth. Rich had received plenty of head in his day, but none like the head Sydney was giving him. The way Sydney maneuvered her tongue up and down his manhood had him weak in the knees. Sydney sucked and slurped until she felt the warm liquid release from Rich's penis coating her tongue. With a smile on her face, she used her hands, jerking on his manhood until he sprang back into action. Standing back to her feet, she lifted her skirt up pulling her lace thong to the side. With a smile on her face, she leaned over the arcade. Making sure she put a deep arch in her back, and throwing her ass into the air. Rich went into his pocket pulling out a gold wrapper, cracking the seal, he slide the condom onto his manhood. He grinned as he eased his head into her entrance. Releasing a soft moan, as her wetness welcome him. Gripping her around the waist, he slid in and out of her, loving the warm tight fit around his penis. Sydney wasn't like the other girls he fucked, she was sexual skilled. She winded her hips with every pump Rich gave her. It didn't take long for Rich to feel the pressure rising to the head of his manhood. Rich whiled out a loud moan, as his semen begged to be released. With one final pump, Rich was ready to release. A loud noise from behind him stopped him.

"We busy over here," Rich said without looking back trying to release his nut. Sydney still was throwing her ass back on his dick.
A sharp pain came across Rich's head down to his back.

"What the fuck?" Rich yelled turning around pissed off. He didn't see anyone. "Who in the hell playing fucking games?" He questioned. No one said anything.

"C'mon baby, I'm tryna get my nut in," Sydney said tugging at Rich's arm.

"Somebody hit me with something." Rich said rubbing his head.

"Who?"

"Shit, I don't know." Rich said walking further into the distance expecting one of his friends to jump out laughing. Playing some sick joke on him. Rich didn't see anyone so he walked back to where Sydney was. Out of nowhere, Rich was struck with a punch to the side of his face, which caused him to stumble. The attacker tried to deliver another blow, but Rich was faster. Rich couldn't see a face, but was prepared to not let whomever it was, get the best of him.

"What the fuck?" Sydney yelled.

"Shut up, bitch!" A deep voice yelled snatching Sydney.

"Let me go," She yelled.
Rich heard Sydney's voice, but it began to sound distance.

"Sydney?" He called out.

"Ani't no Sydney here," A male voice spoke. It was deep and strong.

"Who are you?"

"Don't worry," The voice said. Rich didn't know what happen but, several blows from several hands landed all over him, instantly dropping his body.

"My brother's gone kill you. Whoever the fuck you punk ass niggas are," Rich yelled balling into the fetal position. He could feel the blow and kicks, all over his body. Unable to withstand the pain, Rich passed out.

Land of Snakes

ELEVEN

Sin was beyond furious, it was passed 11 o'clock and Kym wasn't answering the door. So he decided to stagger around to the back of the apartment complex, hoping to get in through her side door. Sin climbed the gate jumping onto Kym's patio. He slide the unlocked glass patio door open. Breaking the flimsy lock on the screen door, Sin stepped into Kym's bedroom. His eyes darted around the room. The room was empty besides the bed. Micah had left the empty closet open, letting Sin see that all of her clothes were gone.

Sin made his way into the living room. An eerie feeling lie in the pit of Sin's stomach something wasn't right, and he could feel it. The fresh smell of weed and the burnt end of the blunt in the ashtray that was still warmed, caused Sin to quickly scan the apartment for any signs of Kym or another man being there, or had been there moments before. Sin searched the house until he found the cordless phone lying on the breakfast nook in the kitchen. Rushing to it, he quickly push the talk button, the strong sound of the dial tone blared in his ear. Sin dialed Kym's number so fast; he had to look at the number to make sure he dialed it right. With each ring of Kym's phone the feeling in Sin's stomach doubled.

"Micah damn now you calling from my house phone? What part don't you fucking get? You got played nigga. Stop acting like a pussy. Man the fuck up, and charge it to the game. Leave my apartment fucking clown." Kym spat. She

97

knew how Micah felt about her, but she didn't feel anything about him.

"Micah?" Sin questioned. "Bitch this Sin. What the fuck you and my brother got going on?" Sin questioned looking at the phone like he had missed something. "Kym where in the hell are you at? And where the fuck is my money?" Sin barked.

Kym paused for a moment hearing Sin's voice on the phone. "Ha-ha," Kym laughed loudly. "Just the nigga I been waiting to hear from. Hey boo, sorry to inform you, but this my money now."

"Bitch! I'm not playing with you. Don't make me break yo' fucking neck. I better get my money in a fucking hour," Sin blared into the phone.

"That's real cute but, like I told your punk ass brother. This is my money now bitch. You and your brother got JACKED! Oh yeah, and I've been fucking your brother, too. His dick game got you beat by a long shot. I'm going to miss that nigga eating my pussy until I bust all over his face. Have a good life Sintrell, and try not to go back to prison," Kym laughed spitefully before hanging the phone up in Sin's face. She had been waiting for his call. Kym was hoping he would call before the plane took off, so that she could disconnect the phone before left, leaving all of California behind her.

"It's done, he still inside," Kym said with a grin wide as the pacific ocean as she powered off the phone and prepared to head to ATL to do damage.

Land of Snakes

Sin was stuck, cradling the phone in his hand; he couldn't believe what just happen to him. All the time he had hustled on the streets, and instilled fear in men, he got stiffed by a bitch. Sin was lost in a daze; He knew if he ever got his hands on Kym she was dead. He would kill her with his bare hands and watch life slip from her. Sin hung the phone up, and prepared to exit Kym's apartment. The phone rang which called him to stop. Thinking it was Kym calling back, Sin rushed to answer it. "Stop playing with me bitch, I want my money and I want my shit now."
A loud laughter roared into his ear. It wasn't Kym's voice, but a male voice, and it sounded so familiar.

"Who the fuck is this?" Sin question.

"It's the nigga behind your stick up," The voice spat into the phone.
Sin stood puzzled by what was really going on. He knew the raspy voice from somewhere, but couldn't place it. "Lucius?" He questioned.

"Charge it to the game big timer," He laughed. Lucius was a cell mate of Sin's for the last two years of his sentence he was released six months prior to Sin. He was the one who introduced him to Kym, as his cousin. Sin had looked out for Lucius when they were inside.
Sin looked at the phone; he knew his ears had to be playing tricks on him. He knew the once pussy ass nigga he had rescue from becoming someone's bitch, and helped couldn't be playing him like this. The loud sound of gun fire rang in Sin's ear as bullets whizzed passed him. Ducking

for cover, Sin reached in his pants for his gun, and began firing shots back, trying to protect his life. He was happy he decided to reload another full clip before leaving the house. The way the shots came rapidly, Sin knew that his life was what they wanted. Sin didn't stop firing shots, as he made his way towards the patio trying to exit, before the police came. Going back to jail wasn't in his future, and neither was dying. Sin didn't bother closing up Kym's apartment. Exiting the back way he crept through the back streets trying to stay low key. He was in another hood, and was a walking target for an enemy who wanted him. "Stupid Bitch!" He yelled. "Fuck," Sin was pissed. He kept looking over his shoulder as he took hasty strides his hand laid on his gun in his pants. He didn't know who all was against him, and not being in his own hood, he didn't feel safe.

****

Micah gripped his steering wheel weaving in and out of traffic speeding to his destination. Reaching his block, he cut off his lights; as he drove pass his target. Parking a few blocks from Turks trap, Micah clad in a hoodie with the hood pulled over his face walked the back streets to where Turks spot sat on the corner. With his held down Micah pounded on the door, like all the fiends did. Turks little worker, Badass cracked the door half open. "What you need?" He questioned not really looking at Micah.

Land of Snakes

"Let me get a dime," Micah said low, with his head still down, not trying to make eye contact.

"Give me a second," The worker said closing the door to retrieve the drugs requested. Micah gripped the gun tucked in his pocket glanced around him, waiting for the worker to come back. The door crack opened the worker stuck his hand out the door. Micah looked around once more. When he saw the coast was clear, he pushed the door open. "Give me everything in the safe," Micah yelled aiming the gun at the young workers head.

"Nigga you sure you want to do this? Turk get word of this you a dead man," The worker spat, his hands in the air. "He already don't like yo' pussy ass Micah. I know only your dumb ass would try to hit Turk's spot,"

"Fuck you and Turk. Just walk me to the safe and pray I will let yo' little ass live." Micah yelled pulling the hood from over his head. The worker walk over to the safe logged the code into the system it popped open. Micah smiled as he saw the stacks of money and product inside.

"Here." Micah said handing him a bag. "Put all of it in here,"
The worker gritted his teeth as he whispered something under his breath. Getting on his knees he packed each stack of money in the bag, followed by the ten bricks of coke they had left in the safe. Standing to his feet he threw the bag at Micah's feet. With a smile on his face Micah bent down to retrieve the bag only to stand back up to the barrel of a gun looking him back in the face.

"You didn't think I was just about to let you walk up out of here with all the money and work did you?" Badass questioned.

"I didn't think shit nigga. Because I knew I was walking out of here with all this shit," Micah spat squeezing the trigger firing a shot right in Badass head, killing him instantly. Micah smiled at the quick and actual shot. He had never hit his intended target, like that before. Micah rushed out the door; briskly he walked down the street to his car. He knew he didn't have much time to count the money and make it to Gators. He didn't know where to go, Kym's spot was out of the question, and his home was playing it to close, being he had just robbed the complex two apartments down. Micah headed to the snotty fox, a motel that rented room's by the hour. Booking the room for an hour, Micah spilled all the contents from the bag onto the bed and began to count the money. Micah had paid attention to Turks operation. He knew Turk bundled his money in five thousands sequences. That shorted down the time for Micah and not having to count every single bill in the seven bundles. It took Micah a little over ten minutes to count the loose change. Add all the money up Micah sighed only coming up with thirty- nine thousand dollars. He was eleven thousand shy of what he owed Gator. And that didn't count for the sudden interest Gator wanted. Micah knew if he could move the bricks he took, he could make an easy twenty-five grand. Which would be enough to pay Gator, and some change on the side for his

Land of Snakes

self .Throwing the money and product back into the bag Micah checked the time and he had less than ten minutes to make it to the boogie joint. Micah was nervous as he whipped the car down the Los Angeles streets. His palms were sweaty; he was ready to be over with Gator. The last year had been hell trying to pay Gator back. Micah arrived at the boogie joint right at twelve he tried to calm his nerves. He knew he had most of the money and Gator was all about his business, so taking the product as payment, should have been equal. Micah thought as he walked inside. He knew Gator wasn't still in the drug game, but knew plenty of people who were still in heavy. Bishop stood at the door, waiting for Micah's arrival. "About time," Bishop said stopping Micah from walking passed him. He didn't like Micah. He knew Micah was shady, everything about Micah told him so.

"What? I'm tryna' get this shit handled with Gator." Micah glared.

"Not before I shake you down. Then I will escort you back there to see Gator.

"What? Now I need to be shook down and escorted?" Micah questioned annoyed. He had been coming in and out the joint for years, and never did he have to be searched, and escorted.

"Just shut the fuck up," Bishop said searching Micah and the bag he was carrying. When Bishop was finished patting Micah down for any weapons, he led him to Gator's office. Normally Micah was allowed to roam freely around the boogie joint. Tonight was different, and that scared Micah.

"Gator, this nigga Micah here," Bishop, spoke in a deep tone, slightly opening the door.

"Give me a few moments, and then send him in," Gator replied finishing up with the young chick that was occupying his office space with him.

"Come in Micah." Gator called out, as the young chick walked passed Micah. "See you later," The women said.

Micah walked into the office, taking a seat in the chair across from Gator, he sat the bag at his feet.

"So you got all my money?" Gator questioned peering at Micah.

"I got your money….but I don't have it all. I wasn't able to move the rest of the product, I had a little family situation to handle," Micah spoke.

"I guess you didn't understand me earlier. I said I wanted all of my money, and I wanted it today."

"Gator it's a little more than half of your money in this bag, plus some product." Micah spoke.

"And what am I going to do with that, I don't deal with drugs anymore. Just money, and you owe me that, and I want my money. The same money I gave you."

"Gator give me a few more days to have Sin move this product, you know Sin good for it. He already has a few deals in place," Micah spoke. He knew it was a lie, but Gator would trust that Sin could flip the bricks for the money.

Land of Snakes

"So Sin is going to move the product for you?" Gator chuckled. Since Sin was a little boy, he had hustled the blocks like the men twice his age. Hustling was in his blood, Gator knew Sin would move the product in no time, it was just he didn't trust Micah. Something told him Sin didn't even know what was going on. Gator sat in his chair, leaning back; he studied Micah face, and the fear that spilled off of him. Gator conspired on killing him where he stood. He was dead weight in the streets, and a coward who pretended to be something in wasn't, trying to follow in his brothers footsteps.

■■■

Sin was beyond furious to know he had been set up the whole time, and that his own blood was fucking his bitch behind his back. With most of the money he had left to his name gone, Sin felt sick, he knew he would have to dive back into the streets, fast and hard. He had money stashed, but it wasn't enough. He had to move his mother out of the hood, and what he had stashed somewhere else wasn't enough to cut it. The streets of LA were about to get real. Sin was on a mission, gun tucked in his pants he walked the twenty something blocks from Kym's house back to his mother's crib. As soon as Sin hit the block, a swarm of people headed his way, Turk leading the pack. From the glare in his eyes, Sin knew Turk was pissed.

Nisha Lanae

"Sin chu' where yo' brother at?" Turk question clinching his semi- automatic in his hand. Murder lye in his eyes.

"What's good? What you looking for my brother for?" Sin questioned looking from Turks gun, and clinched jaws. He knew Turk well enough to know, he was in murderous mode.

"Cuh' yo' brother ran in my spot, took all my dough, my work and killed my little worker."

"You sure? Who told you that? That don't sound like some shit Micah would do."

"My shit may look like a dump, but I got that bitch fully covered with surveillance. And I have your brother on camera coming into my shit and splitting little dude wig back."

"Let me see this camera," Sin said despite him and Micah bumping heads and the latest news he found out, he wasn't about to let anyone dead his brother, that was out the question. Weather he did it or not.

Sin followed Turk inside a small room in the trap house. A CCTV system showed every angel of the inside and outside of the house. Turk hit a button and there Micah was on the screen blowing the young dudes head off. Sin was at lost for words, a small part of him beamed with pride that his little brother had some gangsta in him. Another part of him hated how sloppy his brother moved, to close to home and not doing proper homework on the trap. Now his life was in jeopardy, as well as his families, and that didn't sit well with him at all.

Land of Snakes

"You know he can't walk these streets without feeling some heat for this shit. Brother or not, I have a name to keep, and a connect who gone want his money. So I ask you man to man where is your brother with my shit?" Turk asked,

"I don't know where my brother is, but let me find out what the fuck is going on. I will get with you in a little bit," Sin said walking out the door. Checking the time he knew exactly where he could find his brother. *What the fuck have you gotten yourself into Micah?*" Sin questioned out loud to himself, as he paced down the street looking for anyone who could give him a lift to Gator's spot.

"Sin!" A female voice called out from behind him. Sin turned around cautiously. His hand clashed on his gun tucked in his pants with everything going on around him, Sin didn't trust anyone. It was Keisha, a local fiend who he grew up with.

"What's good with it?" Sin said walking the short distance back up to her.

"You got some blow?" She asked scratching her matted hair. So much had changed about her Sin found it hard to look at her. She had five kids with five different men, who all didn't stick around to see the baby be born. Keisha was so hooked; she would take any drug she could get her hands on. Growing up, she was the smartest in the school, and gave them hope that some could make it out the hood.

"I'm out. but, see if you can get yo' mom's car and run me to Gator's I got twenty for you,"

107

"Okay," Keisha said as she briskly walked the short distance to her apartment where she lived with her five kids, three siblings and her mother. It didn't take long before Keisha came trotting back out the house, her mother's keys in hand. "C'mon Sin," She yelled walking to her mother's beat down 1987 Honda Civic.

Grapping the keys from her, Sin made his way to the driver's side of the car. "I'm driving," He spoke jumping in and roaring the engine before driving like a mad man. His mind was on finding his brother before someone planted a bullet in his skull. Pulling the cell phone, out his pocket he quickly dialed Gia's number. "Stay in the house tonight, and don't answer the door for nobody, everyone who lives there, has a key." Sin spat into the phone. Hanging up, without letting Gia pleaded, or ask any questions.

Turk had a feeling that Sin knew where to find Micah. So when he saw him pull off the block, he knew he would lead him to where Micah was. Although Sin was a real nigga from the street, his blood was thicker than any nigga in the street, and he wasn't going to knowingly lead death to his brother.

■■■■■■■■■■■■■■■■■■■■■■■■■■■■■■■■■■■■

"Let me see this work you have?" asked Gator looking at Micah, he really wanted to laugh at how sad Micah was.

Land of Snakes

Micah picked the bag up from where it sat at his feet, and sat it on Gators desk as he removed one of the tightly wrapped brick out the bag.

As soon as Gator saw the packaging he knew Micah was a dead man. Many didn't know he was still heavy in the drug game, he now operated as the connect to some of Los Angeles heavy hitters, including a small timer like Turk. Even Micah, purchased his product from Gator, he just didn't know it. The naked women plastered on the front was his signature, Black Angel was the name of the product straight from the broader of Punta canna in the Dominic republic.

"And where did you say you got this product from again? Gator pulled the pocket knife he was known to carry around out his pocket, slicing a nice size hole into the package he dabbled his hand in the tiny whole he formed. "This looks like some good quality of work, pure."

"From my mans, and yeah the fiends love it," Micah said not really caring, he just needed Gator off of his back.

"And what's ya' man's name?" Gator quizzed

"Why? That's not important right now. All that is important to me, is settling my debt with you," Micah shifted in his seat looking down at his watch.

"Got somewhere to be?" Gator asked noticing Micah constantly glancing down at his watch.

"Yeah I got some shit to do and pick up a few people. So are we done here?"

"Sydney!" Gator yelled. A tall slender beauty emerged from a door to the left of Micah.

"What's good?" She spoke making her way towards Gator; she stood behind him as her eyes connected with Micah's, a small grin forming across her face.

Micah sat stunned glazing at Sydney. He had met her a few months back at a strip club in Vegas, where she was working at the time. After fucking off and on while he was in town for business she let him know she was in need of some extra cash. Micah agreed to let her run a few errands for him, making a few drops. So that she could make some quick and easy cash. In the midst of a drop, she got held at gun point, and robbed. Needing some money to pay the connect who threaten to kill him; he turned to Gator for a loan. Micah knew Gator, was the only one in town to have that kind of money on deck. From the moment the money touched Micah's hand, Gator had been all over him. Especially when he found out Micah had a huge gambling addiction, and was losing money he owed him all over town; Gator became a pain in Micah's side. It was all becoming clearer to him, from the start he was set up. Here he was trying to get over on his own flesh, and hadn't noticed he was getting played the whole time. Micah moved so reckless to even see the signs that were written on the walls, he was to naïve to see between any lines written.

Gator sat behind his oak wood desk grinning. He told Micah he was moving sloppy. He was too busy trying to fill Sin shoes, but was failing horribly at it. He was too vexed on trying to be better than Sin; he didn't see the trail of mistakes he was making. The drug game wasn't for everyone, and Micah didn't have it, he was filled with hate and too greedy for street fame, just to be recognized.

"I told you little nigga, I run fucking LA. What I say goes; you can't deal on these streets and not give me my cut. Everyone has to pay dues," Gator chuckled.

"So meeting you wasn't a coincidence huh? Nor was the fucking robbery?" Micah could feel his blood boiling. As he stared at Sydney, killing her several times, with his eyes. "You set me up because I didn't pay yo' fat ass no fucking dues on streets I'm hustling?" Micah questioned Gator. When the word had come from inside that Micah had been given the green light to run the block. Gator had a sit down with him. Gator offered Micah, a referral to a connect with super low prices, for Grade A product. Micah declined after Gator, told him he wanted a monthly percentage from his business.

Sydney smiled. "No, not at all. It was all a part of the plan, but it was fun while it lasted, you're a good fuck, that's about it," She laughed "So is your brother. You are weak, you told me too much about you, too easily. Boasting doesn't always make you look good, sometimes it gets you set up."

"So I guess you on Sin, dick to huh bitch?" Micah spat. "Just like the rest of these bitches."

Sydney just grinned as Micah, grilled her.
Walking back towards the door she came from,
she stuck her head in and whispered something
to someone.

"See, I have the powers to make
motherfuckas' lives crumble. You didn't want to
give me my cut, so I shut you down, and in return
you came crawling, just like a bitch right to me.
In need of my help, the same person you refused
to pay your dues to, so yeah, I fucked you raw in
the ass, just like the bitch that you are." Gator
chuckled.

The sound of the door opening made Micah look
to see who was coming into the office. It was
Sydney, followed by another man, Micah hadn't
seen before. He was carrying a body over his
shoulders. All Micah could see was the shoes of
the man, he was carrying. "I'm talking about this
brother," She smiled. As the man sat Rich's badly
beaten body on the ground.

Land of Snakes

TWELVE

Sin was filled with fury, he hadn't been home a full twenty-four hours and his life was spiraling out of control, and he was trying to clean up Micah's mess. A woman he trusted, turned on him, and stole every dime he had to his name, so she taught. On top of that, his brother had been creeping with her. His mother was being sexual violated by her apartment manager, and inside he knew she was dying. They day seemed surreal, but it was reality. Throwing the car in park, Sin quickly jumped out the car throwing two crumbled twenty dollar bills on the seat. He rushed off without saying a single word to Keisha. The Boogie joint was always so live, day and night. But, tonight it was dead zone, and that gave Sin an ill feeling. Using a solid fist, Sin pounded hard on the metal double bolted door. Darby, who was Gator's right hand man, pushed the door open. "I heard they finally let your little crazy ass up out the joint," Darby chuckled.

"Shit you know how that goes, they can't hold a real one down for too long. Where that nigga Gator at? I need to holler at him about something.

"He should be in the back, waiting on your brother to show up," Darby said looking at his watch for the time. "I just walked in, so I can't really call it. But, aye Micah, He into some deep shit, with that nigga Gator."

"That's why I am here. I'm about to head back and holler at him. If Micah show up, tell him go to my spot, lay low, I got it. Just don't go home," Sin said hoping he could dead any issue with Gator, and then handle the issue with Turk before either one of them killed his brother.

"Alright, I will be back there in a second. I gotta' call my young tender, an old-timer need a re-up of that sweet stuff," Darby smiled, digging into his pocket for his phone.

"You still haven't changed a bit," Sin joked as he made his way towards the back.

Sin knew exactly where Gator's office was located. He had got his start in the drug game being a watch out for one of Gators men. Sin quickly made a name for himself and moving his rank up in the operation after planting a bullet in a undercover who was threating to shut their operation down, and taking money out his pockets. It solidified his position in the organization at the tender age of 11, and he had been loyal and dedicated even during his bid inside since then. Sin, was one of those, naturally born for the lifestyle.

As Sin neared Gators office, he reminisced on all the blood that had been shed, between the walls. All the drugs, that followed through the place, and the thousands of dollars they brought in weekly.

Micah couldn't control the anger that was quickly rising. Gator had fucked him, and fucked him hard and raw. With his elbows resting on his knees, his head feel into his hands. He didn't know what he had gotten himself into when he turned down Gator. Micah eyes feel to the floor. His stomach felt like it had dropped to the bottom of his stomach at how badly beaten Rich was. Grapping the gun that he had tucked in his timberlands, that Bishop didn't search. Micah jumped up with the gun in his hand.

"This shit was between you and I. why you bring my brother into this?" Micah roared tears streaming down his face.

"It's all a part of the game. You didn't pay me, so you pay with family. Didn't Sin, teach you this part of the game?"

Micah tears dried up quickly. A devious grin formed on his face. He had nothing to lose. Sin and his mother would hate him for pulling Rich into his mess. "So you pay with yours too," Micah said as he pulled the trigger, a bullet piercing Sydney in the head. Her body weakly dropped, hitting Gator's desk.

"Sydney! You killed my daughter," Gator jumped from his desk reaching for his gun, but Micah was faster. Planting a bullet into Gators, bum knee making him stumble back.

"It's all a part of the game, you fat bastard," Micah yelled. "You fucked me, so fuck you, its payback."

The sound of Micah's voice, followed by the sound of a gun brought Sin back to reality. "Fuck!" He yelled rushing to the office praying Gator hadn't already killed his brother.

Micah heard the door agar, not knowing who was entering Micah fired a shot at the door, he didn't pay attention to who had entered, assuming it was one of Gator's henchmen. Until the loud sound of a very familiar voice yelled.

"Micah!" Sin shouted ducking for cover seeing his brother standing there firing shots at him.

"What the fuck are you doing here?" Micah questioned. Seeing Sin ducked behind the door.

"I'm here looking for you, to save yo' ass. That nigga Turk looking for you, you hit his spot, and killed his mans. The nigga has everything on camera," Sin spat.

"Fuck Turk, that nigga tried to take over while I was down, but that shit all over now. I am the man and I'm gone claim my streets back. These niggas gon' know me, and respect me."

"You sound real fucking dumb, this nigga is out to fucking kill you. All I know is no one in my family better get wrapped up in your bullshit" Sin yelled coming from behind the door, almost losing his footing. Sin glanced at the floor, seeing what almost caused him to fall, and froze seeing Rich's face, beaten so badly. "What the fuck happen to Rich? Micah who did this?" Sin questioned frantically rushing to his brother aide. Rich had a faint pulse. His eyes had been beaten close, and his face was now the size of a bowling ball. The flimsy way his legs laid Sin, knew that he to be broken.

"What the fuck have you done? You stupid motherfucka', look at Rich?" Sin yelled cupping his brother into his arms.

"I don't know. ...I don't know man. This bitch brought him out here like that." Micah paced the floor; he didn't know how he would explain that to his mother. Rich was the only one out of his siblings and himself to actual be doing

Land of Snakes

something good with their life. Walking over to the other side of the desk, Gator lay on his side, the wound to his upper thigh made it hard for him to move his pudgy frame around.

"You tried to kill my brother motherfucka' and know I have to explain that to my mother. What's the code to the safe?" Micah questioned. He knew Gator had a wad of money in his safe.

"Really? Sin yelled. "You worried about fucking money!? This nigga Turk has a bounty on your head and our little brother is lying here fucking dying! And your selfish ass worried about money. I could kill yo' ass myself," Sin spat trying to pick up Rich's body to get him to the hospital.

"Fuck you," Micah spat. "You always thinking your better than the next nigga, Fuck you. That's why I was spending your money and fucking yo' bitch, while your ass focused on not becoming some niggas bitch," Micah spat, focusing his attention back on Gator.

"What is the code to the fucking safe?" Micah questioned, the .45 in his hand aimed at Gator.

"You should really listen to your brother, and stop trying to be better than him. You are not Sin and you will never be. You just don't have it Micah," Gator laughed. Mind fucking Micah, he knew Micah couldn't stand the fact he wasn't respect on the level that Sin was.

"Fuck you!" Micah yelled firing several shots into Gator's body.
Sin managed to get Rich's heavy body up, and

over his shoulder. The dead weight of his body made him heavier then he actually was. Getting him steady on his shoulder, Sin walked out of Gators office leaving Micah alone. He needed to get his baby brother some medical attention before it was too late. Micah would have to survive on his own, he no longer was Sin's concern, Rich needed him more.

Micah searched Gator's office looking for the safe; he knew it was one in there. After ten minutes, he couldn't find it, he gave up. Taking everything dollar Gator had in his pocket Micah griped the bag he came in with. He made his way towards the front; he had to find Turk, before he found him.

Sin got to the front of the Boogie joint, and looked for Darby to see if he could give him a ride to the hospital. Not seeing him inside, Sin prepared to head outside to look for him. When he felt his phone vibrate in his pocket, Sin stopped to answer. "Hey Baby, what time are you coming? A female voice said.

"I'm tied up right now." Sin said walking out the boogie joint. "I will call you once I get to the hospital."

"Are you good?" The women asked.

"Yeah it's my little brother." Sin said struggling to get out the door without dropping Rich. Sin stepped foot outside and was met with Turks deadly glare.

"So now you are following me Cuh'?" Sin questioned.

Land of Snakes

Turk had been sitting out front since he pulled up after Sin waiting for him to leave, he knew Micah owed Gator a large sum of money and possible could be there, and if not, he knew Sin would eventually lead him to him. "I stepped to you like a man. Your brother broke code, and for that he has to pay."

"And you think I'm just gone hand you his head on a silver platter?"

"Yo' bid got you getting soft on these streets, Big Homey. You know the rules. They don't change because it's yo' family," Turk said, his nine sitting on his lap, as he sat on the hood of his car.

"I've been real, since the day my mother spit me out her womb. Ani't no bitch in me, only thing soft is my dick right now. I'm still that nigga, the one who put you on, when no one wanted to fuck with you. The one who laced your pockets when your mother's only care was looking for her next high, and whose dick she could suck to get it," Sin sneered. He could feel his temper escalating rapidly. He knew the codes of the streets, and had played by them most of his life, but when it came to his family he didn't give a fuck about the code of the streets. His blood, bleed Jones; and that's were where his loyalty would lie. If anyone was going to be killing Micah, it would be him. Turk sat on the hood of his Audi tightly clinching the nine in his hand. He studied Sin, his mentor and a dude who looked out for him when he was hungry, laced his pockets with more dough then he would've ever saw in his young 19 years of life. Sin had looked out for him, like no one ever did. Sin had bought him shoes, when the sole on his had more holes then Swiss cheese and put clothes on his back. Turk saw Sin as being weak, no longer was he the cold-hearted man he knew before his bid. It didn't matter who it was, they broke code of the streets, and they had to be dealt with. Sin always instilled that in him; know he was going back on his own words. Micah went against the grain, in Turk's eyes the only feasible punishment was death, a life for a life. Turk knew the smug Sin wore, was the one of death. To get to Micah, he would have to kill Sin as well, because if not; Sin would sure kill him.

"So how you want to play this Turk?" Sin questioned.

"Ya' brother dying tonight cuh'. There is no other way to say it, when I see him, I'm pushing that nigga wig back," Turk spat, death looming in his dark eyes.

"Well, if my brother dying tonight so are you," Sin blurted sitting Rich's body down on the ground. Sin stuffed his phone in his pocket, pulling his gun out. He knew at any second Micah was going to walk out the door. And shit would get real.

"Then that's some shit I will have to live with. But, Micah, he gone feel these hot bullets." Turks said holding his .9 in the air.

Micah was in another world, thinking of how he would get Turk and Sin, out the way. He wanted to own the streets, and they wouldn't embrace him if Turk and Sin were alive. "This shit gone be easier than I thought," He spoke as he witness

Land of Snakes

Turk and Sin standing with guns in hands and deadly scowls on their face. With the gun in his hand, he walked outside. "So which one of you nigga want to go first?"

"Micah what in the fuck are you doing?" Sin questioned puzzled.

"What the fuck it look like? The streets are mine, and you two niggas are the only ones standing in my way.

"So what? You gone kill me?" Sin questioned.

"Fuck you. You always thinking you better Sin, you not better. You not shit, but a fucking jail bird. You should've just stayed in fuckin' jail," Micah blurted as he waved his gun between Sin and Turk. "All my life I had to be compared to you, about everything. I'm tired of walking in your shadow.

"I've never thought I was better Micah. You thought I was better. I gave the streets my blessings to let you carry the torch, and run the streets, but you failed. You failed because you thought you were better than me, then just simply being you. You can never be me Micah, there is only one me, and you should've tried to only be you. You stole from me, when I would've given you my last. You fucked my bitch; and they say blood thicker than water. My brother the fucking snake slowly slithering in the grass, waiting to fucking bite me with a deadly mouth," Sin spoke never raising his voice, but the malice laced around his words could be felt. He was hurt, that his own brother hated him so much.

His eyes told Micah so. "You're my fucking brother. I would've killed another nigga for bring any of the bullshit you have brought to our front door."

"You don't know how to run the streets Micah," Turk said with a slight chuckle that Micah was even entertaining the thoughts of being the king of the streets. "Sin, let me off this snake ass nigga, he a thorn in both of our sides."

"Shut the fuck up Turk. This shit is between me and my brother. If Micah dying tonight, I will be the only one pulling the trigger," Sin interjected.

Turk watched as the brother's ice grilled each other. Micah was the weaker of the two. With Micah wanting Sin dead too, it would be easier to knock Sin off first, since Micah wasn't a challenge.

"So what, you gone kill me big brother? Do it? How will you explain that to our mother? You know she think you a fuck up, anyway."

"You are a fucking snake Micah. Even as fucked up as you are, and all the fucked up shit you did, I wouldn't ever want to see ma' go through that pain, but you. You don't give a fuck about no one, but Micah. Look at our little brother," Sin pointed to Rich's slumped body. "He needs medical attention and you not worried about that. You worried about selling drugs and respect. That is why I am the better man Micah."

"Both of you niggas are weak, and no longer are needed on the streets." Turk said firing a shot, at Micah. Sin watched Micah's body hit the ground, and saw red. Before he could pull the trigger, a bullet pierced him in the shoulder, causing him to stumble and trip over Rich's body. Sin watched Turk move in closer to him, and when he got close. Sin fired several shots into his body.

"Fuck," Turk yelled stumbling back and landing on his car firing wild shots.
Micah checked himself for any signs of being shot, and found none. The bullets had missed him. Micah stood checking himself again, there still wasn't any signs of him being shot. Seeing Turk bent over his car, Micah rushed over to him. Standing over him, Micah locked eyes with him. Turk was losing a lot blood and had dropped his gun, he knew he was dying. "You should've stayed out of it, I will control these streets, you just won't be able to see me," Micah spoke. As he blew his brain out, brain matter splattered all over the car, and Micah's shirt.

"Micah!" Sin yelled from the ground firing several shots that whizzed passed Micah's head causing him to duck and returning several shots of his own. Micah stood, and trampled over a body, it was Darby.

"Whhhat?" Micah stuttered trying to make sense of how Darby was dead behind him, with bullets riddled to his back. When Micah looked down, he could see the blood gushy from Sin's mouth and the two nickel size hole into his chest. Sin was trying to warn Micah, that Darby was behind him, trying to kill him. Micah moved so fast, he didn't see where his bullets landed. He thought Sin, was trying to kill him. Micah rushed over to Sin.

"Youuu shot me," Sin managed to get out.

"That was an accident. I'm sorry about that," Micah kneeled down beside Sin.

"Fuck you Micah, you're a snake. You're not sorry, this was your intention. You wanted me dead.

"It was by accident. I thought you were shooting at me, not trying to protect me. You are right, I'm not sorry. It's only room for one of us at the top, and I'm tired of sharing it with you. Your time has expired big brother," Micah smiled preparing to leave Sin, lying right there in a pool of his blood to die.

"Micah," Sin called out weakly.

"Yeah," Micah replied.

"Let me tell you something. Come a little closer, so you can hear me. Clearly." Sin said using all his might to speak.
Micah kneeled back down, closer to Sin this time.

"Even in my death, you will still never be me. You will always walk behind me. Good luck you snake motherfucka', I'll always remain," Sin said coldly as he spat a glob of blood into Micah face.

"Remember there will always be a bigger snake, more deadly then you, waiting to bite." Micah wiped the blood from his face. "I'll be sure to remember that," He spoke coldly, raising his gun to Sin's head; he fired two shots killing his own brother. Micah stood and looked over to where Rich's body was he knew there wasn't much he could do for him, at that point. Micah

Land of Snakes

could hear the police sirens nearing. Grabbing
the bag he came with, he dashed to his car, and
speed off the street, in the opposite direction.

THIRTEEN

Hours had passed since Micah, had left his brothers bodies laid out on the concrete to die on the other side of town. Micah sat on the bed of the sleazy motel room. The money he took from Turk and what little he got from Gator's pockets spread out on the bed as he totted on the blunt, the half empty bottle of E&J sat on the night stand next to him. The feeling he once possessed about killing Sin, had quickly vanished. It was now occupied with guilt. He couldn't face his mother, to tell her because of his gambling and ego his brothers were dead. With his gun in hand, he aimed at his temple. Micah sat looking himself in the mirror. He thought about all of the fun, he and Sin had as children, before life removed his innocents and he became the man in the streets. He thought about the career path Rich was on, and how it was short lived. His mother would never forgive him, he was good as dead. His family was ruined, and he had no one to blame, but himself. Carrying the title in the street meant nothing, if he didn't have anyone in his corner.

The story was headlines on all of the stations. The scene kept replaying repeatedly in his head, as the news anchor assassinated the character of the person who committed such homicide.

"Fuck you bitch, you don't know me. He should've stayed in jail. Rich wasn't supposed to be there. Fuck!" Micah yelled shattering the outdated television with the butt of his gun.

Land of Snakes

For what seemed like hours, Micah paced the floor, until he couldn't pace anymore. He couldn't bring his self to take his own life; he had too much pride to bring himself to do it. The ringing of his cellphone brought him out the hazy daze that formed. It was Sarina; an older chick he hooked up with from time to time that lived up north.

"Hello?" Micah said lowly into the phone, his voice hoarse from all the yelling mixed with the liquor he consumed.

"What's good Papi? I'm in town for a day or two. Let's link up it's been a minute, I need some of that," She whispered into the phone seductively. Micah wasn't in the mood for sex, but he needed to get his mind together, and off what happen tonight. Sarina was the perfect distraction he needed, she wasn't from around his way, and wouldn't ask a billion questions like most women did.

"Where are you staying at?" Micah questioned.

"I'm lying naked in my hotel room. I'm at the W Hotel in Hollywood. Hurry up, I'm in room 325." Sarina giggled softly before hanging up the phone.

Throwing all the money back in the bag, Micah through it over his shoulder, grabbed the bottle of E&J and walked out the motel. At that moment, he knew being alone wasn't something he needed to be, it would drive him crazy.

Before he made it to the hotel, Micah had parked his truck on a random street. The motel sat in the cut, asking the front desk attendant to call a taxi, Micah made his way to the busy street around the corner to wait for the taxi to arrive. Clad in all black with the hood of his sweat shirt pulled over his head only letting his eyes be visible. Micah stood on the corner, so that he could see all incoming and outgoing traffic to the motel. He had trashed the clothes he had on, and picked up something from a mini mark that sold close to everything. Micah saw a taxi approaching. "AYE!" he yelled flagging it down. The taxi stopped looking Micah over before he unlocked the backseat door.

"Were to tonight?

"W Hotel in Hollywood," Micah uttered, sliding the Indian driver a crispy hundred dollar bill.

 The driver didn't say a word; peering at Micah through his rearview mirror he pulled his taxi into traffic with one hand on the small .22 tucked in the arm of the driver side door. The mixture of weed and liquor reeked off of Micah.

****

It was a quarter pass four in the morning Pamela stood in front of the ironing board, pressing her work uniform. The news played in the background behind her. She shook her head as the news anchor reported another senseless homicide. "Makes no sense, just killing each other up," Pamela said out loud to herself. Setting her clothes on the sofa, she put up the ironing board. Sitting the hot iron on the stove, she grabbed the phone. She dialed Micah's number again for the third time since she had woken up, and still hadn't gotten an answer. "I told them to have my baby home hours ago," Pamela said taking a seat on the couch to watch the news and drink her morning cup of coffee before she started getting ready for work.

A strong solid knock came at the door. Pamela sat her coffee on the in-table, preparing herself to answer the door; the knock came again.

"Alright...I'm coming," Pamela uttered slightly praying that it wasn't Mr. Kirby at her door. Today wasn't the day, and she would surly give him a piece of her mind. She was tired of him. At that moment, she rather take her children's blood money than to let him violate her ever, again. Enough was enough, and she was fed up. Pamela swung the door open; annoyed that someone was banging on her door at five o'clock in the morning. Before her, were two plain clothes detectives. Instantly her stomach began to rumble, she couldn't count how many times the police had shown up to her door, but this time; it felt different. "How may I help you officers?" She questioned hoping Sin hadn't gotten himself in trouble already.

"Yes, we are looking for a Pamela Jones," The tall Hispanic officer spoke. Glancing over his at his scribbled notes on his notepad.

"I'm Pamela Jones. What can I do for you gentlemen this morning?"

"Are you the mother of Richard Jones and Sintrell Jones?" The Asian officer asked.
The mention of her children's name, made Pamela light headed. "Where are my son's?" She questioned.

"Ma'am, can we come inside and talk."

"Where are my sons? What is going on? What are you not telling me?" Pamela questioned quickly panic consumed her heart. She knew something was wrong. *"Where was Micah? Why hadn't they mentioned Micah?"* She thought to herself.

"Ma'am, can we come inside?" The detective who hadn't stated his name spoke. Lightly he touched her arm to lead her inside. Once inside he made sure to close the door behind him. "Take a seat," He said releasing her arm.

"I can't sit. Just tell me. Tell me what happened to my children?" Pamela's spoke weakly her head was spinning out of control at the suspense. She couldn't sit. Her nerves wouldn't allow her to. So she paced the floor patiently waiting for the officers to give her the news, news that something had happen to one of her children.

"Ma'am I am sorry to inform you of this. A little after midnight gun shots were exchanged between a few gentlemen, in the 700 block of West Manchester."

"The Boogie Joint?" Pamela questioned.

"Yes ma'am you know the place?" The officer questioned. Looking at Pamela, she didn't look like she would be in an establishment like the boogie joint.

"Yes, it's run by that low-down good for nothing Gator," She frowned. "What did that son of a bitch do to one of my children? Pamela spat.

"We don't know what happen at this point. We arrived on the scene to four African American males, dead on scene, along with one African American female. We believe that two of the gentlemen found are your sons Richard and Sintrell, according to a witness, and prison identification found on one of the gentlemen" The officer spoke standing at a distance from Pamela.

"We will need you to come down to the coroner's office to identify the bodies Mrs. Jones," The other officer chimed.

Pamela felt her knees become weak, a strong pain shot through her body, as a stream of tears poured from her eyes. Her body went stiffen. Pamela tried to stand but couldn't, her limp body collapsed "Noooooo....not my babies," She wailed loudly. Her hands banged against the floor.

"Ma?" Gia yelled rushing into the living room hearing the loud thump of her mother's body hitting the ground followed by her antagonizing cries. "What's going on?' She questioned taking her mother's trembling body into her arms.

Pamela couldn't respond her heart was too busy aching, to tell her daughter, her brothers were dead.

"What happen? What's going on?" Gia questioned the officers. Tears began to whale in her eyes.

"Miss, are you a member of the family?" The officers questioned.

"Yes, this is my mother. What's going on? Tell me now." Gia demanded.

"We need you to get your mother and yourself down to view the bodies we have in custody."

"Bodies? Gia questioned with a raised eye bray. What bodies do you have?"

"Richard, and Sintrell, Jones."

"What? What do you mean? What happened to my brothers?" Gia questioned heavy tears coated her face, as she tried to make sense of it all. *Was this in connection to Sin's call last night?"* Gia thought.

 With the help of the officer Pamela and Gia were able to get themselves together and get to the corners office. Dreadfully Pamela entered the double doors her feet felt like they were being held down by bricks. Her head pounded as she neared the doors where her children's possible dead bodies could lay. She prayed this was just a mistake. That they were wrongful identified and maybe laying in the hospital waiting for her to come check on her.

"Are you ready ma'am?" The medical examiner asked. "This can be a lot to handle."

"Yes," Pamela replied weakly. She wasn't ready; she would never be ready for something like this. The medical examiner slowly pulled

Land of Snakes

back the black traps; Pamela peered at her son's lifeless bodies lying in the cold room. Rich had been beaten so bad, if she wasn't his mother, she wouldn't have recognized him. It was the tear drop shaped birthmark on his chest, and the two inch scar on the side of his face, he got when he was only a child, which confirmed it was her baby, and her baby boy was gone. Sin's once radiant skin, was so dull. The multiple wounds to his body, could be seen. "Who could do something like this?" She cried as she stared at their lifeless bodies. Her knees buckled, all of her limbs went limp as she hit the ground blacking out. Her worst nightmare had become her reality. Her sons were dead.

"Ma? Ma?" Gia yelled lifting her mother's head from the cold tiled floor of the coroners office. She had been standing at the end of the hallway; she couldn't bring herself to look at her brothers. "Help! I need help!" Gia yelled. Tears ran down her face. "Help!" she cried. She couldn't lose her mother, on top of losing her brothers. She wouldn't know how to deal, they were all she had.

The medical examiner quickly ran to Pamela aide. Signaling for others to help, they whisked Pamela to the emergency room.

FOURTEEN

It didn't take long for the driver to arrive at the hotel. It was almost six in the morning and the freeways were nearly empty on an early Sunday morning. Hoping out the car, Micah slid the driver another twenty dollar bill before slamming the door shut. Micah entered the upscale hotel feeling a little out of place.

"Hello Sir, How may I help you morning?" The front desk attendant spoke bubbly.

"Yeah, can you let room 325, know I am here," Micah said as he nervously scanned the lobby making sure no one was looking at him. It wasn't many in the lobby, but the few people who stood around were all dressed in upscale attire, three piece suits, knee lengths dresses, and cocktail dresses. Micah felt out of place, his pants hung off his ass, he reeked of weed and liquor, and his eyes were blood shot red. His attired looked more like he wanted to rob the hotel. Due to catering to a lot of Hollywood top celebrities the attendant didn't past judgment.

"Sure Sir and your name?"

"Her guest," Micah said focusing on the traffic coming in and out of the hotel lobby. No one paid him any mind most eyes were glued to PDA's, and iPhones.

The attendant frowned at Micah rudeness. But, He did as Micah asked quickly dialing the room's extension. The attendant described Micah. Hanging up the phone after getting the approval he approached Micah. "She is waiting. Third floor to your right, have a great day," The clerk said cheerfully.

"Yeah you to," Micah replied heading towards the elevator.

Micah approached Sarina's room; her hotels door was slightly opened. Micah put his hand on the gun in his hoodies pocket as he peeked in the room. Slowly he crept inside, gun in hand. He didn't know what Sarina had going on, but he had already been tricked by two women in one night, he wasn't settling for a third. Turning the slight curve inside the room, Micah had his gun raised.

"It took you long enough, thought you forget about me, and left me to take care of myself, on this lovely morning." Sarina, spoke as her red stained lips spread into a sexy grin. She laid on the bed with not a stich of clothing.

"Oh I was coming, believe that," Micah grinned as his eyes wondered over her perfect small frame, plump vagina and scrumptious ass.

Micah sat the bag at the foot of the bed, before removing his shoes and climbing into the bed alongside Sarina. She wasted no time sucking his tongue into her mouth as she fumbled with his pants. The sight of Sarina frame had Micah hard as a rock and freed his mine of the murders he committed, and the guilty heart he once carried. All he was worried about, was sliding into Sarinagussy walls, and busting a nut. Sarina pushed him back, flat on his back. Straddling his face, she gripped the headboard and winded her hips, as Micah long tongue explored her wetness.

Nisha Lanae

****

Gia paced the waiting room; she hadn't heard anything since they rushed her mother to the emergency. She was a nervous wreck; she couldn't stop the tears that coated her face. She dialed and redialed Micah's number, but never got an answer. She didn't know where her brother was, or if he was still alive. That drove her crazy, and not knowing the status of her mother only added to her stress.

"Gia," A male voice called out.
Gia turned toward the voice, she prayed it was Micah, but it wasn't it. It was Kenny, her ex-boyfriend.

"What are you doing here Kenny?" She questioned. Not interested in seeing him.

"I heard what happened to your brothers. I came to check on you."

"Why? After all those text messages telling me, fuck me, abort our unborn? That you don't give a fuck about me? Why are you really here?" Gia was annoyed with him. Since the incident with Sin, he had been sending her all kinds of hateful text messages.

"Man that was all talk. I was pissed. Yo' bitch ass brother came at me all kinds of sideways, and you just stood there and didn't say shit, just stood there and let him disrespect me."

136

Land of Snakes

Gia flew into his face. "Watch your mouth. My brother is fucking dead. You are not needed here, so leave before I go nuts on your ass."

"Well fuck you bitch, I tried to come make peace, and be here for you. I see that shit isn't going to work, I tell you about you fucking hoes today," Kenny spat.

"Whatever Kenny, I wasn't a hoe when you was fucking me raw, and eating my ass."

"You were a hoe then and you a hoe now. I don't know what I was thinking; I was on some thirsty shit. Just make sure you abort that baby, hell, it might not even be mine. I'm not claiming shit, that came out that pussy, no way," Kenny spat. He was trying to hurt Gia's feelings he knew it was in fact, his baby she was carrying.

"Are you done?" Gia questioned glaring at Kenny with disgust. "I don't have time for your shit; my concern is with my family." Gia said walking away from Kenny.

"You right about one thing, I came to make sure that nigga Sin, was really dead. I guess somebody got to him, before I did. Word on the street it was your own brother Micah, over there at Gator spot." Kenny said. He knew his words would cut her deep. "That's some cold shit, if that nigga Micah did kill Sin. But, I can't say I'm not happy. Kenny laughed.

"Fuck what the streets saying. I know my brothers, and Micah, wouldn't have killed his own. So fuck you and what them people saying. You talking a lot of shit know that you know Sin, is gone. You wasn't talking that shit to him, ole' bitch ass nigga. First chance I get, I will abort this baby, so I won't have to carry and birth anything with bitch ass DNA, and the end up like you," Gia lashed viciously into his face.

Kenny gripped Gia, by the neck slamming he body into the waiting rooms wall. "Fuck all of your brothers; I wouldn't give a fuck, if all of them were dead. You keep popping off at the mouth; you might be joining them, Bitch!" Kenny spat sternly into her face.

The people that occupied the waiting room began to scatter as the hospitals security barged into the room. "Let her go now," The Security office yelled His hand on the can Taser on the holster of his pants.

With his hand still clasped around her neck, tightly. Kenny turned, to see the few security officers peering at him. "This bitch, not even worth it," Kenny said releasing the death grip he had on Gia's neck. "Make sure you get rid of that baby, bitch."

"Fuck you, you fucking coward," Gia spat rubbing her neck. As decorated her face. Kenny hadn't always been the best to her, but he had never treated her that badly.

The security rushed, and detained Kenny, escorting him out. "Are you okay ma'am?" The Security officer that lingered behind questioned.

"Yes," Gia replied looking at all the people in the waiting room, who stared at her. "What the hell y'all looking at? Mind yo' fucking business," She yelled storming to the desk, she needed to know something. "Excuse me," She said trying to catch the attention of the catty nurses, who were talking about what just happened between Kenny and her.

"How may I help you?" One of the nurses asked breaking away from the crowd of nurses giggling.

"Yes, my mother was brought in almost two hours ago. I haven't heard anything, is my mother okay?" Gia questioned.

"What's your mother's name?"

"Pamela Jones," Gia replied quickly watching the nurse's hands as her fingers glided over the keyboard.
The nurse fingers came to a standstill, as her eyes scanned the computer. "Your mother is in room 216, you can go inside, I will let the Doctor know you waiting to speak with him," The nurse said issuing her a visitors passed and pointing Gia in the direction of the room. Gia dashed down the hall's in search of her mother's room. Her heart pounded as her legs shacked uncontrollably, she didn't know what to expect when she entered her mother's room and that slightly scared her. Locating her mother's room, Gia legs became weak, she couldn't move. Standing in the hall, her eyes didn't leave the bed where he mother was supposed to be, the white hospital curtain was pulled around. Gia wanted to run to her mother, find out if she was okay, but her feet wouldn't allow her, they wouldn't move.

"Can I help you?" A voice asked moving closer to her. Gia could hear the voice, but her eyes were glued on the bed. "Are you the daughter of Pamela Jones?" The same voice asked. The mention of her mother's name, snapped Gia out of her daze. Whipping her head to where she heard the voice. She saw an older white gentleman, sprinkles of sliver covered his head, and bifocals covered his eyes.

"What you say?" Gia questioned. Looking the man over she realized he was a Doctor.

"Pamela Jones, is that your mother?" He asked.

"Yes... Yes, that's my mother. How is she?" Gia managed to get out without crying.

"Your mother is going to be fine. Her blood level rose very high, prior to her passing out. She also suffered a mild heart attack. She is in stable condition right now, but needs plenty of rest, we will be keeping her for a few days for observation," The Doctor said as he glanced back and forth from Gia to Pamela's chart. "I'm Dr. Gary, By the way. I will be her Doctor.

"Okay, but she is okay. She is going to live?"

"Yes, with time and plenty of rest your mother will be fine. I was told your mother passed out at the corners office, has your mother been stressed in the last few months or days?" The Doctor asked.

"Two of my brothers were found dead, this morning," Gia wailed at the words having to leave her mouth. It hurt to the core.

"I'm sorry to hear that, you need to get some rest. I don't want to see you admitted," The Doctor said patting Gia on the back. "We will

Land of Snakes

have your mother moved into a private room; you can stay the night with her. I will let the nurses know," The Doctor said before walking off.

Gia took slow steps, until she stood at the foot of her mother hospital bed. The sight of her mother with tubes coming from everywhere broke Gia's heart. Pamela was always so strong; she raised them without the help of their father. She worked three jobs, to make sure they never went without. Gia knew she would have to step up, and be there for her mother.

Pamela had always been slightly prepared to get the call one day that Sin, was dead. He lived a crazy life, which put his life in jeopardy just walking down the street. It was Rich's death, she wouldn't be able to handle, and he was her baby; her only child that had a future ahead of him.

Gia kissed her mother's forehead, before pulling a chair close, to her mother's bed and took a seat. Her eyes were heavy, red and puffy from all the crying. She tried Micah one more time; still she didn't get an answer. All the crying made Gia tired, her eyes were heavy. Gia, lend on her mother's bed, and quickly fell into a slumber.

****

With a fist full of Sarina's hair, Micah plunged deeply giving her back shots that left her tongue tied. "Yesss...Yessss...Fuuucckkk," Sarina moaned twisting her hips; she brought her ass back matching Micah rough paced.

Micah usually wasn't so rough, but he was still feeling the effects of the liquor and weed, on top of taking his frustration out on Sarina.

Sarina, was a freak, and liked it rough. Micah always gave her the dick good. This time was different, he was great. That, Tony the Tiger type of great. She had already experienced one orgasm and was preparing her body for the tingle that was rising up her spine, her walls clinched as she let her juices exploded.

Micah couldn't hold his nut any longer, the way Sarina sucked him in and out and winded her hips. With a strong grip around her neck, Micah sucked her ear, as he pulled out, pulling the condom off, letting his semen coat her round ass.

"Damn, you were trying to kill my ass," Micah laughed plopping down on the bed.

"Boy please, you were tryna' kill me with them back shots," Sarina giggled pulling out a rolled blunt. Placing it between her thin lips, she sparked it, and let the aroma of the purple haze fill the room.

"What are you doing down here anyway?" Micah questioned taking the blunt out of Sarina's hand and puffing on it, before passing it back to her. Micah picked up his flashing phone, it was Gia, she had been calling him non-stop for the last half hour.

"I made a run down here, you know how it is." She replied.

"Business must be booming up north, shit dry out here," Micah stated. He needed somewhere to set-up shop. He knew Los Angeles, was too hot for him right now.

"Hell yeah, I told you. You should fuck with my peoples. Money flowing, fuck a drought," Sarina smiled. She ran packages for her cousin up and down the coast.

"With all the crazy shit going on, I should head up north and get this money," Micah smiled as a light bulb went off in his head. The dudes up north didn't know him, or what was going on in Los Angeles but what word of mouth was, and he could easily downplay that. He knew Sarina could plug him in with some dudes and get him a few blocks to lockdown. Get money, and restore his name that was slowly tarnishing.

"Let me know if you for real, I know you about your money, so I could easily plug you in with my peoples," Sarina said as she sparked another blunt. "Damn someone must miss you? They are blowing your phone up. Tell them sharing is caring, and it's my time so beat it." Micah looked down at his phone, it was Gia once again. He knew they must have got the news, and was worried about him, but he couldn't face them at the moment. He didn't know the words to speak to soothe the pain he know his mother must have been going through.

"It's just some crazy bitch I use to fuck with, she don't want shit, and I'm not about to entertain her bullshit. Not tonight, I don't have time for it," Micah lied.

"Fuck her ass then, anyways I will plug you in with my cousin, but in the meantime, hit me with

some more of those back shots," Sarinagrinned
as she sucked Micah into her mouth, getting him
back hard. Micah and Sarina smoked, drunk
liquor from the rooms mini bar and fucked into
the sun peaked through the hotel room blinds.

FIFTEEN

After several days in the hospital, Pamela, was finally being released. "Now, Mrs. Jones, you have to make sure you keep your pressure down, right along with taking the proper dose of your medicine. I understand what happened to your sons, I send my deepest condolence to you, and your family. But, you have to take care of yourself, so that you don't join them anytime soon."

"I hear you Dr. Grey," Pamela said grapping her bags. She was beyond ready to get home, and far away from the hospital. She missed sleeping in her own bed, hospitals creped her out.

"You take care too." Dr. Grey said to Gia.

"I will," Gia smiled helping her mother with put her bags into the taxi waiting for them.

As the taxi pulled up to their apartment, Pamela heart raced. The apartment was surrounded with police and the corners department. Rushing to the entrance "What's going on? Is someone dead? Who is it?" She questioned.

"Back up ma'am," An officer said as a gurney was being pulled from the building a body bag strapped down on it.

"I live here, I just want to know who it is," Pamela stated with a pleading urgency in her voice.

"Kirby Steel, the apartment manager," The police replied. "You all will be let in the building shortly. In the meantime, I need you to back- up ma'am."

Pamela knew it was wrong, and had always been a firm believer in not wishing harm on anyone. But, a sign of relief overcame her. All that he had done to her, in the last months, she was happy to have him out of her hair. "Gia have you heard from Micah?"

"Nah, I keep calling, but I never get an answer. Once you get settled, I will ask around," Gia replied. She knew her mother would continue to stress until she knew the whereabouts of Micah. Gia was upset with her brother. It had been a long time since she had been this mad at him. He had better been dead in the hospital, or in jail unable to call. If he was alive, and just ignoring her she was prepared to give him a royal tongue lash. Gia thought. Her mind pondered on what Kenny said, and the last call she got from Sin only an hour before his reported death. She didn't feel the need to tell her mother, she had spoken to Sin, and that he wanted them to stay in the house, she wouldn't even dare tell her what Kenny implied, it was ludacris. She didn't believe it, Micah couldn't do such a thing. He probably was just scared, and in hiding until things died down.

"Okay," Pamela replied as she watched the police carry out several large bags from the building. After an hour, the police had finally gathered everyone's name, and contact information and allowed them to enter the building. Pamela rushed inside she was starving and needed to call her job. Gia had informed them, that she would be out on leave for a while

to deal with everything. Pamela didn't want to stay at home, she couldn't stay in the house all day, knowing her children would never walk through that door.
****

Since arriving at her hotel room days prior Micah and Sarina had become inseparable. Micah tagged along as Sarina traveled to Arizona, Vegas. They speed down the 15 freeway leaving Vegas to head back into the city. Micah had made plans to head up north with Sarina, once they hit back into the city. While in Vegas he was able to move some of the product to some dudes Sarina knew, and introduced him to.

"You ready to play with the big boys?" Sarina smiled from the passenger's seat in between totes of the blunt in her hand.

"I've been ready. I'm just happy the opportunity has arisen finally, it's about time.

"Well get ready, cause we about to get this money, and I do mean a whole lot of it." Sarina said. After making her last few errands in Los Angeles they jumped on the freeway headed up north with nothing but the clothes on his back, Micah said a temporary good bye to LA. He still hadn't spoken to his mother, the calls from Gia, had slowed down. Other people from his neighborhood had called him a few times; all of their calls also went unanswered.
After a little over five hour drive, they had finally made it to Sarina's plush two bedroom condo.

"You can crash here, it's my extra place. For the times that I just need to get away and clear my head."

"So where do you stay at, if you don't stay here? Micah questioned looking around the plush resident.

"I have a house on the other side of town, where I live with my Grandmother. I help her take care of my little nephew, and cousin. You might want to get some rest. Pablo wants to meet you before sun up."

"Sun up?" Micah questioned making sure he heard her correctly. "Who does business that damn early? Micah questioned.

"Pablo. Most of his business is done before sun up, he is an early bird. But, I'm out. I have to pick up medicine for my grandma, before the pharmacy closes, since I have been out of town. I will see you around 3am."

"Damn that's early; I'm used to getting home at that time, but okay."

"There are towels in the hallway closet, and some extra toothbrushes in the bathroom cabinet. If you get hungry before I come back, there are some hot pockets in the freezer."

"Cool, see you in a few hours," Micah said looking round the condo once again. He was looking for any sign of another man being there in the past.

Sarina grabbed her bags and walked the short distance to where her car was parked. Just as she climbed into her car, an all-black sedan pulled alongside her. "He is inside, make sure he doesn't

Land of Snakes

leave here, at all unless it's with me," Sarina said to the driver of the car, before she drove off.

    Micah showered, and slipped into some basketball shorts he had picked up during the time they were traveling. Finding a cold Budweiser that was in the fridge, Micah sat on the couch, trying to catch the last of the game. The constant beeping of his cell phone caused him to focus on the multiply messages, and missed calls he had. Most of them where from Gia, a few chicks he fooled around with, and a few hustlers' friends of Sin's, that knew him. He decided to check a few voice messages from Gia, to see what was going on. His heart almost stopped when he heard Gia's whimpering voice telling him that their mother was in the hospital. Micah wanted badly to call and find out the state his mother was in, but he didn't know the words to say. His guilt forced him to not be there for his mother, when she needed him the most. Micah couldn't control the few tears that happen to fall from his eyes, he was lost and didn't have a soul to confine it, and everyone would look at him differently if they knew his part in his brother's deaths.

Micah scanned the phone trying to clear all the messages. He couldn't help it, he clicked on Gia's name, and brought the phone to his ear, but all it did was ring, until Gia voice from her voicemail kicked it. Micah hung up opting to not leave a voicemail. Micah decided to power off his phone. He hadn't slept in the last few days. Every time he closed his eyes, he saw Sin's face, and the

149

sinister grin that was on his face, before he killed him. *"You will never be me, even in my death. I'll always be the better man."* He heard Sin's voice clearly. Micah jumped up and looked around. "FUCK!" He yelled. He knew it was his guilty conscience, and it would hunt him for a while. Micah lay back down, only to hear Sin's voice again. This time he didn't react. He lay with his eyes open, and hoped to get a few hours of shut eye.

****

Gia stood in the doorway of her mother's room, as Pamela sat with her back towards the door. She was kneeled down, at the foot of her bed praying. Gia knew her mother was going through the emotions, with her brother's deaths, and Micah missing in action. Her drama would only add to the stress her mother was going through. Gia prepared to walk away from her mother's door, and save her situation for another day.

"Gia." Pamela called out. "Come in, what's on your mind?" Pamela asked putting her bible up. She faced Gia waiting for her to enter her room.

"Oh nothing ma, I was just checking on you." Pamela knew she was lying. "Come take a seat next to mama." Pamela said patting the space next to her.

Gia made her way over to her mother, taking a seat on her bed next to her.

"So what's bugging you Gia?" She questioned.

Land of Snakes

"Nothing mama, just worried about Micah, no one around here has heard or seen him since that night."

"I know you are. I am too. But, it's more to it. You are my child; I know when something is bothering you. How far along are you? Pamela questioned.

"Huh? Gia questioned baffled. She glanced at her mother.

"Like I said, a mother knows her child. I know more about you children, than you all think I know. I listen and pay attention when you think I'm not. So how far along are you?"

"13 weeks,"

"And what does Mr. Kenny have to say about this? I hope he is prepared to be a father."
Gia burst into tears. "He told me, to get rid of it. He doesn't want to have a baby by a hoe,"
Pamela was pissed by Kenny's words. She looked at her distraught daughter, and became more pissed off at Kenny. She knew Gia loved Kenny and was heartbroken. "I never sleep with anymore else when I was with him. How can he say that about me? I did almost everything he asked me, and he calls me names, and puts his hands on me," Gia cried.

"Look at me," Pamela said gripping Gia by her chin. "Kenny is a boy, and that's how a boy lashes out, but he had no damn right to put his hands on you. When I see him, I will give him a piece of my mind. What he isn't going do, is hitting on a child on mine. You don't need no man to raise no child. It's nice to have a man step up and do what he should, but it doesn't always work out that way. I don't believe in abortions, but if that's something you choose to do, as your mother, I will support you and be right by your side. If you want to go forth with your pregnancy, I'm here, and will always be by your side. We don't need him, but having a baby doesn't make you a women, and isn't an easy job at all. I'm willing to help any way I can, but understand this by no means am I a live in baby sitter."

"I'm not sure what I want to do. I don't know if I want to bring a child into this world, and have to go through life knowing my child will never have a father, because I made the mistake of dealing with a no good dude. I don't want that for my child.

"Well the choice is yours; you will be the only one who has to live with whatever you decided to do.

"Ma' what about our daddy? What happen there? He didn't want us?"

"No, that wasn't the case there; I'm the one to blame about your father not being in you and your brother's life. You were young, and probably don't remember, but you father was there for you all. He wanted you children, but I didn't want to be with him anymore, and I refused to leave you all behind, no way would I. So you not having a father, active in your life is my entire fault. I made that choice and I have to live with it."

"You don't give up easy ma', so I know it had to be something bad for you to walk away."

Land of Snakes

"It was, and I just couldn't take it anymore. That's why I want better for you Gia; I don't want you to fall for a damn fool, like I did. Go to school, get your education, travel the world live life baby," Pamela said on the brick of tears.

"I hear you ma', I promise to not let you down. I know I have in the past, but I promise to try and correct that. I'm tired, I'm about to lay it down." Gia said giving her mother a hug.

"Don't worry about letting me down, worry about letting yourself down. That's the most important person, you. But go get some rest. I'm going to finish reading my book, until I fall asleep, it's getting good." She laughed.

Gia lingered for a moment before she headed to her room. The flashing light of her cell phone caught her attention. Her eyes almost bulged when she say who she had missed a call form. Gia practically ran back to her mother's run "MA!" She yelled.

Pamela's heart began to race as the loud sound of Gia's frantic voice and feet coming down the hall.

"What's going on baby?" Pamela questioned.

"It was Micah, he called me back. I missed his call, he has to be okay, ma' he called." Pamela's heart fluttered. "Thank you Jesus, call him back."

Gia redialed Micah's number, she didn't get an answer, so she tried it again, but still she got no answer. "He isn't answering, damn," Gia yelled upset she had missed his call.

"If he called back once Gia, he will call again, when he is ready. Don't beat yourself up about it, remember you are with child; and what you go through, your fetus goes through too, no stress."

"Okay," Gia said walking back to her room trying Micah one more time. She had so much to ask Micah. She needed to speak with her little brother; she wanted to know if he was okay, what had happened to their brother?

Pamela went to the kitchen and made her a pot of coffee. She couldn't sleep, so she turned on the news. As she watched the news, she seen they had moved on to another headlines. There wasn't a single word or update on Rich and Sin's murders, and that sadden her. She knew because they were inner city African American boys, and where the crime took place, her son's murders would go unnoticed and unsolved, like so many others. Glancing around the walls and all the pictures that lined the walls, of her children brought a smile, along with a single tear down her face. She couldn't bear to be in the room, she missed her son's. Sin had just come home from being gone so long, and now he was gone again, this time forever. Pamela turned the Television off and went to lie in her bed, until sleep found her

SIXTEEN

A sudden bright light blared in Micah's face causing him to jump up.

"Wake up, it's already 3am, you were supposed to be up already." Sarina said standing over Micah.

"I'm up," Micah said sliding on some clothes you up mighty early looking all good."

"Thanks, and good morning to you," Sarina smiled. She was dressed in a short form fitting black dress, and all black stilettoes. Her hair had been pulled up, to a high bun. "I brought you some breakfast," She said sitting the McDonalds bag on the bed.

"McDonalds? That shit ani't no damn breakfast, that's bullshit,"

"It's better than nothing. So eat up, so we can hit the road, and get business took care of." Micah took the bag, and quickly scarfed down the Muffin quickly, chasing it down with the watered down orange juice. "I'm ready," Micah said coming from out the bathroom from washing his face and brushing his teeth.

"Well let's go, you have the product right?" Sarina questioned as they made it to the car. Sarina eyed the black sedan that sat in the corner. Signaling them it was okay to leave.

"What you think this bag is? I'm well prepared. I told you I been wanting this for a while now," Micah said getting into the car.

"Good, that's what I love to hear," She smiled as she pulled out the apartment complex into traffic.

"So what can you tell me about Pablo?"

"What is there you want to know?"

"He yo' peoples right? Micah questioned. He didn't trust many; he wasn't trying to go into a set-up so he wanted to know a little background on who he was going to meet with at the crack of dawn. He had made that mistake before, not knowing who he was dealing with, he couldn't make it twice.

"Nah, but he cools peoples. My cousin does business with him, and has been doing business with him for a cool minute."

"What's this thing with meeting so damn early?"

"That's Pablo, and how he does his business." Sarina replied as she switched in and out of lanes flooring the gas pedal.

"We here," Sarina said as she pulled her car around the back and parked.

"We are getting on a boat?"

"Yeah, it stays docked. What you scared of a little water huh?"

"Nah, just some different shit, I'm not use too."

"Different is always good." Sarina said climbing out the car.

Micah and Sarina walked the short distance to where a lined of boats sat. They walked to the end where a lavish yacht sat.

"Damn. What kind of money is he getting?" Micah questioned admiring the yacht. He had never been on a boat. He was in awe of it.

Land of Snakes

"Let's just say it's long. Very long" Sarina replied. As she then Micah climbed onto the yacht. Two husky men armed with gun stood at the entrance.

"Here to see Pablo, he is expecting me. Sarina, plus one."

Sarina and Micah were searched before being escorted to the lower level of the yacht. Sitting behind a glass table was a middle aged man. His olive skin was so radiant. His hair was perfectly slicked into a ponytail that hung to his shoulders. Clad in a tan lien shorts, and a white bottom down, that showed off his tanned chest.

"Hola Pablo, How are you?" Sarina greeted extending her hand out.

"Hola Senorita," He spoke with a heavy accent as he showered Sarina's hand with kisses.

"You're looking very lovely, like you always do. So who is this you have with you?" Pablo questioned as he looked Micah over.

"This is a dear friend of mine, Micah."

"What can I do for you Micah?"

"He is new around these parts, and looking to make this home for a while, and get some money." Sarina spoke up.

"And what brings you this way?"

"It's somewhat of a drought in my city. And I'm looking to elevate and make some real money."

"So I hear you have some product on you that you're trying to get rid of?"

"Yeah," Micah replied going into the bag to show Pablo what he was bringing to the table.

Pulling out a few of the brick he had brought along, Micah sat them on the table.

"Black Angel?" Pablo said noticing the label on the product. "Where did you say you were from? Because I only know once person, and place that pushes this product."

"I'm from Los Angles. I use to cop from Gator," Micah replied nervously. He hadn't expected Pablo to know of Gator, let alone know his product on sight.

"He still pushing bullshit, I see. How many more of this weak shit you have?"

"10," Micah replied.

"So, this is what I can do for you. In exchange for all 12 of these, I will give you 8 of the purest form straight off the boat from Cuba,"

"That's not an even exchange," Micah said ready to turn down Pablo's deal.

"For the quality, it's not, its better. You getting a better product, and I'm not charging you. Hell, that's better than anyone will give you, around these parts. Plus, I run Oakland, Richmond, and San Jose. But, you get my point. I supply the product around here.

"Sounds like a good deal to me," Sarina spoke up.

"Wait, what about re-upping?" Micah questioned. He wasn't the type to just jump on the first thing coming his way. He done it before, and got himself into a world of bullshit, it wasn't going down like that this go round.

Land of Snakes

"That all depends on how fast, you can move the product. At that time, we will discuss that. You just worry about getting this off,"

"So when can I get the product?"

"I will text Sarina, with the time and location for the exchange. Nice too meet you Micah, hopefully this is the beginning to a healthy business relationship." Pablo said as he and Micah shook hands.

"Likewise, and thanks for looking out."

"Sarina, your rep with me relies on him doing well, and not fucking me over. Tell Hector, I haven't seen him in a while, he coping somewhere else? Or he just got too big to deal with a small timer as myself?" Pablo chuckled.

"Micah got this, and I will extend the message to Hector. You take care; we will be waiting for that message." Sarina smiled as she followed Micah out.

Micah had mixed emotions about the whole ordeal. Pablo was just too cool for him. "Is this dude the real deal? Because, if not I'm good. I don't have the time or energy to deal with bullshit."

"Since you met me, I've always been about my money. Pablo is the connect and is very well known. I knew you wouldn't want to work under the trap boys, since you use to moving product. So I linked you up with the connect directly. I know a few blocks that money is waiting to be made. Hector, who is my cousin, has given me the blessings to let you set up. The only thing is. He wants twenty percent off of everything.

"Twenty percent and I'm bringing in my own product? That's bullshit, I'm not some fucking mark, and I can smell bullshit."

"You have to remember this isn't Los Angeles, you don't have any pull here. He is giving you a whole fucking block to run, and willing to lend you some workers until you build your shit up. You are an outsider around these parts, these niggas won't hesitate to off you, for trying to take money out they mouth." Sarina said with a slight attitude.

"Okay, I'm gonna' trust you." Micah said as he climbed into the car.

"You think I'm just gonna' stick my neck out for some bullshit, I'm about getting money."

"So where are we about to go now?" Micah questioned changing the subject. He could tell Sarina was beyond annoyed with him, and the situation. He was just wary of everyone since everything happened.

"I'm about to take my nephew to a football game and to get him some new shoes." Sarina replied whipping through the traffic.

"You stay busy, shit, I thought we could get some drinks, and explore the city."

"I've been gone for two weeks. I'm playing catch up, maybe later. We can go for drinks and I show you around my city."

"I'm down with that, just don't flake on me, like you are known to do. I'm just ready to get this money, I can't sit for too long, and not do shit."

Land of Snakes

"Hector, will be back into town tomorrow. I will take you by there and show you where you can set up at. Then we can get to the money, and keep you busy."

Sarina pulled up to the Condo, and popped the locks to let Micah out.

"You not getting out?" Micah questioned seeing she still had the car in drive.

"Nah, I'm tryna' beat the traffic, and get this done, I will see you later."

"Alright, hit me before you come back this way, so I can get something to eat.

"Okay," Sarina said pulling off.

Sarina made it to her destination quickly. Briskly walking into the run down building, she constantly looked over her shoulder. Sarina quickly slid the key into the door, and made her way into the apartment.

"What's new?" A male said with his back toward her. He sat watching several monitors.

"We met with Pablo today. I'm waiting for his text to come through for the date and location of the exchanged. You are due back in town tomorrow, so we will be meeting you as Hector, my cousin and a big timer dealer who is giving him a few blocks to slang from, on the strength on me." Sarina rambled from the loveseat.

"When can we rap this shit up, and be done with these low-life? Put they're ass where they belong, in prison. Caged like the animals they are."

"It won't be long, all we need to do is get them all together in one room making a large transaction, and we got them,"

"And how much longer will that take? I'm pissed I lost all that damn evidence. This shit would've been over." Detective Ortega said angry. During transmission of evidence they lost all of the evidence they had gained against Pablo.

"Give or take maybe two weeks to a month. Micah is eager to get money. Pablo wants to see what he can do with the eight keys, he going to give him. Micah has a chip on his shoulder, and something to prove, it shouldn't take him long."

"I just can't wait for this shit to be over. So what should I know about this dude before tomorrow? I ran his name, but didn't get any hits for a Micah James. I guess he never had any run in's with the law, which I find to be odd."

"He is very egoistic, like I said he has something to prove. Micah wears his emotions on his face, so he is very easy to read. I have a doctor's appointment to go to, and I have to spend at least some time with him so he doesn't stray. I have people sitting on him. I will hit you, when Pablo gets with me," Sarina said preparing to leave. "Oh, and Pablo said what's going on, you too big for a small timer like him, he hasn't seen you in a while," She laughed.

"Fuck Pablo," Ortega yelled.

****

Land of Snakes

Pamela and Gia sat in the cemetery making the arrangements for the boy's home going. It still seemed so surreal to Pamela. One day she is hugging her son's, and seeing their big smiles. Next she is picking out their caskets and tombstones. It was all too much for her.

"Mrs. Jones, did you hear me?" The funeral home director asked.

"I'm sorry, I just had a moment." Pamela replied trying to focus on picking everything out and making sure the boys were laid to rest like she knew they would've liked.

"That's okay. So that will be gold caskets for both? And you want them to be buried together in a double crib?"

"Yes, and I don't want them on the ground, in the wall."

"I will look to see what we have available. Do you know the day and time you want to have the service? And where you want to have it? Do you have a church home?" She questioned. She could tell it was taking a toll on her. Pamela couldn't stand focus on anything lately.

"I have a church home, but my children don't. I couldn't get Sintrell; into a church in lord know since when." Pamela chuckled. "I prefer to have it, in a chapel. A very nice size one would be nice. They had a lot of friends, so something that can accommodate all their friends."

"Okay, let me check what we have. I will be right back." The woman said grabbing some papers; she left out the room, returning moments later. "Okay, we have the next four Thursdays, and Fridays available for our large chapel."

"We can set it up, for next Thursday."
Pamela said as a single tear escaped her eye. "Are we almost done?" She questioned. It was all taking a toll on her.

"Yes ma'am, I think we have everything we need at this time. If we need anything else, I have your contact number. Once again, I'm sorry for your lost."
Pamela quickly gathered her belongs and rushed out the office, with Gia hot on her heels.

"You okay ma'?" Gia questioned. She knew her mother would lie and say she was, but she could see she wasn't.

"Have you heard from your brother?"
Pamela asked bypassing Gia questioned.

"No, he doesn't answer, or return any of my calls or text messages."

"What have the streets been saying? Is anyone talking about did this?"

"The streets?" Gia laughed she hadn't ever heard her mother talk about the streets. "What you know about the streets ma'?"

"You know what I am talking about. What are the people saying?
Kenny's words rang in her hear, on top of a few other rumors that were circling around the hood.

"No ma', I haven't heard anything from anyone," Gia replied.

****

Land of Snakes

Micah hadn't realized he had fallen asleep until he heard a voice coming from the living room. "Sarina?" He questioned fishing for his gun.

"Yeah, it's me," Sarina replied quickly ending her call and meeting Micah in the room. "You finally up sleepy head, I been here for over an hour. I spoke with Pablo. He set up the exchanged for tonight, at the Doc's. He won't be there, it will be just a simple exchange, and then I will take you to meet my cousin Hector."

"Cool, but in the meantime can a nigga slide into something tight and wet. You got me horny ass shit, the way you handling business and shit," Micah smiled pulling Sarina close.

"I guess, only if you promise to hit me with some of those back shots."

"You know I only aim to please."
Sarina pulled her panties to the side, freeing his harden dick from his pants, she straddled on top of him sliding him into her warmth.

SEVENTEEN

After the exchanged, Sarina dropped Micah back
off at the condo, and rushed to the apartment
where her partner sat waiting for her arrival.
Sarina sat next to her partner, Detective Ortega
as they applied the undercover wire. Detective
Ortega prepared for his meeting with Micah. He
had been undercover as a drug dealer, by the
name of Hector for the last two years.

"You ready?" Sarina questioned.

"Yeah, ready to get this shit over with."
Ortega spoke. He had a deep rooted hatred for
going undercover, especially when he had to deal
with low-life drug dealers who ruined lives so
they could live lavish and flashy lifestyles.

"It will all be over shortly. I will see you at
the meeting location." Sarina said trying to get
away from Ortega before he went on a rant.
Sarina speed back to the condo to pick up Micah,
so that they could head Sarina was slightly
nervous. She had been undercover plenty of
times, but this time was a little different. She was
ready to end this case, for many reasons. For the
last three years she had been working closely
alongside Pablo to retain as much information
she could about his operation. It took over a year
to get in good and then introduce Ortega as
Hector, an ambitious drug dealer on the rise.
Over the time they had been working with Pablo,
they had established a solid case against Pablo,
which would send him away for nearly a decade.
Sarina had a personal vendetta against Micah,
and decided to add him to the mix. So when

Land of Snakes

Ortega wasn't around, she stole some of the most incriminating evidence they had on Pablo. Without the evidence they didn't have a case against Pablo. Until they re-gathered the information they once had. Sarina pulled in the parking lot of the condo; she tapped on the horn a few times to signal Micah she was outside. Moments later Micah rushed down the stairs and slide into the car.

"Let's get to it," Micah spoke cheerfully as he climbed into the car with Sarina. He was ready to get back to making money. Granted he still had a hefty amount from the money he took from Turks spot, he wanted more.

The exchanged went better than Micah had attended it too. Pablo had included two more bricks into the deal. In the past he had made some mistakes, everyone had done so. In his mind you had to stumble around before becoming one of the great, and that was his plan. He was ready to prove he knew how to get money, and run an operation just like any other nigga getting money.

"I see you in a better mood, I guess good pussy, and knowing paper coming can do that," Sarina smiled as she sped off. "Now let's go see the final piece to get this shit started."

Sarina took a deep breath as she parked the car in the restaurant parking lot. She stepped out the car looking like she was going on a date to Mr. Chow's then to a business meeting. The sound of her heels clicked against the cheap tile floor of the Mexican restaurant, as she led the way Micah staggering right behind her. "Hector?" She called out nearing the back office.

Ortega sat in the back of the Mexican restaurant descried as being one of the many business he owed. There weren't any people inside but the undercover police in the kitchen recording the conversation. "In here," Ortega spoke.

"Well look at you, how was the vacation?" Sarina smiled leaning over the desk to embrace Ortega.

"It was lovely. I didn't want to come back, but business has to be attended too. And when we're talking money, you know I'm all ears." Ortega smiled glancing in Micah direction then focusing his attention to Sarina. "How is Abuela? And the little one, but he is getting big." Ortega asked with a wide grin.

"They are good, you have to stop by more often, but let's get down to business. I know you have other business and things to attend too. This here is my friend Micah," Sarina spoke pointing at Micah who stood inches from her looking around the room.

"So Micah, it looks like my dear cousin Sarina is smitten by you. What brings you to these parts of town? And what do you expect to gain?"

"Money. I'm all about getting money, I have a family to look after, and money around my area seemed to have slowed down," Micah replied.

"I can respect that. Sam!" Ortega called out. A tall slender white gentleman entered the office.

Land of Snakes

"What can I do for you boss?" The man asked clad in chef attire.

"Search him for any wires," Ortega said pointing to Micah.

"Hands behind your head," Sam spoke. He began to frisk Micah. He was working undercover alongside Sarina and Ortega.

"What's this shit?" Micah questioned looking over at Sarina, then to Ortega.

"You can't be too sure. I don't know you, but what Sarina has told me. For all I know you can be the police, a women can be blinded by dick, and not see the odd signs."

"I can feel that but, what about you? You can be the police," Micah spat.

"You are coming to me, not the other way around."

"He's clean boss?"

"Thanks Sam, you may be excused. Now that we have that covered, and don't take it personal. In this line of business you can't trust everyone, even your own flesh, will fuck you over." Ortega said glancing over at Sarina. "I usually don't do business with those who aren't from around here. Sarina, put in a good word for you, and I trust my family. So I'm going to give you a chance to make us, both some money. There is about three blocks that are unclaimed right now. They were once controlled by a man name Spank, but since someone aired him and his whole crew out, the streets have been unclaimed. I'm losing money, with them being dry. So I'm going to allow you to serve your product on those blocks, and provide a little man power for you, unless you have your own crew?"

"Nah, I don't. I roll solo," Micah said.

"Well I can handle that with a few of my most trusted. I want my twenty percent monthly dues just like the county recipients, I want my funds on the first of every month." Ortega said.

"It sounds all good in all, but twenty percent. That's a lot when I am fronting my own product. I can just go out and slang slimy rocks hand to hand, and keep my twenty." Micah spoke.

"I don't know how y'all in Los Angeles do it, but here in the Bay. We do shit different; by all means you can go out there and set up shop and serve hand to hand transactions, and fuck around and lose your life. This isn't a game; it's a lifestyle, which many cherish, and people die for." Micah sat and pondered. He had already stirred up enough drama in Los Angeles, he needed a clean slate. He would obey by Hector's rules, for the moment. He wanted everything, and everywhere. His mind was on takeover, so until he learned the area and everyone, he would play by Hectors rules.

"Okay, I'm down. But, say after six months of me doing well, which I am confident that I will do. We will get together and discuss lowering the percentage.

"We will see. We can't say what can or what cannot happen in six months. Only time can reveal that," Ortega smiled. He knew he wasn't going to allow Micah to roam the streets in six

Land of Snakes

months. He planned to have him sharing a three by three by that time.

"We sure will," Micah spoke. He stood followed by Ortega. Micah gripped his hand, to give it a shake. It was something about him, he didn't like. He couldn't put his finger on it, but he knew it was something.

"Well I look forward to doing business with you," Ortega gave him a half smile turning his attention to Sarina. "You know how everything goes down.

"Likewise," Micah replied slightly puzzled by Hectors words to Sarina.

"I know," Sarina replied gathering her purse. "Thanks for helping my friend out. I know this is only the beginning to some major power moves."

"You know I will always look out for family, until you fuck me. Now, everything he does is a reflection on you, you brought him into this operation. Maria will be waiting for you,"

"I understand. I have never brought harm your way, and don't intend to now. I'll kill him myself, if he was to ever double cross you." Sarina said eyeing Micah.

"Thanks for looking out, again." Micah said as he and Sarina made their way out the building.

"What does he mean by you know how everything goes down? Micah questioned Sarina when they got to the car.

"He was saying I know where the location you will be sitting up at, and all of that."

"Oh, why he couldn't just say that."

"I don't know, but let's head over there."

"Something isn't right with him, I just feel it. Something is off."

"He is just cautious, it comes with the game. He didn't get this far, on good faith."

"If you say so," Micah replied sitting back and putting his game plan together. "You know where I can buy a little cool low-key car, where they not gone be all in my business and shit."

"My home girl has a plug at the police auction. She can get you a descent car for the low."

"Hell nah, I'm not fucking with a damn police auction. I don't fuck with the police, and damn sure not gone drive a car that they have information on, fuck no!" Micah sneered.

"Well shit, I was trying to help you. Calm yo' ass down. It's a street not too far from here, there's always car parked along the curb for sale. Find a fiend, and have them put the car in their name, for some work." Sarina suggested. "What you on the run or something?" She questioned.

"Nah, I am good. I just don't want shit in my name. right now, I'm tryna' stay low-key." Micah replied.

"Let me know, if you see any cars when I pass," Sarina said cursing down the street bypass a row of cars for sale.

Micah looked at the cars, looking to see if he saw any that was cool enough for him, but saw none.

"Nah, I don't like any of these."

Land of Snakes

"Okay." Sarina said turning up the music. She could tell Micah was not in the mood for conversation and was thinking. She wanted to know what he was thinking, but couldn't put too much pressure on him.

Micah scanned the area of the street Sarina had turned down. It was dirty. Fiends, stray dogs wondered the streets and the entire building look like they were hanging on their last piece of good wood.

"We here," Sarina said pulling in front of a duplex. "It's these two buildings here, and the very last one on the right of this block." Sarina pointed. Sarina and Micah stepped out the car. Micah scanned the area again. Hector, said the block had been unclaimed, Micah was looking for anything that stood out. He had enough streets sense to know either Hector aired the dude Spank out, or someone did preparing to takeover.

"What you looking for?" Sarinia asked noticing Micah lagging behind her.

"The area, and for anything that seems out of place. Hector said the dude got aired out, that can only have been two ways. Gotta' play it safe, I'm not tryna' get aired out." Micah said walking up on Sarina.

"Maria is the look out, so you can always count on her being your second set of eyes and ears," Sarina said as the approached the font house of the duplex. "Maria," Sarina yelled banging on the door.

A short older Hispanic woman came to the door.

173

"Sarina, long times no see. Hector told me you have a new friend in the neighborhood?" Maria said eyeing Micah.

"I know I have been super busy. This is Micah. He will be moving in, I need you to be his eyes and ears. Like always, Hector, will take care of you."

"Okay. Welcome Micah. Just let me know how I can be any service to you." The women spoke with a half-smile. Maria was the neighborhood watch. She worked closely with the police, and helped out anytime she could. She had been in the community for over 30 years, with her family. Five years prior her husband was gunned down, by a drug gang that controlled the area at the time. Her husband had grown tired of them standing and hustling in front of his door, and trying to get with his daughters. A heavy argument turned into a fight, and Maria husband being shot nine times, dying in front of their house, in front of his daughter. A year later, her daughter killed herself. From that moment on, Maria vowed to help the police bring drug dealers down.

"Nice to meet you Maria and thank you for any help you can provide. Please never hesitate to let me know if you need help with anything." Micah said extending his hand to Maria, who gladly shook it.

"Oh no, I'm fine. Hector takes very good care of me," She replied. "Here are the keys to all the buildings." Maria said digging into her moo-moo handing Sarina several sets of keys. "I have to go,

Land of Snakes

I have food on the stove, and Sarina don't be a stranger."

"I won't," Sarina said as they headed to the apartments. "Here are the keys to every apartment, in all three buildings. You can pick where you sitting up at, and get to it. I suggest you use more than one apartment, you don't ever want someone to know everything, you never know when someone is watching your every step." Sarina smiled as she led the way into the building.

"Thanks Sarina. You a real bitch, you my nigga fo' sho," Micah laughed taking her into his arms, planting a juicy kiss onto her lips.

"I told you, I got you."

EIGHTEEN

Gia sat in the waiting room of the Planned Parenthood awaiting her name to be called. She was plagued with a ray of emotions. She knew it was only right she terminate her pregnancy, but deep down, a small part of her wanted to carry and give birth to the child she created. But, she didn't want to end up, like so many of her friends from high school, bringing children into the world, who wasn't wanted. She didn't disclose it to her mother, but growing up she hated to see others with their father, because she didn't have one. She didn't want that for her child. Kenny, had been calling her non-stop threating to kill her, if he found out she kept the baby. He would sit outside her house into the wee hours, to see if any other men were showing up. Without any of her brother's around, Gia was scared he would actually harm her. She knew he didn't have it all, especially when he choose to pop molly's and consumed several cups of lean, on the daily. Gia glanced over at her mother; she knew she had to do it. She was all her mother had, and bringing this child into the world, may change that, and she couldn't chance it. "Ma, I'm scared. Can you say a prayer for me?"

"It's already been done Gia. I'm always praying for you." Pamela said glancing over at her daughter. Pamela didn't believe in abortions, but she understood why some women went through with them. Pamela said a prayer for Gia, as well as one for herself. She didn't admit it to Gia, but she was happy she wasn't going through with the pregnancy. She believed in marriage before children, and wanted that for her daughter. On top of that, she didn't care for Kenny at all; he wasn't what a mother wanted for her only daughter.

"You don't have to go through with this, like I said the choice is yours,"

"I have to do it,"

"All you have to do is pray that God will take all of your troubles away. I hope you're not doing this only to please Kenny? Like I told you before, only you Gia Jones has to live with the end results."

"Gia Jones," The nurse called out.

"Right here," Gia said standing and following the nurse inside. Her stomach fluttered as she walked behind the nurse.

"Room 3, I will be back in a few." The nurse said sitting her chart down and walking back out. Gia looked around at all the different baby informational posters all around the room. Tears began to pour from her eyes.

"Are you okay?" The nurse said coming back into the room.

"Yes," Gia replied clearing the tears from her face. I'm just a little scared.

"First abortion?" the nurse questioned.

"Yes,"

"I know it may be hard, but this isn't your only choice."

"I have to do it," Gia said

"May I ask why?"

"It's either this, or my life. I don't want to bring a child into this madness, or without a father."

"Single mothers have done it for years, alone. I know it's not right, but its life .I'm sorry to intrude,"

"It's okay," Gia said.

"I know you said this was your first abortion? But is this your first pregnancy or do you already have a child?"

"No, this is my first,"

The nurse took Gia's height and weight, blood pressure and then escorted her to the operation room. "Would you like to be put to sleep?"

"Yes, please."

"Okay, once it's done, you will be in recovery for about half hour to an hour. Is there anyone here with you, or do you need to call a ride?"

"My mother's here with me, she is in the waiting room waiting on me."

The Doctor sedated her, and before Gia knew it. She was waking up in the recovery room, it was over. With the help of the nurse Gia, made it to the waiting area, where Pamela rushed to her side. "How are you feeling?" Pamela asked taking Gia into her arms.

"I just want to go home and lay down," Gia replied weakly.

"Okay, the taxi should be pulling up shortly," Pamela said as they made their way outside.

It didn't take long for the taxi to arrive. The short ride to their apartment was filled with silence.

Land of Snakes

"C'mon let mama get you upstairs," Pamela said as she paid the taxi driver.
Despite the abortion going quickly, Gia was left tired and emotional drained and riddled by guilt.

"Gia," A male voice called out from behind them as Pamela and Gia climbed the stairs of their apartment. The voice caught the attention of both women, it was Kenny. "Can I talk to you for a minute?"

"No, I'm not feeling well right now."

"It will only be for a few minutes," Kenny pleaded.

"And I said no! We don't have anything to talk about. I had the damn abortion, now leave me alone." Gia said nervously. She knew Kenny wouldn't try much with her mother around. She couldn't be sure the way he neared the staircase where they stood.

"Well fuck you bitch," Kenny sneered his ego was busied she didn't want to speak with him.

"Now wait one got damn minute!" Pamela yelled. She rushed down the few stairs so that she was close to Kenny. "You better get your ass way from here, and I do mean now! If you ever in your damn life, but your hands on my child," Pamela pointed to Gia. "Again, you will feel a raft, like never before. I don't need my sons, to handle you. I have a Louis Ville Slugger that has your name on it. Make me use it, you gone wish all I did was call the police." Pamela said sternly staring Kenny in his eyes.

"No disrespect Mrs. Pamela, but this shit has nothing to do with you. It's between Gia and I."

"Gia Jones is my daughter, and she doesn't want to talk to you. So go find someone else to talk to, because she isn't it. I'm not gone tell you again, to get away from my house, and to stay the hell away from my daughter." Pamela said gripping her purse, just in case Kenny tried something.

Kenny glared back at Pamela, he knew she was serious. She wasn't backing down, and there wasn't a sign of fear in her eyes.

"I don't have time for this shit," Kenny spat backing away giving both Gia and Pamela a dirty look.

"That would be best, because you not prepared for this war. "Pamela spoke as she watched Kenny rush off and jump into his car. She waited for Kenny to drive off, before she finished retreating up the stair's into her apartment. "You want something to eat baby?"

"No, I'm tired and in pain. Imma' go lay it down for a few."

"Okay."

"Ma?" Gia called out.

"Yeah," Pamela turned to face Gia.

"Thank you,"

"For what," Pamela questioned.

"For being by myself always, I know you don't believe in abortions."

"You are my child, I will always be by your side, when you are right and even when you're wrong helping you correct you wrongs, and get it right. Now get you some rest." Pamela smiled.

Land of Snakes

NINETEEN

Micah sat in deep thought, Sarina laid next to him, naked in a light slumber. It had been a few days since the meeting with Hector, and Micah couldn't be happier. Just like Sarina had said, the streets of Richmond had money to be made. The fiends quickly took a liking to the product, and the money came to him in abundance, it made Micah even hungrier for the takeover he knew was in his future. Through the grapevine he had heard his brother's funeral would be coming up. He hadn't thought much of them, and was torn on whether or not he should show his face at the funeral. He knew the streets were in rage about Sin and Rich's deaths, but hadn't heard of anyone pointing in his direction. Not even in the case of Turk, or his spot.

"Micah!" Sarina called out for the third time.

"Yeah," Micah replied finally hearing Sarina yell into his ear.

"What the hell? Are you okay? Your damn phone has been ringing nonstop. That shit woke me up," Sarina said throwing his phone onto his lap. "It was Maria, she said they out over there."

"Okay," Micah replied getting up to put his clothes back on. "Can you run me over there; the dude had to change the starter in the car." Micah said he had finally found a car he liked, and purchased days ago, from a friend of Sarina's.

"Yeah, let me shower real quick," Sarina said making her way towards the bathroom. Micah sat on the bed, waiting for her to get ready, still in deep thought. Sarina had noticed the last few

181

days he had been distance. She needed to know where his head was. Sarina quickly showered and slipped on a maxi dress. When they got to the car, Sarina glanced over at Micah, who looked out the window. "You good? You been zoned out all day, shit, for a few days."

"Yeah, I'm good. I just have a lot of shit on my mind."

"You want to talk about it? You know I'm here for you."

"Not really," Micah replied.
Sarina didn't bother forcing him to tell her what was going on with him, she knew in time he would, she needed to always know his moves. As they neared the apartments Micah turned the loud music down. "Next week, imma' be gone for a few days. I'm gone need you to hold shit down," Micah said never looking at her.

"Where are you going?" Sarina questioned staring at him.

"Remember that night you called me?"

"Yeah,"

"I told you I wanted to get out of LA, because it was a drought. Well, that wasn't the full truth of why I wanted to leave. That same night, I saw my brothers get killed, and feared for my life." Micah paused. "There funeral is coming up next week, and I need to be there. My mama doesn't even know if I'm dead, or alive. He spoke low never giving her direct eye contract.

"Oh my! I'm sorry to hear that. I couldn't even image losing two siblings and seeing them be killed. My sister was killed almost three years

Land of Snakes

ago, by her husband. I know the feeling." Sarina tried to sympathize with Micah. In reality, Sarina didn't even shed a tear when her sister was killed. Sarina felt she deserved it, because it was her ex-boyfriend that her sister married.

"This shit been eating me up, I try to not think about it, but it's hard. I know my mother is going through it. My little brother was on his way to college. I gotta' be there for her." Micah said. Deep down Micah was more scared of how his mother would treat him, if she knew it was his entire fault, which was digging at him, not the actual loss of his brothers.

"I can go with you, if you need me to."

"Nah, I got it. It something I have to do, alone. I need you here, holding shit down. It's only been a few days, but shit looking bright

"I got you, don't worry. Just go handle your family, and get back," Sarina smiled.
Since the night he went to her hotel, Sarina had been right by his side. She had showed him another side of her. He never really cared for a chick; he used them for what he could get out of them, and then was onto the next. Besides Kym, he had never entertained the thought of cuffing a chick. Kym was everything he could've wanted in a woman, but she was never truly his. She was Sin's, and after the grimy stunt she pulled. It proved she was a bitch he didn't want to cuff; she was fueled by a niggas stash. Micah never saw the signs, because he was blinded by her big ass, and good pussy, and the fact that he had something that was Sin's. Sarina, on the other

hand was different. She was born to a family of hustlers straight from Puerto Rico. She knew how to be a woman and hold down her man. Not only was she drop dead gorgeous, loyal and down with his lifestyle. She cooked, cleaned and fucked him on the regular.

"Thanks, you really be looking out for a nigga. When shit gets right, I'm gone make sure I spoil yo' ass," Micah said gripping her face stared in her eyes before kissing her. "I'm gone chill here for a little while."

"Well then, I'm gone run to my grandma's. Call me when you're ready."

"Cool," Micah said checking his surroundings before stepping out the car and heading into the building. Sarina waited until Micah stepped into the building before she pulled off headed to the undercover spot which was a few blocks away.

"Juan," Sarina called out walking into the apartment that Detective Ortega hung out at. She didn't see him, or the unmarked town car he usually drove. On the several monitors, she saw the condo, where Micah had been staying and a few of the apartments where Micah handle his business.

"What's good?" Ortega said coming out the bathroom with the towel wrapped around his wrist. His ripped chest still, drenched with water.

"Damn! Have you been working out?" Sarina questioned as her eyes roamed all over his body. Ortega stood at 6'4, with a rippled chest, a 6 pack, broad shoulders and strong muscular legs. He was eye candy. He was a mixture of both The Rock, and actor Omari Hardwick.

"Oh. You noticed?" He grinned. "I thought your little boyfriend had you all caught up, over there with them back shots," He laughed. "Yes! Right there!" He mimicked.

"You know I'm always paying attention. You get a kick out of watching me fuck another man?"

"It's fun to watch, especially since I know, he can't fuck you like I do."

"So you say."

"So I know. What's up with this dude anyway? We really don't need him for this case. We still have all the wire taps at Pablo's. We just need to get Pablo on their sitting up a meeting with who he gets the product from, and him getting a shipment."

"Don't worry about him, I got that part, he will go down right alone with Pablo and his connect. How about in the meantime, you come show me how you fuck me better than he does." Sarina smiled.

"Oh I can do that, and when I'm done I want you to tell me, I did that." Ortega spoke pushing Sarina up against the wall. Like a magnet their lips connected. In one swift motion Ortega slid Sarina's short maxi dress up, over her head, and had her legs up on his shoulders. "Damn!" Sarina laughed at how fast he picked her body up.

"Don't get excited to fast, you gone be begging me to stop in a minute," Ortega laughed as he smacked his tongue against her dripping pussy, enticing her.

"Stop teasing me," Sarina yelled shoving her pussy into his face.

"What you talking about?" Ortega laughed smacking his tongue again. Bringing her legs up, Ortega gripped her by the back of her thighs, by her knees, until her plump ass was in his face, slightly spreading her legs, so he was eye to eye with her pussy. He made sure to pin her against the wall, so she couldn't move as he greedily devoured her pussy. Sarina winded her hips to the movement of his tongue. She couldn't help but to push his head deeper into her pussy, the way he sucked on her clit, sent a shock over her body. "FUCK! FUCK!" She yelled grinding on his face. Sarina didn't know how much more she could take before she squirted all over his face. Ortega dropped her legs down, cuffing her into his forearms, dropping his towel from around his waist. Positioning his massive harden penis, at her opening. Sarina gladly slid down, welcoming him into her dampen vagina. With a slick grin on his face, he wasted no time stroking in and out of her pulsating pussy. With her legs pent back locked in his forearms, she couldn't move, just like he wanted. Ortega plunged deep and hasty into her pussy. All she could do was holler out of ecstasy, as her fingers tugged into his back. Spent, and out of breathe, Sarina was happy when Ortega decided to let her down.

"We ani't done yet, go bend that ass over,"

Land of Snakes

Sarina bent over the sofa, throwing her ass into the air. Ortega wasted no time sliding back inside her. Gripping her by the nape of her neck Ortega slammed into her making her ass create a wave with every stroke.

"Who fuck this pussy better?" Ortega questioned squeezing her neck tight.

"Yoouu..."

"I can't hear you. Who fuck this pussy the best?" Ortega questioned smacking her ass. Beads of sweat dripped down his body.

"YOU!" She moaned throwing her ass back.

"Yeah throw that ass back, fuck me back." He yelled as he palmed her ass. "I want to hear you tell me who fuck you better."

"You... You fuck me the best. Shit," Sarina moaned sliding back and forth on his dick. Ortega pumped faster and faster until he released himself. "Damn. I needed that shit more than I thought," Ortega said. "I know you better be fucking that nigga with protection. Don't let me catch you fucking him raw again," He snapped smacking her ass hard.

"Damn, that shit hurt," Sarina yelled trying to catch her breath as she stretched out on the couch. "That was only that one time and we were drunk."

Still fully naked Ortega took a seat at the desk.

"What's wrong with your little punk ass boyfriend? He looks a little down. Imagine if he knew the real you." Ortega spoke hawking at Micah on the screen as he sat under surveillance in the apartment he used as his stash spot.

"His brothers were killed a few weeks ago, their funeral is coming up, I guess he's emotional,"

"Who are his brothers? What gang is he from? Most of those damn young dudes from Los Angeles ripping' some streets that was their before they were born, and will be there after their death with the same name."

"I'm not sure. He didn't give me any names, just said his brothers."

"You're the damn police, you can find it out. What's his name again? I heard that name before but I can't place it right now."

"James is the last name," Sarina said lying. "Micah James."

"I'm going to have someone at the station look again. I know he should have some arrest record, then again, he look like a bitch."

Micah sat at the table. His mind was everywhere. He was feeling the effects of the lines he snorted mixed with the cheap liquor he consumed. He didn't want to admit it, but he knew he was a fuck up. Here he was surrounded by niggas' he didn't know, moving enough product to send him to prison for the rest of his life. He knew if Sin was alive to see him, he would really clown him, everyone that knew him would. This was the life he wanted, but now that he had almost everything he wanted, he battled wether it was worth it. Micah could hear a creak at the door. "Who is it?" Micah questioned wiping his nose for any residue. No one answered. "Who the fuck is it?" He yelled. Rushing to the door, but

Land of Snakes

no one was there. "Damn you tripping' nigga," Micah said to himself busting into laughter. He sat back at the table and snorted another line. He could hear Sin's laughter. With each sip of the liquor Sin's wicked laughter grew louder making him hate him even more. Micah needed to hear his mother's voice; she always made whatever he was going through better. Slowly Micah dialed his mother number, the ringing of the phone made his heart race. He didn't know the words he would say. He didn't know if she was mad at him, or if she hated him.

"Hello?" A voice called out. Micah was in deep thought and hadn't realized that someone had answered. "Hello?" The voice said again. "Micah? Is that you son? Micah?" Pamela questioned.

Micah wanted to answer, but the words wouldn't come out. "Son I know it's you. I can feel it, come home. Or at least let me know you are okay, I have been worried sick," Pamela said into the phone trying to hold back her tears.

"Ma, I'm okay." Micah said weakly as the tears streamed down his face. "I love you ma," He said before disconnecting the call. Micah called Sarina to pick him up.

When Sarina arrived she noticed Micah was out of it, fumbling with his words, and stumbling. He told her he had consumed too much liquor. His pride wouldn't allow him to tell her, he had just snorted a gram of the purest form of cocaine. When they arrived at the condo, Micah fucked Sarina long and hard until his body went limp and he fell asleep. Sarina lay next to him; she knew he was on something more than liquor. She just hoped it didn't get out of hand, before her plans came into effect.

Land of Snakes

TWENTY

The days seemed to past fast. Micah tried to keep busy so that he wouldn't go through an emotional rollercoaster. Some days he was up, and felt good about the choices he made. Then other times he felt the guilt of his actions. Micah sat at the foot of the bed, packing a small duffle bag. He hadn't snorted any coke, from that day, but he wanted to, but knew it would cloud his judgment.

"What's that?" Sarina asked coming into the room.

"I decided to catch the train down to LA tonight. The funeral is Thursday, I wanted to get there early and check up on some things, and help my mom's and sister out." Micah said.

"How long will you be gone?"

"Just until like Saturday. You can hold it down until then right?" He questioned pulling her in close.

"Of course I can." Sarina said slightly stepping back. She hoped Micah wasn't trying to fuck before he left. Between Ortega and him, she was tired and her pussy needed a rest.

"Well I want to run by the spot and go over a few things with you. Just to make sure you good, while I'm gone."

"What time does the train leave?"

"In about three hours."

"And…. When were you going to tell me this? When you made it to LA?" She questioned pushing Micah away from her. She searched for her cell phone. She needed to know his whereabouts at all time. She hoped he wasn't getting suspicions.

"It's not like that. I got the call this morning and booked the first thing down that way. You weren't here and not answering your phone. Thinking about it, where were you all morning and why didn't you answer any of my calls?" Micah questioned.

"My uncles are in town, I had to run them around and then clean my grandma's house. I left my phone at her house and once I saw you called, I was already on my way here." Sarina quickly lied. She hadn't expected him to question her back.

"When am I going to be able to meet the family and this grandma you always talking about? And what does your grandma think when you are gone for days at a time?"

"My grandma knows that in order for me to take great care of her, and my nephew I must work. And my work requires travel, and for me to be on the go. You worry about being there for your family in LA, right now. When you get back we will talk about you meeting my family. Since I couldn't come to LA, to meet your mom and sister," Sarina said.

"Okay, I got you. If it was under better circumstance, I would've loved to take you with me and introduce you to my mom's and sister. My mom's would like you, I don't know about my sister, that's another story."

"In due time, we will meet each other's family when the time is right."

Land of Snakes

"You right. I'm gone take a nap, before we leave to head to the apartments."

"Okay," Sarina said slipping her phone into her hand when Micah wasn't looking and making her way into the bathroom. It had been buzzing since she walked through the door. She knew it had to be Ortega, because it was her work phone.

"Hello," She said into the phone above a whisper.

"Get your ass here NOW!" He yelled into the phone. "We have a crack in the case, big time. Meet me at the apartment."

"Okay. I'm tied up, I will be there as soon as I finish." Sarina said hanging up. She flushed the toilet, and washed her hands. In the hallway, hung a long mirror, Sarina stopped glancing at herself. At 32, she still could pass for early 20's. Along the way she had accomplished a lot for herself, but she wasn't sure it was enough. She wanted simpler things, like the undying love of a man. She thought she had found it before, but like every other man, he left her heartbroken and pregnant. Now she settled for what little a man gave her, like sleeping with her partner knowing he was a married man. Ortega wasn't discreet about his cheating ways. He had slept with over a dozen female officers.

"Sarina?" Micah called out noticing how she stood staring at her reflection.

"Huh?" She questioned facing Micah.

"You okay?"

"Yeah, I just was looking at myself. I need to get back in the gym, I'm getting fat." She replied.

"I don't know where, cause you still fine as shit," He laughed. "I'm good on that nap, so whenever you ready is good with me."

"Okay, well we can go now. Once I drop you off I'm going to head to my grandma's spend time over there, while your gone."
The car ride was silent as Sarina wonder what big crack did they have in the case. Lately she couldn't read Micah, and she didn't like that. She had to know what he was thinking, his moves and what he had planned. "You good?" Sarina asked putting her personal feelings about her life to the side.

"I'm good, just thinking that's all." Micah replied. "In these last weeks, you have been a real great friend. I didn't think your kind existed. I can't tell you how thankful I am."

"You already told me that, you are welcome."

"You don't understand how thankful I am though. I will keep telling you."

"You my nigga, I just couldn't leave you down and out."

"Is that all, I am just your nigga?" Micah questioned.

"Where is all this coming from? You know you my nigga, been my nigga for a while now," Sarina said nervously, she knew where the conversation was headed.

Land of Snakes

"I've always found you to be beautiful as hell. Within these last weeks of us kicking it super tough, I have saw you are more than a pretty face with a banging ass body that I fuck from time to time when we run into each other. I see you as a woman, a woman I want as my woman."

Sarina glanced over to see if he was serious, and he was.

"For real?" She questioned puzzled. The Micah she had met, and grown to know, wasn't into cuffing any chicks. All he wanted to do was get money, and fuck.

"Why would I sit here and lie? You are every man's dream women. Hood, but classy, beautiful and I promise I can go on," Micah laughed. "What man wouldn't want a woman like you, to be his?'

Sarina became extremely nervous. She didn't know what to say. She never had a man really speak to her like that before. She knew Micah really didn't know her. If he knew the real person she was, and her motives for him. He would run, fast and far from her. "There is plenty that you don't know about me,"

"And I'm sure there is shit about me, you don't know about me. Isn't that how relationships go? You learn as you go and develop?"

"Yeah, but you wouldn't look at me the same," Sarina said putting her head down. She didn't want to feel wanted by him, it was wrong. The last time that happened, she almost lost everything she worked hard for, and she still was

195

left without his love. "Let's not rush anything, and give it some thought. Make sure it's something we both want and can handle. I don't want to have my heartbroken again."

"I'm not looking to break your heart, but possibly mend it. I promise that is never my intentions to hurt you. Life is short; I want someone to spend my crazy nights with. All I ask for, is that you remain true to me at all times, and I will run it back a hunnit' fold,"

"We will have this talk more, once you back in town, and your mind is clear. I know right now you are emotional, not saying you trying to run game to me. I just have seen the change in you, within these last few days. If you still feel the same, when you get back we will talk about taking us to the next level," Sarina smiled throwing the car into park.

"Okay, I'm telling you now a nigga not working on emotions." Micah said as they both climbed out of the car. Micah checked in with Maria like he always did, letting her know he would be out of town and to contact Sarina, for everything and she would call him. When they finished with Maria, Micah broke down how he kept everything separated and where everything was located and made sure the young dude he had working under him, knew Sarina and that she was in charge. It had taken only days for Micah to find some young and hungry workers. He still used a few of Hectors guys for muscle, but planned to change it when he got back into town.

Land of Snakes

"You run a pretty tight ship, to be a drug dealer."

"I learned from watching my older brother, he was no joke."

"You must really look up to him?"

"Something like that."

"So we're good on product?" Sarina question

"Yeah we should be good, unless you trying to move major work, in a few days? Micah chuckled.

"Hey, you never know what I could do. Remember this is my city. Never underestimate the power of a woman. We do anything; including making a man look good." Sarina said clicking the alarm on the car.

"Okay woman, based on what we been moving on a daily, we should be good for the next few days. "

"Okay," Sarina said as she parked alongside the curb on the train station. Micah reached over and kissed her, like never before. He kissed her with so much passion, her clit jumped. It was like he really wanted her.

"See you in a few days," Micah said getting out of the car.

"Be safe," Sarina said watching him walking up to go into the train station. Soon as she saw Micah, go inside Sarina raced off. Ortega had been blowing her phone up non-stop for the last hour. Sarina darted in and out of traffic trying to get to the safe house.

"I'm pulling up now, shit." Sarina yelled into the phone quickly hanging up before Ortega was even able to say something. She knew all he was going to do is bitch. Sarina pranced into the apartment, prepared to have it out with Ortega. He was always so vexed about everything, and controlling.

"About damn time, I have been here waiting. I have actually been here working, while your over there fucking that young punk." Ortega ranted eying Sarina.

"Whatever Juan," Sarina sighed. "Just fill me in on why you have been blowing my phone up, non-stop," Sarina snapped back.

"While you were out fucking your little boyfriend," Ortega said again. "I was here listening and reviewing the wire taps. I overheard a conversation between Pablo and Hussein. The drop is happening the day after tomorrow, early morning like Pablo, is known to do. I have already contacted the Captain, he is waiting on our arrival, and he also wants to speak with you about a case you worked in Los Angeles."

"Okay, well let's head there now." Sarina replied dryly already headed for the door.

"I've been ready. I was waiting on you. You were too busy probably letting that young nigga run inside of you," Ortega spat for the third time in less than ten minutes.

"Do you have anything you want to say to me? Spit the shit out and stop pussy footing. You have repeated the same damn thing three times. Do you want to know if I fucked him today? The answer is YES! And I loved it. Is that what you want to hear?" Sarina questioned. She was at her wits end with Ortega.

"Yeah I do. You are more worried about fucking that damn drug dealer, then focusing on the biggest bust of your career. Haven't you learned about fucking with those young punks? Or do I have to show you again?" He smirked grabbing his jacket.

"You know what, fuck you! I'm a detective, and a damn good one at that. I'm undercover. Fucking him is about my cover, to get my job done."

"And what about fucking me? Since you are bouncing your ass between the both of us. Shit, you might as well hop on the corner with the rest of these low budget hoes."

"You're just fun and a good nut. Some shit, I wouldn't ever let be known in public," Sarina spat bypassing him and making her way downstairs to the unmarked car he drove.

Ortega wouldn't admit it. He didn't like the fact of Sarina sharing her goods with another man, especially a low- life like Micah. In his mind, she belonged to him, and he should be the only one fucking her. Ortega climbed into the car; he could tell Sarina was pissed about the things he said to her out of anger. "I'm sorry I lost my cool. I had no right to disrespect you."

"Whatever. Can we just head to the station, so we can get this shit over with," Sarina said looking out the window. She was beyond fed up with Ortega outrageous temper. She wasn't his woman, in fact he was married. He didn't have control over his wife anymore, so he tried to force control on Sarina. She was looking forward to the case coming to an end. She was tired of working alongside Ortega. Months ago, she put in for a transfer back to Los Angeles where she had started. She was ready to end this chapter of her life, and start fresh after handling Micah. Like always they arrived to the station, and it was a madhouse. People were scattered everywhere, the holding tanks were full of people waiting to be booked, and some waited to be transported to the county jail. Sarina strolled through the station headed to the Captains office, Ortega followed closely behind.

"Is the Captain in his office?" Ortega asked the sergeant of the day.

"Yes, Detective Ortega He is inside with two detectives from Los Angeles," The short pudgy sergeant responded.

"Detective Ortega and Lopez," A voice said from behind them. "If it isn't the best duo still trying to take down the infamous Pablo and his army I hear?" Detective O'Hara smiled coming out of the Captain's office. She was a lead Detective out in LA, and she despised the ground Sarina walked on. When O'Hara entered the force years prior she was partnered with Ortega. She was new and wanted to fit in, and was willing to do anything to be liked by her fellow officers. Like so many other female officers, she found herself lusting after the handsome Detective Ortega. Just like he had done so many other women officers. He fucked her a few times, and was done with her. O'Hara didn't like the feeling of rejection and being used. When Ortega wouldn't fuck her again, she reported him to I.A.B for sexual harassment in the workplace. After a short investigation, they deemed O'Hara scorned and transferred her to Los Angeles's Homicide unit.

O'Hara's only beef with Sarina was Ortega. She hated the fact it wasn't a secret that Sarina and Ortega had been fucking on and off for a while. She was upset Sarina was getting what she couldn't. O'Hara made it her duty to get under Sarina's skin. To let her know, she wasn't anything special, that she had already been with him along with a slew of other female officers.

"O'Hara, what are you doing here? You don't work in this jurisdiction any longer, have you forgot?" Sarina questioned with an attitude. Whenever the ladies were in each other's presence the tension was thick. So thick it would require a special butcher's knife to even peek inside.

"We are here because we have some possible leads on some cases that occurred here, as well as in L.A." O'Hara said.

"What cases? Are these murders?" Sarina questioned again.

"They are kidnappings that have been happening all over east Oakland. We have had three within this week alone. Two happened in the very same area in south bay, and one on the north side of Long Beach. With the information we have gained, and the pattern. It looks like it's the same man. Hispanic male 5'8 to 5'10 medium build dark colored hair. I know you worked a similar case a few years back. It looks like they are kidnapping people the very same way."

"Did they get a license plate number or a partial plate number?"

"From an eyewitness we got a partial of JM6, but she isn't sure in what order she saw them."

"Have we gotten this information out to patrol?" Would the witness be able to give a sketch? Or know the make and model of the vehicle?" Sarina questioned. In the last couple of months it had been a string of kidnappings throughout the bay area. Almost all leading to finding the victim found dead, days after being kidnapped from a public place.

"We ran it by the captain. We are waiting for them to fax us over the one a woman in Los Angeles gave us last week.

"Well in the meantime I will find someone who can help pull up any suspect that fit the profile and have previous offenses." Sarina spoke leaving O'Hara where she stood to search for an officer on desk duty to assist her. "O'Hara," Sarina called out signaling for her to join where she stood. "This is Officer Reed." Sarina pointed to the young officer setting at the desk. "Reed, this is Detective O'Hara from the Los Angeles Bureau. We are looking for a kidnapping suspect, we need to cross reference with those latest kidnapping and the suspect description," Sarina spoke to the young officer. "Have we gotten the sketch yet?"

Land of Snakes

"No. it hasn't come in as of yet," O'Hara responded.

"Well can you give him the suspect's description until the fax comes over?" O'Hara sat the folder she was cradling in her hand down on the edge of the desk, as she quickly rambled through other sheets of papers she had in her hand for the paper she wrote the suspect's description on. In such a rush she bumped her leg on the desk, causing the folder to drop and her papers to scatter. "Shit," She grunted.

"It's okay, I got it. Just find the paper," Sarina said kneeling to pick up the scattered papers from the floor, and nearly choked on her own spit.

"I found it," O'Hara spoke looking down at Sarina who was stuck.

"Oh okay," Sarina said racking up the papers and standing to hand them over to O'Hara.

"You good? Is something bothering you Detective Lopez?" O'Hara questioned noticing the slight change in Sarina's demeanor.

"Yeah, it's just one of those mug shots looks real familiar to me, I'm just trying to place it." Sarina said quickly thinking of something. It was a mug shot of Micah, it was quite old, but he looked the same. Written in O'Hara handwriting was all of Micah's known hangout spots. She needed to know what information O'Hara had on Micah. She had come so close; she didn't need O'Hara coming to mess up all her hard work when it was falling into the right places.

"Which one?" O'Hara questioned anxiously to gain new information on a suspect.

"I think the last name was Jones."

"Where do you think you have seen him before? He is a suspect in a drug related homicide out in L.A. I have checked a few places he was known at, but it seems he is in the wind," O'Hara said handing Sarina Micah's picture. Sarina examined the mug shot like she was trying to place it. "Look's so familiar but I can't place it."

"LOPEZ!" The Captain yelled.

"Let me know if you get any hits, let me go speak with the captain."

"Okay," O'Hara said turning her attention to Officer Reed. To give him the information she had brought with her.
Sarina hurried off to the captain's office, hoping O'Hara didn't bring up Micah's name and mug shot around Ortega.

"Good Afternoon Captain Deed's," Sarina smiled closing the office door behind her.

"Afternoon Lopez. Feel me in on what's going on with this case. I wish you two hurry up, I could use you two on another case. We are swamped here." The Captain grunted out of frustration.

"Well you know we have been investigating a major drug related case on Pablo Marino and the Mexican cartel."

"Ortega! Tell me some shit I don't know. I know who case you're working on. Get to the

good shit, like why you are in my damn office."
The Captain yelled.

"Well yesterday while listening to the wires
we have placed in a known meeting place for
Pablo's people. I overheard him having a
conversation with Hussein."

"And?" The Captain asked.

"Are we talking about Hussein as in the
biggest drug supplier straight outta Cuba?"

"That exact one. They puzzle around it, but I
think a big shipment will be coming along with
him. He is in talks of helping Pablo make more
millions."

"And how can you be sure, it's actually
him?"

"Because," Ortega smiled sliding a small
recorder onto the desk. "I have his voice to prove
it." Pushing play on the recorder they all listened
closely to the interaction between the men.
Instantly when the distinctive voice blared on the
recorder, Captain Deed's blood rose. It was a
voice he would never forget. Captain Deed's had
been after Hussein for more than fifteen years.
He had tried almost every angle on busting
Hussein, but it never worked. He would find
some loop hole in the case, and slid right out of
the charges. A wide grin formed on the captain's
face. He wanted nothing more to throw Hussein
into a federal prison for the rest of his life. With
what he heard on the tape, he knew after years
he would finally have his opportunity to lock
Hussein away.

"I will get a team together, some of the best. Play this one, by the book, as much as we can. You know the history with Hussein. Let's make the last time we go after him. Good job detectives, now let's lock this piece of shit up for good. We will have a briefing five hours before the meet is supposed to happen, here at the station and be in place at least three hours before the meeting is supposed to go down, understand?"

"Understood Captain," Sarina and Ortega said in union as they exited out of the captains office beaming with pride. This was the kind of case they needed under their belt. Sarina hooked a left coming out the Captains office to make her way towards O'Hara and Reed. Who was still at Reed's desk "Any lead yet?" Sarina asked walking up on the two.

"We have narrowed it down, based on prior convictions and arrest. We are still waiting on that damn sketch," O'Hara responded slightly agitated.

"Well good luck, I'm out. If you happen to stumble across any around these parts, the sergeant knows how to reach me," Sarina said walking off to catch up to Ortega.

Land of Snakes

TWENTY- ONE

After a five hour train ride with hollering kids
and tourist that didn't speak a lick of English
Micah had finally arrived to LA. Something about
being in Los Angles made him slightly nervous.
Micah constantly looked over his shoulder as he
headed to the bus stop. Patiently he waited for
the bus to arrive, concealed under his hoodie; he
stood away from traffic and the crowd of people
also waiting to broad the bus. When the bus
arrived, Micah rushed on, finding a spot in the
back of the long bus. As soon as Micah, saw a
motel sign he hopped off the bus. He didn't want
to stay too close to his stomping grounds in fear
of running into someone. Running into the liquor
store Micah grabbed a bottle of liquor, a pizza
from little Caesar and settled in the room. As
much as he loved Los Angeles, in the same
breathes he hated it. It left a sour taste in his
mouth. Being in LA reminded him he wasn't
anything but a wannabe Sin, and that angered
him. In the last few days leading up to coming to
Los Angeles Micah had been an emotional mess.
A small portion of him was guilty for what
happen to his brothers; a larger part felt Sin,
deserve to be killed. He no longer had to be
tucked under his big brothers wings, didn't have
to be looked down on anymore.
Had it just been Sin, that night, that didn't live
Micah, would have felt better about it. So he
chooses to not think about Rich, at all. It was too
much for him to bear with. Sitting alone in the
motel room made his mind wonder. Micah

grabbed the .45 from his bag tucked it in his waist and wondered into the streets. Micah walked down the dimly lit street with no real destination in mind. He just wanted to clear his mind.

"Micah? Is that you?" A voice asked. Micah instantly reached for the gun on his waist becoming nervous. "Who you?" He questioned not able to see the faces clear.

"It's me, Sam. What you doing over here in my hood?" The voice asked coming closer to Micah.

"Oh shit what's good?' Micah said shaking hands with his old high school classmate. Micah and Sam were friends from high school; it was actually Sam who Micah first started hustling with when Sin wouldn't allow him too.

"Where you been? Niggas been looking for you and it ain't been good. I heard what happened to your brothers that shit fucked up. How yo' mom's taking it?" Sam asked.

"I have been ducked off with my chick. What niggas looking for me for?" Micah questioned. "I don't fuck with none of these niggas."

"Tuck squad, nigga that video been all around your hood. Shit, we even saw that shit. Niggas was trying to air us out over that."

"What tape? Micah questioned.

"Nigga they have you on camera blowing that nigga badass head off. You haven't heard? It's a price on your head."

"Nah, but fuck everybody I'm not hard to find, and I'm always ready." Micah spoke

Land of Snakes

"I don't know why you sugar coating shit for him," A voice laughed coming from inside the car.

"Who the fuck is that?" Micah questioned looking at Sam then back to the car.

"That's Kdog ass, don't mind him. That nigga gone off that lean and them bars,"

"Kenny? Micah questioned.

"Yeah it's me, and like I said I don't know why this nigga Sam sugar coating shit for you like he Willie wonka and shit. Everybody knows it was you who killed Sin. Everybody knows you were in bed with Gator."

"Did you see me pull the trigger? No. so shut yo' bitch ass up. How this nigga get put on y'all hood? He makes y'all look fucking bad. I can't see what Gia see in yo' weak ass," Micah spat eyeing Kenny.

"This dick down her throat, and the way I had that hoe hollering," Kenny spat back. He knew Sam wouldn't allow Micah to do shit to him, so he talked reckless.

"What you say about my sister?" Micah questioned not sure if he had heard Kenny right.

"Yo' chill dog." Sam tried to interject. Sam saw the gun in Micah's hand.

"Nigga you heard me. Yo' sister loved this dick I was giving her ass, bitch crying now because I cut her ass off this DICK!" Kenny chuckled. Shit, I might be fucking yo' moms next with that fat ass," Kenny laughed. Before Kenny knew it, Micah was up on him, pulling him out the passenger window. Using the gun he had Micah, smack Kenny across his face.

"Now what was that you said you was going to do to my mom's?" Micah questioned. Kenny hadn't anticipated Micah wigging out like he did.

"It was a joke," Kenny pleaded.

"A joke? Fuck a joke, nigga you wasn't joking. You thought Sam was gone save yo' pussy ass?"

"Micah chill, the nigga fucked up him just talking crazy," Sam pleaded with Micah to take the gun out of Kenny's face. "Plus nigga yo' name dirty ass fuck in the streets. Nigga' is saying you got both of your brother's killed."

"I don't give a fuck what nigga's saying."

"Micah, you my nigga and shit, and we go way back, but that's my relative. This not even on some hood shit. Blood my family. I can't let you just kill him over some petty ass words."

"Blood? Nigga fuck yo' relative. You ani't heard I killed my own brother, so why would I give a fuck about this bitch ass nigga?" Micah questioned. He had already made up his mind he was killing Kenny.

"You pull that trigger, you not gone make it off this street. And that's a promise." Sam said sternly.

"Imma' walk off this motherfucka' just like I walked onto this bitch, fuck you and him." Micah spat letting a bullet spit from the chamber. Sam hit the floor winching in pain.

Land of Snakes

"AHHH!" Kenny yelled watching his cousin's body fall to the ground.

"Shut up bitch," Micah yelled riddling Kenny with bullets on top of the car. Micah didn't stand around to see if they were dead. Turning back around Micah pulled the hoodie over his head and walked back the way he came, headed back to the motel.

TWENTY-TWO

The weeks seem to move slowly. It had been close to a month since the day she had gotten the dreadful news two of her sons were dead. It all seemed so surreal to her. Pamela stood in the mirror, glazing at her reflection in the mirror. The last few weeks had aged her. Her once almond shaped eyes that shined so bright, now were sunk in, heavy dark bags surrounded them. Most nights she stayed up crying and praying for sleep to come, to take her agony away. Pamela applied a light coat of lipstick to her lips and headed toward the front of the apartment. She stopped at the room, once shared by her sons. The door was shut, and had been that way since the day Sin closed it last. Pamela put her hand on the door, her mind drifted to Micah, she hadn't saw him, besides the call. No one knew his whereabouts, or had heard from him. Several people came looking for him, she never knew what to tell them. Gathering herself, she opened the door, slowly stepping inside. The room still smelled of Rich's chrome cologne. Her mind drifted to the last time she saw her child's face, his big brown eyes, and deep dimples. A single tear rolled down her face. She quickly cleared her watery eyes and walked out the room closing the door back. She was prepared to honor her son's life, and lay their bodies to their finally resting place.

Dark clouds lingered in the air; the day was gloomy and humid. The chapel was filled to capacity as swarms of friends filled the pews to see Sin and Rich be laid to rest. Clad in all black, dark shades concealed the sadness that lingered behind as Pamela and Gia stepped out the limo, they were the center of attention. Everyone eyed them, offering them sympathy with their eyes. Trying to hold it together Pamela and Gia scanned the faces not making direct eye contact with any of the people, as they were escorted to the front pew of the chapel. Pamela's body stiffened, as she came face to face with her son's casket. It all seemed like a hazy nightmare, she still hadn't let the reality sit in, her sons were gone, and Micah wasn't around. Pamela stood for a moment, before taking a seat as the service began.

****

Micah sat in the rental car, he had a chick he knew rent for him, in her name. He sat on the other side of the chapel. The dark tint concealed his identity. Sipping on the fifth of Takka gin he purchased from the liquor store before arriving at the cemetery. He needed something to coat with his emotions.

A slight form of jealous lied within Micah, as he watched the dozen of mourners enter the chapel to say farewell to his brothers. Sin was the hoods royalty and had been since a young age. Flocks of hustlers came out to show their love, respect and say finally farewells to the city's young hustler.

Nisha Lanae

 The whole football team and high school
marched into the chapel wearing t-shits with
Rich's face plastered on the front. He was the city
all-star and champ. Micah knew he wouldn't
ever receive the love that was shown for his
brothers, and for that he hated them, and was
overjoyed, that they were dead. "They always
praising them niggas, nobody give a fuck about
me," Micah spat angrily taking another swig of
the liquor.
 Micah thought of just driving away, he had been
a ghost for the last few weeks and thought of
leaving it just like that. When he saw his mother
exit the limo, followed by his sister and the
stressful look of damsel on their face, could be
seen despite the large shades. He knew he had to
at least let her see his face, to know he was okay.
Micah waited until everyone filled into the chapel
before he stepped out the car. Clad in an all-black
hoodie, which had become his new normal
standard attire. He pulled it over his face so you
couldn't really tell if it was him. Micah made his
way inside the chapel. The pews filled and the
walls were covered with mourners crying as the
pastor read the obituary for Sin and Rich.
Micah lingered in the back, as he waited for the
pastor to finish. A young girl, who went to school
with Rich, took center stage opening her mouth
belching her take on Tamela Mann's latest song
"Take me to the King" her soulful high pitch voice
caused the whole chapel to shed tears. Micah
looked around at all the crying faces, he couldn't
take it. All the crying toyed with his emotions.

214

Land of Snakes

Micah walked slowly to the front of the chapel, eyes began to watch him carefully. Micah neared his mother she looked so sad, not like the fearless women he had always saw growing up. It stung a tad bit, that a major portion of her pain, was caused by his actions, and she didn't even know it. Kneeling in front of his mother, Micah dropped his head onto her lap. As he had always done so many times, as a child, when something was wrong. Pamela didn't have to look down; she knew it was her child. A single tear slid from her eye, as she softy stroked his head, like she had done so many times when he was a young boy. When he laid his head on her lap she knew something was wrong with him. Pamela silently thanked god, for retuning at least one of her sons back to her, unharmed. Pamela wasn't in denial she knew Micah was troubled. Micah could hear his mother's light whimpers and it got to him, he couldn't take it. He worshiped the ground beneath her feet. Seeing her so fragile, so weak was too much for him. He was use to her being so strong, brave, and fearless. There wasn't much that could break her. Micah rose until his tall frame towered over his mother. Micah removed her shades, revealing her puffy red eyes. Gently he wiped away her tears, before returning her shades to her face. Micah planted a kiss upon her cheek. "I love you ma," He spoke softly just above a whisper before turning and heading for the door. He didn't feel the need to view his brother's body; he would remember them in his own way.

215

"Micah?" Pamela called out as she rushed behind him.

The sound of his mother's cracking voice, and the clicking of her heels against the tile floor rushing behind him, caused Micah to stop in his tracks, even though he wanted to run out the chapel.

"Micah where are you going? Where have you been? This is the time to be with family," Pamela pleaded soft tears decorating her face. "At least stay to see your brother's be placed in their finally resting home.

"Ma, I can't do that. Plus, I'm sure they wouldn't even want me here, or seeing them be placed in the ground with dirt thrown on top. I just came to tell you I love you, and I will be gone for a while, but I promise to keep in touch with you," Micah stated.

"What do you mean they wouldn't want you here?" Pamela questioned unsure of what Micah was trying to say. "Those are your brothers. They loved you; they would've wanted you here with Gia and me, right now. Where are you going? I need you right now," Pamela burst into tears.

Micah took his mother into his arms, embracing her tightly, he let her cry. He could feel the hurt in her tears.

"I wish I could take away your pain," Micah said. "I can't take away your pain, and if I stay, I will only add to that pain. I have to go ma', I will be okay."

The chapel had become quite, as the people watched the motherly son bonding moment.

Land of Snakes

Micah could feel eyes watching him, and that made him nervous. Kenny's words from the night before played in his mind as he watched the hateful looks he got from some of Sin's friends. Quickly releasing his mother Micah raced towards the exit trying to invade his mother's antagonizing cries, and the few dudes that slowly crept out the pews. Almost everyone in the chapel knew who Micah was, and half of them knew the truth behind the deaths of Turk, Gator and his brothers. Micah rushed to the rental without putting on his seatbelt, Micah floored on the gas smashing out the cemetery just as he heard the sound of gun fire. He glanced in his rear view mirror to see Sin's closet friend Wako, doing the shooting.

Pamela stood frozen as her eyes jumped to the door as she and the whole chapel heard the loud gun shots. Everyone ducking for cover, as others ran outside with guns drawn. Pamela stood as everyone scattered she tried to put the pieces together, but nothing made sense. She couldn't control the tears that flowed from her eyes, she was hurting. She knew Micah was troubled, a mother knew her child and something was wrong with Micah. The look in his eyes told her so. He wasn't the same, something in him had changed. Pamela tried to dry her face, everyone in the chapel eyes laid on her, as if they were waiting to see her unfold. Pamela refused to do so in front of everyone. The Pastor got the chapel back into order, and continued with the service. Gia took her mother's hand into hers; squeezing it tightly. "He will be okay," She spoke giving her mother a weak smile.

The service came and went, as the slew of people passed viewing Sin and Rich bodies for the last time and offering Pamela and Gia their condolence. Pamela waited until most of the people cleared out the chapel before she stepped foot in front of the gold plated caskets. She glazed at both of her sons. She knew not to questioned god, but she couldn't help but think why her? Why her son's? Their lives were cut so short. Pamela didn't know god's purpose but she understood his reason, we were all here on borrowed time, and their time had expired. "Watch over me, your brother and sister," Pamela spoke as she kissed both of her son's cheek. Pamela felt a hand rest on her shoulder

"Hey Pamela, I just want to extend my condolence, and let you know I'm here if you need anything," A male's deep voice spoke. Pamela's eyes grew wide, the voice made her stomach cringe. She hadn't heard it in years, but nothing about it had changed. Pamela was furious as she turned, flinging the heavy hand from her shoulder.

"I don't need shit from you, I haven't in damn near eighteen years, and will never," Pamela sneered. "Why are you here? How did you find out about today?" Pamela questioned looking the husky man up and down. His 6'5 frame towering over her.

"Nice to see you too and I am here because Sintrell is my son too," The man replied.

Land of Snakes

"Just because you donated some sperm, doesn't make you a father. I have raised my children by myself, without the help of any damn man. So don't mosey your ass in here, trying to be here for me. If you wanted to be here for your children, you would've done that years ago," Pamela stated scowling the man. Pamela had forgotten she was in the chapel. Benny brought out the worst in her, the very ugly side of a woman she never wanted to be.

"As I remember it Pamela, you took Sintrell, Gia and Micah away from me in the middle of the night and fled to the states," The man spoke

"Don't sit here, and act like you don't know why. Yeah I took your money and our children and moved, to make a better life than you were giving us."

"You and the kids had everything money can buy."

"I didn't want what money could buy, what I wanted was free. For my husband to not sleep around with every woman who smiled at him, to not sell drugs, kill people. To love me, and not treat me like his sex slave, whore and a punching bag. But, you couldn't give me that," Pamela exhaled. "It was just too much to give."

"It was the life I lived, you knew that."

"It was the life you choose to live, you weren't forced. You wanted to live that life. So what do you want now?"

"To stand up, and correct my wrongs, to re-build relationships with my estranged children and to check on my wife." He smiled

"Let's get this straight. I don't need you, or anything from you. Please don't refer to me as your wife, because I am not."

"By law, you still are," He grinned.

"Oh, it will change, trust me it will," Pamela said hating to hear him say it.

"Well why hasn't it? It's been eighteen years."

Pamela didn't have an answer for him. So she just glared at him. She only kept it, so the kids never questioned why her name wasn't the same. They always though she had given them her last name.

"They are grown, so you try and figure that out, you're too late for these two," Pamela pointed to Sin and Rich's casket's that were being carried out. "You just leave me alone," Pamela said sternly making sure he understood she meant it.

"Ma, you okay," Gia asked approaching her mother, and the unfamiliar man.

"Yes baby, just was getting my final look," Pamela stated as she watched them load the caskets into the hares.

Gia stared at the unfamiliar man. He looked familiar, she just didn't know from where. She looked at him closely. Studying his facial features, when it clicked, it was Sin. The man resembled her brother Sin, a lot. Was this their father? She wondered. She saw herself and each one of her brothers in the man's features.

Pamela turned to face Gia directly. She could see her daughter staring at the man before her; she couldn't lie to her child. There was no denying it, even if someone tired. Sin was the spitting image of Benny, like he spit him out himself. As she looked at Gia, then back to Benny. She saw so much of her in him as well. She looked back at daughter.

"Gia," Pamela said clearing her voice." Baby this is Benny, your father."

Gia stared unable to speak, his features were strong, and Sin resembled him in every sense right down to his demeanor.

"You are beautiful. You turned into such a lovely lady." Benny said as he looked her all over with a smile on his face. "You remind me of my mother, your grandmother. The way your eyes are shaped. You have her strong high cheek bones. Your grandmother would've loved to meet you," Benny beamed looking at his daughter.

Gia didn't know what to say. She just stared at him. She wanted to ask so many questions, she wanted to hug him. As a child she and her brother longed for a father. Pamela did everything she could and they never felt unloved, but it always nagged at them about their father. Here he was, and she was lost for words. She didn't know where to start. She didn't want to hurt her mother's feelings; by being giddy he was in front of her, in the flesh. Her mother raised them alone and Gia knew it was for a reason. Gia couldn't even recall a time when her mother had even mentioning his name. All they knew was, they were born in Jamaica and that Pamela, packed them up as small children and uprooted them to California.

Pamela saw right through Gia, she wanted to speak to Benny, but she didn't. Pamela knew it was because Gia wanted to protect her feelings.

"C'mon baby, let's go see them put your brothers into the wall," Pamela spoke breaking Gia's focus. Pamela knew she would have a lot of explaining to do, and finally she was prepared for it. She knew this day would eventually come. Pamela and Gia walked out the chapel hand and hand, followed by Benny. Just as Pamela made it to the chapel's double doors to exit, she locked eyes with her mother. Pamela hadn't seen her mother since the night she left Kingston, and hadn't spoken to her in more than five years after an ugly argument over her choosing to not come back home, and not letting Benny and her into the children's lives.

"Pamela," Her mother scolded with a look of disgust.

"Mother," Pamela replied coldly.

"How dare you not even call us? To let us know dem' bwoys done got killed?" She questioned in a heavy Jamaican accent. "And you thought dis' place better and safer? Hump," Her mother blared.

"Mother, I don't have time for this, I did what I thought was right for my children, and I have to live with that. But, right now I'm dealing with the fact that I just lost two of my kids, and I don't know what's wrong with another one of mine. So right now, that's where my mind is. If you want to beat me down, judge me or whatever takes it somewhere else, because I don't have

Land of Snakes

time for it. My children need me. How about asking how am I? How are my living children doing? For Christ sake I just lost two children they lost brothers that mean the world to us."

"You look just like any other mother would if they just lost a child."

"Sometimes I forget that you have no emotions mother. As much as I would love to get some sympathy from you, my mother I know it won't happen. But, know this. I have God on my side and my faith in him, will get me through this. Like it got me through the relationship you forced me to have with him," Pamela paused as her eyes drifted to Benny. "And the horrible marriage I had with you. I would give my life for my kids, but sometimes I wished I lay down with someone else and conceived them."

"Ma, you did a good job with us," Gia interjected not liking how they were treating her mother. "Forget what these people have to say about you, they don't know our life. You have your health to worry about, so let's just finishing laying my brothers to rest, and let them go back to where they came from." Gia glanced at the people whom were supposed to be her father and grandmother. She didn't even know them, and she despised them for trying to badger her mother in such a fragile time.

"You are so right," Pamela smiled at Gia wiping away the few tears that managed to fall from her eyes. She turned with a smile on her face she looked at her children's father, and then to her mother "Have a great one," She spoke.

Nisha Lanae

This time Pamela gripped her daughters hand
and walked out the chapel and into the waiting
limo, with a smile on her face.

"I love you ma. This is hard, but we will get
through this, together. You always said there isn't
a handbook manual on being a parent, so don't
let them questioned your parenting. You can't
blame yourself for the life Sin, Micah and even I
choose to live. You raised us with the foundation;
it's our choice to build on it."
Pamela just smiled at her daughter. She wouldn't
admit it to her but, she did question her
parenting to her children. Was she not strict
enough, could she have done more, providing
them with more. The questions swarmed her
brain, just as those words left her daughters
mouth. She couldn't help but beamed with pride
hearing the reassurance from her child.

"Thank you baby. Know that I will always
support you, and try to protect you," Pamela
spoke beaming with pride as they arrived to the
grave site. With pride Pamela held her head up as
she watched them release two single white doves
into the air, then slid Rich and Sin's casket into
the crib where the shell of their bodies would
remain. "Rest well son's, I know your spirit is
here with me, watch over me." She smiled the sun
had burst through the clouds, shining brightly.
Pamela turned to leave knowing she had put her
sons to rest the best she could, and she was
satisfied with that. She wasn't up for a repass or
having tons of people around asking her if she

Land of Snakes

was okay, she just wanted to go home and be alone.

****

Micah sat on his old block, though it had been merely a month since the whole ordeal went down, the block had changed drastic. There wasn't anyone hugging the block, besides the flock of kids playing football in the middle of the street. Turks old trap was bored up, surrounded with caution tape. Since no one was serving on the street, fiends migrating to other areas where drugs were more accessible for them. Micah just stared, so much hate lived in him for the streets that he grew up on. Guzzling down his second can of 211, his mind was racing and his emotions were stuck on top of the rollercoaster, and he couldn't get off the ride, no matter how hard he tried. The ringing of his cell phone snapped him out his dazed slightly startling him. "What's good Pablo?" He asked into the phone spilling the rest of his 211, on himself.

"Micah, I have been hearing great things about you. I have some new exclusive product coming into town. Meet me at the Doc at 4am," Pablo spoke into the phone.

"Like 4am coming up? Micah questioned.

"No, next week, of course like 4am in the morning. See you then," Pablo said hanging up, not giving Micah a chance to speak another word. Throwing the can out the window, Micah cranked the engine and floored on the gas. He knew he

Nisha Lanae

was too drunk to try and drive himself back to
Richmond. Rushing to the motel room he had
been crashing at. He picked up his little of
belongings and speed to the train station,
jumping on the first train headed to Richmond,
leaving the rental in the parking lot, with-out the
decent to call the girl who rented it for him.

Land of Snakes

TWENTY- THREE

Sarina paced the floor of the condo she semi shared with Micah. He had called her multiple times within the last hour, so did Ortega. She ignored their calls, she need to get her mind together. She needed to sort out her next order of plans, and just how she was going to play them. With the biggest bust of her career going down in just a few hours, Sarina couldn't help but be nervous. She had finished the academy on top, outdoing almost every male in the class. Since the day she stepped foot into the force, she had to work ten times harder than her male colleagues to prove she was just as good as them, or even better. In the beginning she loved it, showing out letting them know she could hang with the best of them, and that she was an excellent police officer and that she had earned her spot on the force. Since she was young, she wanted to follow in her mother's footsteps and become a detective, but along the way she lost the sight of the real reason she wanted to be a cop. While trying to play with the big boys, she found herself walking on the thin line between doing what was good, and enjoying everything that came with the bad. That included falling for the bad guys and the lavish lifestyle they could provide. The trips oversee and shopping sprees on Melrose, that she would never be able to afford on her salary. It was everything every girl could want, until reality set in and the guy she had fallen head over heels, face came across her desk. For months she provided him with everything the police had on him, or could find on him. She always kept him two steps ahead of any harm coming his way, until one day Ortega played hard ball and withheld information from her. Rushing to tell her lover they were expecting a child, she found out her balling boo was caged to a cell, facing years in prison, and no longer wanted anything to do with her, when she couldn't help get him released. Sarina was heartbroken and felt betrayed by the man who once sexed her crazy, and gave her the world. From the moment Sarina swore off men, she refused to be heartbroken again. She turned her focus on being a great detective, one that she knew her mother would be proud of, and raising her child on her own, with the help of her grandmother. As much as she wanted to deny, she wanted that sensual feeling only a man could bring. One day while working undercover one thing lead another and she found herself tangled in the sheets with Ortega. That was four years ago. Sarina had been sexing Ortega on the regular anytime, anyplace she could despite knowing he was married, and had a wife sitting at home battling with fertility issues. Sarina wanted to feel bad for her, but she didn't. It was the game called life, if it wasn't her getting all of his nine inches, it would've been the next chick. Ortega was known for slinging dick around. Sarina was convinced his wife had to be doing her, because she didn't nag like most and she would be a damn fool to sit at home waiting on him to change and hang his player hat up. If she

Land of Snakes

was waiting, she would be waiting forever and bitter for it. The ringing of her cell phone brought Sarina back. "Chill fuck," She yelled picking up the phone from the bed to see it was Ortega calling yet again. This time she sent him to voicemail to let him know she was ignoring him. Sarina hadn't realized how long she had been in another world and pacing the bedrooms floor until the voicemail from Ortega ran across her screen. "Fuck" Sarina yelled quickly throwing something on, and rushing out the door.

The briefing had already begun when Sarina walked into the conference room surrounded by dozen of her peers who would aid in the biggest bust the 52nd precinct had in a very long time. Ortega ice grilled her as he watched her hanging in the back of the room.

"We have you all set up in teams; each team will have a leader and a zone where you will need to be. Don't take these men lightly. They have managed to escape police and drug charges for many years now. They will rather be killed, then sent to prison for the rest of their lives, and taking some of us down with them, would make them happy. These men are heavily guarded my skillful killers, who will take great measures to insure their safety. We are a team, a family so let's make sure we are alert, and please make sure your weapons are cleaned," Ortega paused and scanned the dozen of officer face before speaking again. "We will meet at the location at midnight, which is in about five hours from now. At that time we will go over everything. They are meeting at four o'clock in the morning, in the time that I have worked undercover with this guy; he is prompt and take all security measures. He arrives hours early to make sure no danger is looming. We have to be in place, so that we are not seen, or we risk losing the bust. If you don't arrive on time here, don't mind showing up, we will be sitting up at midnight," Ortega spoke looking at Sarina. "See you all later on tonight, back here and ready." Ortega concludes ending the briefing. The officers spilled out the conference room mentally preparing themselves for the night fall.

"I'm glad you were able to join us Detective Lopez, wasn't sure if you enjoyed being a Detective anymore."

"Whatever Juan, I had some family issues I had to take care of and lost track of time." Sarina stated.

"That's hard for me to believe. You never had a problem answering the phone before. I know you were with that low-life, but that will be coming to an end, and you can step back into reality and realize you're a fucking detective, an employee of the state. Your job is to protect and serve. Not be some hoe from the hood hanging onto these drug dealers' nuts."

"You mad?" Sarina questioned peering at Ortega. "Because another man can make me cum, until my body convulse?" Sarina grinned stepping closer to Ortega. "Or is it because, you're not the only one hitting this sweet...tight...gushy shit. You're jealous." She whispered in his ear letting her tongue slide down the side of his warm face from his ear to his chin. "Remember you're fuckin' married, and this is my pussy and I choose who I fuck, and who I don't. See you tonight," Sarina snarled storming out the station leaving Ortega stuck where he stood as her words lingered.

****

Pamela followed behind Gia as they exited out the limo and walked up the stairs leading to their apartment when they were greeted by two plain clothes officers.

"Mrs. Jones?" The taller of the two asked

"Who are you?" Pamela questioned eerie.

"We're police ma'am," The shorter one said flashing his credentials.

"How may I help you?" Pamela questioned her stomach began to rumble. Any time she came in close contact with the police within the recent weeks with all that had happen and Micah still being out in the world alone, it did it. Her nerves were bad.

"We are looking for a Micah Jones. We were told he is your son and resides here with you.

"That is my son, what is this about? She questioned.

"I'm Officer Wade. And this is my partner, Officer Diaz," The Officer spoke handing her a business card. "It's very important that Micah gets in touch with us, immediate. He has the next twenty-four hours to contact either one of us, before we issue out a warrant for his arrest," Officer Wade spoke.

"I haven't seen my son," Pamela lied. "What is a warrant being issued for? Why are you looking for my son?"

"Ma'am if he happens to stop by or call advise him to turn himself in, before this gets worst," The officer said turning to walk away leaving Pamela confused as to what was going on.

"I don't know what this child is into lord, but please cover him in your blood," Pamela said out loud trying to prevent herself from crying as she made it into the apartment.

Gia watched her mother's moves as she made it down the hallway into her room. She had heard the rumors from the streets that Micah was responsible for the murders at the boogie joint and there was a video going around the hood of him killing Badazz at Turks spot that night. She didn't believe any of it, and would have to see the video with her own two eyes in order to believe it. She couldn't even entertain the thought that he would have anything to do with their brothers getting killed. Gia didn't feel the need to bring the bubbling rumors to her mother's attention, she was already taking everything hard, and she didn't need to plant those ugly rumors into her heads as well. She needed to speak to her brother; she had to hear it from him ask him about the rumors going around. Rumors spread like wild fire in the hood, she knew eventually

Land of Snakes

her mother would hear them, and they would sure enough crush her. No one wanted to confirm it, but she knew Turks close friends were gunning for Micah. The gunshots at the funeral, that everyone ignore right after Micah's departure. Gia knew where aimed at her brother, and that scared her. She couldn't lose another brother. From her room Gia could hear her mother praying and that toyed at her heart. Closing her door she picked up her phone and dialed Micah's number. The phone rang and rang until the automatic voicemail kicked in. "Micah this is Gia, and your ass needs to call me be back now, and I do mean right fuckin' now," Gia blurted into the phone before hanging up.

It was well after 10pm when Micah had finally arrive back into Richmond after several delays and having to transfer onto another train. He had tried calling Sarina multiply times, but all of his calls went unanswered. Micah hailed a taxi to the condo, hoping Sarina was home, sleep and hadn't heard her phone, but the condo was empty. Micah showered grabbed a cold one and hit the sac until it was time to meet up with Pablo.

TWENTY- FOUR

Sarina, Ortega and the rest of the tactic team were in place awaiting the arrival of Pablo and his men. Sarina kept checking her phone; Micah had been blowing her up all day. She knew she was blowing her cover, by not being there for him during his mourning. She could feel Ortega's eyes burning a hole in the side of her face every time she looked down at her phone. They hadn't spoken two words to each since the spat in the station. Ortega just smirked at her, he knew she was holding something back about Micah, but so was he. He failed to mention to Sarina that he overheard Micah on the wiretap, being invited to tonight's gathering.

****

Micah awoke from his brief nap, checking his phone to see if Sarina had returned any of his calls or text, which was kind of odd to him, after all this time she would've called back, or came home. He wanted her to attend the meeting with her, but since he didn't know her whereabouts or how to contact her besides the number he had, he would have to role solo. He did make a mental note to get her grandmother info from her, just in case of an emergency. Micah had arranged for the car he purchased to be dropped off to the condo while he was gone, leaving the keys under the mat. Micah hopped into the car, he wanted to stop by the apartment and see how his operation was doing before heading to the dock.

Land of Snakes

When Micah pulled onto the block, an uneasy feeling overcame him. The block was empty. There wasn't a corner hustler nor a fiend in sight, the scene was odd to Micah, normally the street was filled with people all times of the night. Maybe they took a lost and got raided. Was Sarina in jail? Is that why she wasn't answering the phone? Were the questions that swarmed around in Micah's head. Micah parked and headed for Maria's. If something happened she would've known about it. Micah banged and kicked on Maria's door, he needed her to be there, to fill him in, on what was going on.

"Stop banging on the damn door" She yelled swinging the door open. Her face was a sight to see to Micah.

"I'm sorry to be beating on your door so late Maria, but where is everyone? It's so dry. I just got back. Did we get raided?" He questioned. Maria looked out down the street before she spoke.

"I don't know," She shrugged. "I haven't seen anyone all day. Nobody has been around since last night, no Sarina and no boys. I called Hector, but he no answer." Maria said looking up and down the street again.

"Okay, well I have somewhere to be, but I will be back to find out what the fuck is going on, and I will try and contact Hector, myself." Micah said.

"Okay," Maria replied closing her front door before Micah could even make it off her stoop.

Micah searched every apartment for some clues as to what was going on around him and got none. The apartments where empty. There wasn't a drug or single dollar in sight. Micah walked back to his car confused, and pissed at himself.

****

From across the way Sarina and Ortega watched a small speed boat approach Pablo's Yacht. Pablo's security stepped off first and headed inside to check for any danger that may have been looming. Once the coast was cleared Pablo, was helped off the small boat and lead inside, as the speed boat dashed back into the night fall.

"Pablo has arrived," Sarina said into the small earpiece they all were wearing.
Forty minutes passed before another speed boat pulled up to the Yacht. Pablo's security helped a man off the boat, before searching him and his men and leading him inside.

"That there ladies and gentlemen is Mr. Hussein the biggest drug supplier in the united states, Guam, and Cuba," Ortega blurted through the ear piece.
A slight smile crossed Sarina's face as she watched the men with the binoculars exchanging warm welcomes. Everything was coming into place. After tonight she would look like a hero, as a detective for bringing down two of the most deadly and biggest drug dealers in her generation. Sarina's palm's sweated as she thought about throwing the cuff on Pablo, and

revealing her true identity to him, that was until she heard an officer mention an African American male was making his way through the dock. Sarina instantly searched to see who this male was, and almost lost it when she saw Micah taking cool strides towards the Yacht. *"What is he doing here,"* She whispered panic riddled her face. In just an instant her plans were crumbling. Sarina was confused and upset at herself for not answering his calls. *"He is supposed to be in fuckin' L.A,"* She thought to herself watching Micah near the Yacht.

Sarina didn't have the guts to face Ortega; she could feel him watching her. She knew this had his name written all over it.

"Oh, I forgot to mention that your little boyfriend would be attending the meeting tonight, his black ass going down tonight like the rest of them," Ortega smirked.

"That's hard to believe you dirty bastard," Sarina spat, walking off. She couldn't let him see her sweat, even though she was sweating bullets. Sarina approached another officer "Can we hear inside clearly?"

"Yes, and everything is being recorded as well." The Officer replied.

****

After being fully patted down by Pablo's hound dogs Micah was finally escorted inside. Sitting at the table was Pablo, and another older gentleman who was accompanied by two beauties with the most deadly scowls on their face that Micah had ever seen coming from women.

"Micah I'm glad you could join us. Where is Sarina? I thought she would be right by your side."

"Nah, she is tide up with something else."

"Well have a seat; can I get you anything to drink?"

"No thank you," Micah spoke taking a seat.

"This is a good friend of mine Mr. Hussein," Pablo said pointing to the man sitting at the table to the left of Micah. "Hussain, this is Micah a new client of mine,"

"It's a pleasure to meet you Micah, from what Pablo has been saying in the short period he has known you, you moved quite a bit of product." Hussein spoke peering at Micah.

"Likewise, like I told Pablo weeks ago, I'm hungry and a lion always needs to eat."

"Well that's why we are here. I have always dealt with the purest form of cocaine. Well my dear friend here has brought it to my attention that I am missing out on millions of dollars by not pushing heroin. He has offered to attend some product to use to test on the streets," Pablo said looking at Micah.

"And so I'm guessing you want me to test it out?" Micah questioned. Heroin was a very powerful drug many didn't indulge in. "A lot of my customers only smoke cocaine."

"They are users; they will smoke anything to get high. I've been around for a very long time, and seen many drugs float on the market as well as fiends. As long as you have a quality product, they are going to buy it." Hussein spoke. His voice was so demanding yet he talked so calm.

"I agree a drug is a drug to someone who is riding the wave and trying to knock off the edge," Pablo chimed.
Micah sat and pondered what was being laid out before him. Where he came from he didn't know many that dealt with Heroin do to the lengthy sentence that came along with it if caught. Micah was looking at all the money he was sure to gain by slanging it, and how he could flood the streets of L.A. with it. Micah wanted to takeover, to rule and had just found the plug to put him in the position to do so.

"I'm game; I will try it on my customers and see how they take to it."

"Good, Good. I'm sure they will be coming back for more."

****

With her ears glued to the wire listening to the conversation between the men, Sarina stood with the binoculars clasped to her eyes as she watched the men nursing their drinks having idle talk about drugs, but none were present. "

"It looks like they are just having a meeting. We can't do anything without drugs being present. They will just bail out, and know that we are onto them, and ruin the whole operation and everything we worked for in these last three years," Sarina said

"Give it some time, I know there is some drugs somewhere on that fuckin' boat," Ortega snapped. He was determined to take all three of them down, he was tired of waiting, it was happening today.

The sound of a helicopter nearing could be heard.

"What's that noise?" Micah questioned nervously looking around.

"That's my people," Hussein grinned. "I hope you didn't think I was carrying it on me." Hussein signaled for the girls to go and retrieve the goods.

The girls, followed by Pablo's men exited the room, returning moments later to with two duffle bags; they slid in front of Hussein and took their place behind him "This my friend is Black Tar. It can be sniffed or taken orally and is very potent. It will give them an instant rush, quicker than cocaine, even the purest form can." Hussein schooled them sliding each of them a small vital filled with the substance.

"So how much do we stand to make off this shit, if they do grasp towards it?" Micah questioned looking at the tiny vital.

"Those go for a hundred a pop, you do the math."

"And how many are in the bag?"

Land of Snakes

"There is five hundred vitals in the bag. Once you're done with that we can move forward on prices and quantities."

"It shouldn't take me, but a day or two. I mean it's only freebies." Micah spoke.

"Well then we are done, let Pablo know when you're done and what the results are, and then we will meet again and talk real business." Hussein spoke.

"We got'em! MOVE IN! MOVE IN!" Ortega yelled through the ear piece nearly causing Sarina to scream.

"Well I will see you men in a few days," Micah said shaking Pablo's and Hussein's hands as he turned and left to exit. Micah's eyes grew wide as he stepped foot off of the Yacht seeing the dozen of officers nearing him. "Fuck," He yelled bolting the opposite way. He didn't know where he was going but he refused to be caught with five hundred vitals of heroin on him.

"We have an African American suspect on the loose, with five hundred vitals of heroin. He's wearing a black shirt, blue pants and drives a blue regal. Don't let him leave this dock," Ortega yelled into the earpiece. Ortega turned to say something to Sarina and noticed she was gone. "Fuckin' bitch," He yelled following behind the dozen of officers who were still swarming in.

When Sarina noticed Micah making a beeline, she gave chase. Rushing around the building hoping she ran into Micah.

Micah ran until he no longer could hear the sounds of the police. Winded Micah stopped to catch his breath as he tried to figure out a plan to get out of there, safe and alive. Micah had thrown the bag into the water, just in case the police apprehended him, he wouldn't have any drugs on him. Heading for what looked like a pathway to the street, he saw a small figure looming in the darkness behind him. Micah sped up his pace a tad bit, he didn't want to appear nervous, or like he was up to something.

"Micah!" Sarina called out. She had noticed the built of his body from behind.
Micah was so nervous he thought his mind was playing tricks on him.

"Micah," Sarina called out again this time a little louder trying to gain his attention before swarms of officers covered the whole area.
Micah froze the second time he heard his name called. "Fuck," He blurted. He knew he had been caught and would be hauled off to jail. There wasn't anywhere for him to run. He could hear the footsteps getting closer. Turning to face his capture, he was at lost for words.

"Sarina?"

"Yeah, it's me," She replied.
When she came close, Micah could see the sparkle of her shield, the gun in the holster on her side her clothes where plain, not sexy like he was used to seeing her in.

"What's all of this?" He questioned looking her over again. He felt weak.

"It's what it looks like," Sarina replied.

"You're the fuckin' police?"

"Yes. I'm an undercover detective."

Land of Snakes

"So everything was a lie. You don't give a fuck about me. This wasn't about helping me, but about fuckin' me over. You snake ass bitch. I could kill you," Micah yelled lunging towards Sarina, who quickly reached for her gun and drew down on him.

"Calm down, let me explain." She said with her police issued weapon aimed at his chest. She was prepared to shoot if he tried anything "This was never about you, and I haven't lied to you, at least not about how I feel. I couldn't tell you I was undercover, you would've stopped talking to me. I wanted to help you, that's why I plugged you in with Pablo. I needed to bring him down, and I knew you needed a connect."

"And what about Hector? Huh? Is he really your cousin or another undercover? Because I went by the apartments and everything is dry, and Maria said she hadn't saw you."

"All the workers that were working for you, that Hector sent, were all police officers."

"And Hector?"

"Hector's real name is Detective Juan Ortega, he is my partner." Sarina admitted.

"This whole fuckin' time you been playing me bitch. FUCK YOU! You must gone kill me, because I'm not going to nobody fuckin' jail, and that's a promise." Micah said peering at her before walking off.

"Micah," Sarina called out giving chase after him. "I'm not here to arrest you, but to free you. I'm sorry I deceived you, that was never my intent, but I knew you wouldn't go along with my plan. Hopefully one day we can sit down and talk about this. The police will be looking for you, so get out of town." Sarina said handing him a key.

"I don't believe anything coming from your mouth. Everything else has been lies," Micah spat.

"This is to a storage unit in an unknown name. It's a car inside, that can't be traced and a few thousand dollars. Enjoy your freedom."

"Why are you doing this, what are you getting out of letting me go?" Micah questioned.

"I'm not getting anything out of this. I told you, I care about you, and I meant that. I never intended for you to get caught up in this mess, you weren't supposed to be here tonight. I thought you were still in L.A."

"If I find out, you on some other shit Detective Sarina. I promise I will hunt you down, and kill you." Micah spoke his voice was cold.

"I understand. If you keep straight," She pointed ahead. "It's going to take you through an open field, which leads to the main street. Hurry, this place is about to be filled with police and the sun is about to rise."

Micah didn't feel the need to respond. He turned and ran as fast as he could towards the direction she pointed him too, he hoped she wasn't setting him up.

Sarina waited until she no longer saw Micah before she turned and headed back the way she came. Halfway back to the front, she saw Ortega creeping around the building.

"Where did your little boyfriend go?"

Land of Snakes

"I couldn't catch him," Sarina said bending over pretending to catch her breath.

"Yeah right quit the fuckin' lying. This is the same shit you did before, falling head over hills for some young dumb drug dealer. Who probably doesn't even have a GED let alone a high school diploma. No real future but ending up in a six by six or 6 feet under. Where is he Sarina? Be a fucking cop for once in your life." Ortega yelled. "You aren't going to fuck this bust off for me." Sarina could feel his breath piercing the side of her face, as his vicious eyes peered at her.

"Fuck you!" Sarina yelled looking him dead in his face. "Like I said, I don't know where he went. I gave chase and lost him. End of story." Sarina barked walking off.

"You aren't going to fuck off this bust for me. I've worked hard for my career, and I'm not going to let some silly bitch hung up on some dick to ruin it for me. LOPEZ! WHERE IN THE FUCK IS HE?"

"This is all about you, like always. The almighty Detective Juan Ortega. If you care about taking him in so bad, won't you go look for his ass. Call me another bitch, and this bitch will show you how she truly can be a bitch and ruin your life. Remember I know where that sweet little precious wife of yours lives." Sarina spoke low and maliciously.

"You wouldn't dare say shit to my wife, if you knew what was best for you."

"Oh, but I will." Sarina said slowly with a smile creeping upon her face. "You don't scare me, you have ruined my life enough, there isn't much left you can do. Now get the fuck outta' my face, so I can finish doing my job," Sarina spat brushing past Ortega. He could feel his temper rapidly rising. Gripping Sarina by the arm, he flung her around bringing the back of his hand down on her face.

The unexpected powerful slap caused Sarina's petite frame to spend, as she clutched her stinging face and the blood that quickly began to trickle down her lip.

"I tried to play nice, but you want to play hard ball, that's fine with me. I will put word on the streets to narcotics, the fiends and anyone else I have to, that he is pushing black tar. Remember this is my city, you're just a visitor. His ass will be brought down, keep fucking around, so will you."

Sarina chuckled as she slowly lifted up her pants leg, pulling the.45 from her leg holster.

"Fuck you and this mu'fuckin' city," Sarina yelled coming up with the gun in hand. "I've been waiting for this moment for a while. I'm tired of acting like I like your bitch ass. You ruined my fucking life, my child's life."

"And I saved your career. You weren't thinking with your head, but with your pussy. He didn't want you, as soon as he got locked up, he dropped you." Ortega said. "Your child was better off as a bastard, then to have that loser as a father."

"Only after you visited him, to tell him you were fucking me. Oh, didn't think I knew that?

Land of Snakes

You're a fuckin' clown. I only started fuckin' you, to get close to you. So that I could kill you but never found the right time. The time is now. You should've minded your own business." Sarina smirked as she heard the bullet slide into the chamber, and land into Ortega's chest. "I'll be sure to let your precious wife know that you loved her dearly, and make sure she doesn't find out about your five kids, the ones you had on her." Sarina laughed planting another bullet in his head. Quickly sliding the .45 back into her ankle holster she grabbed her nine and let off several shots running to the other side of the building. "OFFICER DOWN!.... OFFICER DOWN!" She yelled. Firing several shots creating the perfect crime scene for the crime she had just committed. The area was filled with officers. It didn't take long for swarms of officers to rush to Sarina's aid after hearing the shots. "Search this fuckin'place, he is here somewhere," She said rushing over to where Ortega slumped body lay on the concrete. "Is he okay?" Sarina questioned.

"He's gone," The young officer spoke his voice cracking.

"What? What do you mean? Sarina weakly asked tears forming in the corners of her eyes, and slowly coated her face. "Get his wife down to the station, she needs to hear this from us and not the morning news," Sarina spoke her voice was light, as she took several breaths before each word. She put on her best impression of a concerned partner, but inside she was smiling

247

hard, finally plucking the stinging thorn from her side.

Land of Snakes

TWENTY-FIVE

Micah walked and walked until he found a small diner, he had been walking for what seem hours ducking anytime he saw a police car and he didn't really trust Sarina. He had known her for over two years, and hadn't expected at the very least that she was a police officer. Micah sat at the table sipping his coffee racking his brain for any signs he may have overlooked, and couldn't come up with any, she hid it well. With each passing day, it seems that nothing was as it appeared to be around him. Everyone had some type of motive Paying for his meal, Micah crept back into the streets, careful watching everything around him. Micah stopped by the corner store grabbing him a pint of gin. Fishing in his pockets for some cash, he felt the keys inside. Paying for his drink, Micah looked at the tag that was attached to the keys; he studied it, and thought of going to check it out.

"Where is Rick's Storage Palace?" Micah asked the cashier.

"Not too far from here. " Are you driving?" The older black man asked looking Micah over.

"Walking."

"It's about five blocks up, once you hit the dead end, you can only going left, and it's about three blocks from there."

"Thanks," Micah said grabbing the brown paper bag and headed out the store.
The sun beamed brightly, shining down on Micah's face as he took hasty strides down the street, glancing around him often. Everyone

looked suspect to him. Micah moved so fast, it didn't take him long to arrive at the storage unit, it sat in a back, and if you didn't know it was there, you would miss it. Micah stood in front of the storage facility. He was slightly afraid to go inside. He didn't trust Sarina, everything she had told him up to that point, had been a lie, why would this be different. Micah thought to himself. He didn't know if the police would rush him, as soon as he stepped foot into the building. *"Fuck it,"* Micah said out loud. Retrieving the car was his only way to back to LA. He couldn't risk taking the train, a plane or renting a car was out of it.

"Good Morning. I'm looking for unit 264," Micah read off the number on the key to the young girl who sat behind the counter.

"The two hundred units are in the far back, 264 should be on your right hand side." She replied with a soft smile on her face.

"Okay, can I go right back out this door?" Micah questioned pointing to the door that he used to come in.

"Yes. I can have someone drive you back there, if you want?"

"No, it's okay. I will find it, but thanks." Micah said heading towards the back of the facility where the young girl pointed him too. The walk was long, and extremely quiet. Micah didn't like it; it was like a scene out of a scary movie. It took him a minute, but Micah finally found the storage unit number. As he stood in front of it, he looked around for any suspicious activity, anyone

Land of Snakes

looming around looking out of place, but there was no one, it was like he was the only person in the facility. Slowly Micah unlocked and opened the unit. His heart race a million miles a second, his palms were drenched in sweat. Expecting a swarm of police officer to jump out when he opened it, Micah inhaled, then exhaled before throwing the door up, and there wasn't a police in sight. Sitting inside was a 96' Chevy impala. Micah walked around the car, expecting it, to see if anything was out of place, seemed extra, again he didn't find anything. Flipping the driver's seat matt over, laid a single key. Fishing in the glove box, Micah found an envelope with close to ten thousand dollars inside. Micah was more confused about what was really going on. Cranking the engine Micah flew out the unit with the money in his hand. Once he let the car run for a while, he was sure there wasn't a bomb anywhere in it. Micah pulled the car out, locked the unit and speed to the exit.

****

After being questioned several times of what went down, giving written and verbal statements, and writing her report for the arrest of Hussein and Pablo. Sarina was finally able to go home, and be on leave for the next 6 weeks due to her witnessing the murder of her partner, and the suspect still at large. Sarina was making her way to leave, when she saw the distraught Isabela, she was Ortega's wife. Sarina made her

251

way over to where she stood talking to the captain.

"Isabel, I'm sorry for your lost. Juan was a very well respect detective and his murder will not go unsolved, and that's a promise, he was the best partner I ever had," Sarina spoke sincerely. The sound of Sarina's voice caused her skin to crawl. Isabel looked at her.

"Oh I bet you will," Isabela spat walking off.

"Well fuck you too, bitch," Sarina whispered to herself watching Isabel sashay across the room.

"Are you okay Lopez?" The captain asked.

"Yeah I'm okay."

"Well go home, and enjoy the next 6 weeks off. Go out of town, enjoy your young years."

"I will try that, I'm out of here, and my head hurts." Sarina spoke walking off.

"Lopez!" The Captain called after her.

"Yeah," Sarina turned.

"Good job. We lost a good man and a few others but, we took down two. Juan was a good detective and that will always live on. Don't be so hard on yourself."

"I know, but it still hurts." Sarina smiled as she turned and continued to walk out the station. Since Ortega wasn't alive. All praise went to Sarina about the bust, and bravery. As Sarina neared the door she couldn't help but stop when she saw O'Hara cradling Isabel's weeping face in her arms. "What in the hell is going on?" Sarina laughed loudly gaining the attention of O'Hara, who just smirked at her. Sarina continued her

Land of Snakes

laugh as she made it out the station putting
O'Hara, Isabel and Ortega behind her.

TWENTY – SIX

The funeral was over but Pamela's emotions were still scattered. She tried to not cry, but that was easier said than done. She hadn't expected Benny and her mother to show up, she was actually puzzled that they knew what was going on in her life. Pamela was curious to know, but her pride wouldn't allow her to call and ask Benny. Pamela sat in the living room, the television watching her, as she pondered on her life. What life would be like without two of her four heartbeats?

"Who is it?" Pamela yelled out hearing someone knocking at the door. So many people had been coming to check on her, and ask Micah's whereabouts she stop answering the door. "Go away; just leave us alone, right now."

"Pamela it's me, Benny. Open up the door," Benny yelled from the other side forcefully tapping on the door again.

"What in the world?" Pamela questioned jumping up to peep through the peephole. Sure enough Benny was standing at her front door clad in a double breast custom Italian thread suit. Pamela swung the door open, enough was enough. She wanted to know how Benny knew all that was going on in her life, and where she rest her head. "How in the hell do you know where I live?" She questioned her hands rested firmly on her hips as she glared at him.

"Can we do this inside? Benny questioned looking down the hall at the Hispanic women sweeping the hall. "I need to speak with you,

Land of Snakes

about something important," Benny stated sternly. Pamela could hear the seriousness in his voice, and became nervous. Pamela stepped aside, and allowed Benny inside.

"How do you know where I live? Or about what's going on in my life?" She questioned as she closed the front door. She just had to know.

"Pamela. I know almost everything about you and my children. I've known where you lived for a very long time. It isn't like you moved since you came to the states," Benny stated talking a seat on the couch.

"And what is that exactly supposed to mean?"

"You packed up and left like a thief in the night. Just up and left with my kids, you didn't think I would come looking for you? You know me, better than anyone, I am well connected, and when I want something, I get it."

"So you hired a private detective?"

"All of that doesn't matter. I'm here, because I hear Micah's in trouble, as his father I am here to help him. I don't want to see another one of my sons dying on these streets. Where is Micah?"

"I don't know Micah's whereabouts."

"C'mon Pamela, I know you know where he is."

"Come on my behind. I don't know where my son is, because if I did. I would go get him, and drag him home. I've lost two children to these streets. Do you think I want to lose another one? Like hell I don't. I don't wish that on any mother."

Pamela spat her voice was beginning to raise, and become shaky.

"I want to take him back home with me. So he doesn't end up, in prison or dead like Sintrell."

"You're not taking my child a damn place, especially not back to Kingston. What? So he can be a drug dealer like you?

"In case you're in denial Pamela. Micah is a drug dealer, just like Sintrell was. He just does bad business and that's why he is into this mess. Face it; your son's sold drugs to make a living, just like their father."

"What? You get a kick out of knowing that? Pamela questioned angrily at Benny's ignorance. The streets talked, she knew what her son's did, and she didn't agree with it.

"I'm just speaking the truth. I've lost one son on these California streets, that's enough. Let him come back home with me, where he is safe. You and Gia, can come back home, your family miss you."

"Did you just say one son?'

"Yes, Sintrell, my son,"

"Wait one damn minute. Richard was your child, too,"

"How is that so?"

"What in the hell you mean how? So now you must have amnesia. You don't recall the months leading up to me leaving? I can vividly remember them, oh to well. The beatings, the being forced to have sex with you, that's how it happened. I left you when I found out I was with child. I couldn't stomach bringing another child of yours; into that mayhem you called a house.

"How was I supposed to know he was mine? You left me with Charles in the middle of the night. When I located you, you had a small child. I thought maybe he was his, or hell another mans."

"Don't stand in my face and tell me Richard isn't dead on Sintrell, who is a spitting image of you, like you spat him out yourself. You don't have to claim him, because he was mine, they are all mine. Pamela was furious at Benny.

"I didn't come here to argue with you Pamela. I just want to save our son."

"Whatever Micah has gotten himself into, he has to face it like man, and get himself out. What I am not going to do, is let my son think running from problems, is the way to solve them."

"You ran away from your problems instead of facing them." Benny reminded her.

"No, I ran away from you. I left to give my family a better chance at life, because I would've killed myself or you if I had stayed with you. I don't regret it for a minute."

"So you say."

"Screw you, now you can get out my house. I don't know where Micah is. I pray my child can stand up like a man, and face whatever foolishness he has gotten himself into, and deal with the outcome of his actions."

"Hasn't the police come to your house looking for him, a few times?"

"So? His brothers were just killed."

"Have you stopped and really asked yourself why the police are looking for Micah? I know you have been hearing the chatter amongst these people around you."

"What are you talking about?"

"His brothers just were killed. At that very same location so was three other people, at a location he visited frequently, and now the police are looking for him."

Pamela stood repeating his words in her head.

"What are you implying? That the killers can be after Micah? Did the police kill my son's?"

"Pamela if you hear from Micah please tells him to give me a call." Benny stressed standing and heading for the door shaking his head. After all the years of her being with him, and raising three boys, she still didn't get it.

"Do you think you can come in here, and say I'm your father let me help you flee to Jamaica and run away from the problems you caused in LA. I'll teach you more about the drug game, because I run shit in my town," Pamela mimicked following behind Benny. "He doesn't know you. He doesn't need you in that way. Help better him as a man, not a coward."

"I've let you fill their heads with whatever you wanted about you leaving. But, I've been looking out for them. I've helped Micah, Sintrell and Richard and they didn't know anything about it, and I made sure of it. Like I said, I've known where you laid your head. Out of respect, I kept my distance. But, I've been helping out like when Micah was over his head down at the gambling shack. It was me, who paid them dudes off. When Sintrell wanted to step into the game, it was me who insure he had quality product and reasonable prices. I made sure he was connected to be his own man, and not under another man. When Richards's scholarship wouldn't cover his tuition, it was me who paid the school off. I didn't even know for sure if he was my child. For my baby girl, I sat up an account with 100k in it, for when she left that young punk alone, and got her life together. So I have done for them, I just didn't let you know." Benny advised. "You tell them the reason I wasn't allowed to be physically in their lives."

"I'm fully responsible, and will own it."

"I'm serious. Tell Micah to give me a call," Benny said slamming the door behind him.
Gia had been listening to the conversation the whole time when she heard Benny leave; she walked into the living room. "Ma, can I talk to you?" She asked taking a seat on the couch.

"Sure baby what's on your mind?"

"I want to know more about Benny, my father. Since the funeral I found myself thinking about him, and what life would have been if we had our father in the house.

"Ummm...Okay," Pamela exhaled she knew soon the questions would be asked. "I met you father when I was 17, at that time I wanted nothing to do with him. He was loud, arrogant and I wasn't into dating at that time. Your grandmother was good friends with his mother, who was fond of me. I wasn't like most of the

women in my family or around the area I stayed
in the books. They tried for some time to get us
together, but it didn't work. On my 19th birthday,
him and a few friends came, bearing gifts and I
got to know him, more and liked what I saw. He
was different with me, not trying to be all tough.
One year later, we got married and nine months
after that, we had Sintrell.

"So where did things go wrong and make you
leave?"

"I never really knew what Benny did for a
living. I was so naïve then, all the signs were
there, that he was into illegal dealings. I wanted
no part of that, my father, your grandfather died
of drugs, and I wanted no parts in a man who
was in that life. I was already married and
pregnant with you, so I stayed. After I found out,
he felt it was no longer a need to hide it from me.
Along with that life came the women, plenty of
women who called the house in the wee hours.
Late nights of him staying out, coming home
reeking of alcohol and other women. Yet I stayed,
because I loved him, but once the beating started
to come on the daily, I wanted out. I didn't have
anywhere to go; my mother told me it was life, to
stay. Stay for you and your brother, I tried, but
when you and your brother would jump from his
yelling and the fighting, I knew I had to leave. I
was tired of caking make-up to cover busies; I
was tired of being tired. After giving birth to
Micah, I went to live with a friend for a while, but
that didn't work. Your father would come all
times of the day and night, making all sorts of

ruckus. Benny is a very persistent man, and what he wants, he wants. My friend's home became a target. Men patrolling and sat outside daily; it wasn't fair, so I left. Without anywhere else to go, I went back to your father, only this time, things were worst. When I found out, I was pregnant with Richard, enough was enough. I couldn't let him kill me. You guys needed me. When a childhood friend said he could help get me away, I went with him. He helped us sneak into the states, and we have been here ever since," Pamela spoke to her daughter wiping the few tears that decorated her face. "I don't regret it, even with what happened to your brothers. I did what I thought was best, for you all. So if you hate me for not having a father, I'm sorry."

"Don't cry ma, he didn't deserve you," Gia spoke leaning over to comfort her mother. "I could never hate you. I understand you wanted to live, and be a mother to us, and you did that.

"That's why I always instilled in you, to be strong and not need a man for anything. You want a man, he is not needed. Men will do only what you allow, the first time he hit me, I stayed and allowed him, so he continues to push and push. Don't ever let a man, belittle you, or put his hands on you," Pamela spoke, she knew she couldn't tell her daughter all the hell Benny had put her through, the several kids he had on her.

"Well I'm proud to have you as my mother, you are strong. You worked, and made sure we never went without," Gia beamed, she knew her mother was beating herself down because of her brother's. She wanted to make sure her mother, knew she had given them enough love, and she had nothing to do with the way they choose to live their life. Pamela didn't have to say it, Gia looked beneath they strong exterior of her mother, she was hurting. She heard her every night, praying and crying.

Pamela smiled, and was about to respond, when a loud knock came at the door. The loud sound caused Pamela's heart to skip a beat. It seemed every time a time a knock came at her door, it was the police bearing bad news. Pamela looked at Gia, who instantly picked up on the nervousness of her mother. The knocks came again, this time louder.

"I will get it ma," Gia said, with a smile. Gia was nervous, as she went to the door. Peeping through the peephole she could see the police on the other side. "Hello officers?" Gia spoke as she opened the door to find half a dozen of los angles finest lingering in the hall, with their guns drawn.

"We have a search warrant to search the place, are you home alone?" The first officer

"No...No, my mother is also home," Gia fumbled with her words. Seeing all of the guns faced at her.

"We are looking for Micah Jones, is he home?" The officers asked coming into the apartment.

"No what is this about?" Pamela asked.

"And who you are?" The only women officer asked with too much attitude for Pamela liking.

Land of Snakes

She was dressed differently than the others who entered her apartment.

"I'm Pamela Jones, Micah's mother. Where is this search warrant you have? Why are you looking for my son?" Pamela questioned.

"We are looking for Micah in connecting to several homicides." The women officer said.

"Homicides?" Pamela gasped.

"Search the house top and bottom, ma'am will you ladies step outside with me. I need to ask you some questions," The woman officer spoke.

"Why? I don't have anything to hide. My son isn't here, and I haven't seen him," Pamela lied.

"Ma'am you can step outside to speak with me, or I can have you escorted to the station, the choice is yours. We will be searching this apartment today, like now."

"Search my house, my child isn't here. I just buried two of my children, if I am not a suspect to hell with you all, I'm not going a damn place," Pamela snarled taking a seat back on the couch. The women officer had become vexed at Pamela disrespect for the law. She stormed out the apartment, only to return moments later with a tall husky white male detective.

"Hello Ms. Jones. I am Detective Gill. My partner Detective O'Hara meant no harm, your son," He paused checking the small pad he had in his hand. "Micah, he is in a lot of trouble. We have linked him to more than six murders, including the deaths of your other sons Sintrell and Richard," The detective spoke.

Pamela felt herself getting light headed, her heart raced. "Wha-at? No.... no that isn't true, don't lie on my son. Micah... Micah" She stuttered. "He would never kill his own brothers, or let anyone kill them," Pamela utter. Pamela's mind began to race, as she replayed Micah's final words. *"I'm sure they wouldn't want me here anyway."*

"Ma'am breathe," The Officer said. "We also believe your son's Micah, and Sintrell murdered the apartment complex manger Kirby. We have reviewed the camera's he had in his home; your son's were the last two to enter his apartment, before the system went out. While investigating Mr. Kirby's murder we found dozens of video surveillance of women, here in the complex." Detective Gill spoke gently.

"Including you," O'Hara spat.

"Kirby has a camera in my house? Where? He has been watching us?" Pamela's eyes shifted around the room looking for anything that looked like a camera.

"Well, we found all of the recording of what seems to be your bedroom. We also have found several tapes with you two engaging in sexual activities." Detective Gill spoke.

"Tell us the truth. We're you and Kirby sleeping together? And your gangsta sons found out, and killed him? O'Hara blurted trying to get to the bottom on it.

It was all so much for Pamela too take in. First they are saying Micah had something to do with his brother's death. Now finding out Kirby was recording himself belittling her. She was at a loss for words, until she heard Gia's voice. She had forgotten she was in the room.

"Ma? You and old ass Kirby was creeping?" Gia questioned. "Ewe that's nasty."

Pamela became furious that the Detective didn't have the slightest courtesy that her daughter was still within inches of them. To make such statements.

"NO! We were not sleeping together; he was forcing me to sleep with him, for extra time to pay my rent. I fell behind, and that was the only way he wouldn't evict me. So if you have surveillance it should have told you that. I wasn't enjoying it, I hated it. It made me feel dirty, like a whore. I AM NOT A WHORE!" Pamela yelled as the tears screamed down her face. She hated that, all she seemed to do was cry these days, slowly she was unraveling. "How dare you ask me a question like that in front of my child? That's disrespectful and I will make sure your captain here's of this shit, rude ass women. My son's maybe whatever you try to label them, but that isn't how I am, or how I see them. Now please leave my home." Pamela sneered looking at Detective O'Hara.

"I'm sorry to hear you had to go through that ma'am we recovered over three dozen video, from the women tenants in the building, who he was also doing it to." Detective Gill spoke trying to break the tension.

"The house is clean." An officer spoke walking back into the living room.

"Thank you for your corporation Ms. Jones and I offer my symphony to you and your family with the loss of your sons. If you happen to speak with your son Micah, convince him to turn himself in, and make this a lot easier on him. He is in serious trouble." The officer spoke as his team began to clear out. The officer stood to his feet, extending his card to Pamela. "Here is my card, if you talk to your son, tell him to give me a call. I'm also sorry for my partner, and how she dealt with the situation."

Pamela sat the card down, on the couch next to her. She didn't have anything else to say to the police. She just wanted them out of her home. Pamela sat staring into space; she didn't know where Micah was, and what he was into. With everything going on around her, it made her sick. The sudden urge to throw up, overcame her, as thoughts of Kirby recording himself taking advantage of her.

Gia rushed into the kitchen to grab a bag. "Ma, you okay?" She asked. Pamela lay balled up on the floor mixed in a pool of vomit and tears. Pamela couldn't stop crying. She never intended for life to end this way for her children.

"Children are supposed to bury their parents, not the other way around." She cried.

"I know, but sometimes God has other plans. It's that what you always told us?"

Pamela couldn't answer. All she could do is cry. It took Pamela over twenty minutes to gather her thoughts, and pull herself together. Gia left her

Land of Snakes

mother there, she knew she needed to let it out, she had been holding it in for so long.

"I ran you a hot bubble bath ma," Gia said helping her mother up and out of her clothes, and into the tub. Gia bathe, clothed and put her mother to bed. To keep her mind occupied she cleaned the house from top to bottom. The only smell in the house was the smell of lemon pine-sol and the glade candles burning. Her heart was hurting. She was hurting for her brothers, their lives were cut short, and Micah was lost in the world trying to find a place to belong. The pain her mother felt. Would never be erased, and she knew it. Gia walked down the tiny hall that separated her room, from her brothers the strong urge to cry bolted through her body. She had a relationship, personally with each of them; her life would forever be changed without them near.

TWENTY-SEVEN

It was in the wee hours of the night. The freeway was clear as Micah coasted down the I-405 freeway. The city of Los Angles limits sign brought a smile to Micah face. Despite not knowing the trouble that lingered in the city, He was more happy be in his neck of the woods, where he knew the in's and out's .Micah wanted nothing more to wash the grim from the day off of him, and just chill. But, the money he had was burning a hole in his pocket. Micah checked in the double tree hotel in downtown Long Beach. He had a hook-up there where he wouldn't have to show ID. He had grown tired of the run-down cheap motel rooms. Quickly showering and throwing on some clothes he picked up along the way. Micah was in and out.

Micah parked the car, into the underground parking and made his way to the underground gambling shack. The owner Jesus Ramos was an ex- baseball player who got injured and was forced to retire. With the money, he bought a family business .trying to capitalize off the business he   converted the basement of the Mexican dinner into a gambling shack. Micah had been invited from another patron of another place he visited often.

Micah banged on the steel door twice. A small door slide open. "Code?" A husky voice asked.

"Duce G," Micah replied giving his entrance code. Each member was giving a significant entrance code based on their minimum bet. Micah's was always two thousand. The small door shut, moments later you could hear the deadbolts turning. The steel door slide open, and Micah strolled through the doors like he owned the place.

"We haven't seen you in here, in a while. Since you lost all that loot," The husky security chuckled peering at Micah.

"Well I'm back. Can you just sit me up at a table, and I want Alysia as my waitress. Thank you." Micah stated walking off. The gambling shack was sit up, like a mini casino and bar. Micah walked to the bar, glancing around the room to see if he knew anyone. "Let me get a Hennessey and coke, no ice."
It didn't take the waitress long to fulfill his request. Sliding the drink in front of Micah, she smiled and walked off to help the next.
In two gulps Micah swallowed down the liquor slamming the glass on the table. "Let me get another round."

"Don't worry about it, I got it." A sultry voice came from behind him. Micah turned to see Alysia standing before him in her skimpy waitress uniform. "Hey there stranger, table 10 has a seat for you." She spoke patting Micah on the back.
Micah stood and followed her lead. The table had five others who were engrossed into the game. Micah took the seat, dropping his money on the table. "Keep them coming." Micah told Alysia, smacking her on the ass.
It didn't take long for Micah to still the show. He was on a winning strike. With shot after shot

coming to the table around the clock, Micah's mouth got reckless. "Yeah I'll take all of that. Tell the wife I have a big black cock she can sit on, since you just lost all the money." Micah rambled as he took all 100k, of the money on the table. Micah boasted seeing as he was the second person to get up from the table empty handed, losing all their winnings to Micah "Bring me some more liquor. Hell, bring me the whole fucking bottle." He yelled.

Jesus emerged from the back, where he had been watching everything. He didn't like a lot of commotion and Micah, was being too arrogant for his liking.

"Micah, my friend I see you are winning. You must tone it down, or leave this establishment. You know I don't allow all of that."

"Jesus, man you tripping. I'm winning. They can't fuck with me." Micah laughed. "Who's next? I'm ready to kick some more asses. Who wants some of the nigga?" he questioned loudly causing everyone to look at him in plain ignorance. "Alysia where is that damn bottle of Hennessey?" Jesus walked off. He needed Micah out his business he was running people off and making too much attention.

"Let them in; tell them to get him out of here, before he is dead. I don't want him back in here. And don't let him leave with that money," Jesus said to the husky security that stood at the door.

"I got you boss," The security said allowing an entourage to gain entrance. "He is at table ten."

Land of Snakes

With steady strides the men walked over to where Micah sat at the table still babbling at the mouth.

"He is good. He is cashing out now." A heavy voice spoke landing a heavy hand on Micah's shoulder.

"Who in the hell are you? I'm not cashing out until I'm good and ready, and I'm not ready." Micah slurred discombobulated Flinging the heavy hand from his shoulder. "So nobody want to play now?"

"We need to talk."

"So talk."

"In private," The voice said.

"Look, I don't know you, and you must don't know me. If you did, you would get out of my face. I'm trying to get this money, drink and enjoy myself.

A tall lanky man came to the table. "I bet 50k," He spoke dropping his money looking at Micah.

"He's out," The voice said to the dealer sternly.

"I don't know this nigga, don't listen to him. You said 50k, here." Micah said sliding his money to the dealer.

"Micah" Alysia called out approaching. "How much longer are you gonna' be here? I need a ride to my house and some of you?" Alysia smiled groping Micah's manhood as she sat another shot down.

"Shit when you ready?"

"Now. I just have to clock out and get my stuff."

Nisha Lanae

"I'll be waiting." Micah smiled as he watched the sway of her hips, and the exposed cuffs of her ass in the little uniform prance off. "It was fun, but winning all this money got my dick hard. So as much as I wish I could stay and take some more of your money. My dick is ready to be taken care of. CASH ME THE FUCK OUT!" Micah yelled. Micah stumbled out the gambling shack with over three hundred thousand dollars in his pocket. He was so intoxicated to see three men following behind him and Alysia or to notice the man who approached in the gambling shack had disappeared. Alysia tussled with the zipper of his jeans trying to free his manhood.

"Wait... Wait I need to enjoy all of this. My hotel room right down the street." Micah smiled cranking the engine of the car bolting out the parking lot. By the time they got into the Hotel's parking lot it was too late. Alysia had a grip on his dick in her mouth that felt too good for Micah to pull away at that point. Pushing the seat back, Micah gripped her by the hair, pushing his dick deep in too her mouth.

Alysia slid down and bounced on top of Micah's harden dick that plunged inside of her raw, caught up in the bliss he forgotten to slide a rubber on. Alysia hissed as she moved her body in circular motion loving the raw feeling of Micah's huge dick inside of her. Micah could feel the tension of his nut brewing, and loved every minute of it. Alysia knew how to do him right. A tap came at the window, slightly startling Micah.

Land of Snakes

"Go the fuck away. Don't you see me in some pussy" Micah yelled. His hands gripped Alysia around the waist as he prepared to enjoy his nut. The tapping came again, this time much harder, causing the windows to rattle.

"Micah." The strong voice called out. "I need to speak with you, now."
Hearing his name brought Micah to halt, as he because nervous. His eyes jumped around the outside of the car. The car was surrounded by men, all in black, and men he hadn't ever seen before. Micah's heart raced, but he knew he couldn't show an ounce of fear and weakness.

"Who in the fuck are you? And what do you want?" Micah questioned pushing Alysia off of him.

"Micah I'm scared who are these people?" Alysia questioned as she looked around. "Do you have a gun? Micah I'm really scared. Don't let them kill me." She whined.

"Shut the fuck up, and let me think."

"Get rid of the girl, and come take a ride with me."

"Nah, whatever you have to say to me, can be said right here. I'm not going nowhere with you" The liquor was beginning to wear off, due to his nervousness.

"I'm not going to hurt you Micah."

"How do you know my fucking name?" Micah questioned glaring at the man. Micah didn't know what was going on.

"That doesn't matter. I am a friend of your mothers and she told me you are in a lot of trouble. I offered to help you."

"My mother?" Micah questioned. "My mother doesn't have friends. Fuck you!" Micah yelled cranking the engine and smashed on the gas forcing the men to get out his way. "They are trying to rob me. My mother doesn't know about this place or my whereabouts." Micah shouted trying to get out the hotels parking lot. The sound of guns being fired at him from behind mixed with him being scared caused Micah to almost hit the curb trying to duck.

"Why are they shooting at us? Who are these people?" Alysia cried trying to duck shots.

"Shut up," Micah yelled trying to invade, the shots that came rapidly, but couldn't. They had shot all of his tires causing him to lose control of the car and crash into the fire hydrant. The men quickly filled around the car pulling Micah and Alysia out of the car.

"Get them out of here, now." The man yelled. Micah swung hitting one of the men in their face. The man only smirked delivering his own blow to Micah's face knocking him out cold, on impact. Alysia couldn't stop yelling. "This wasn't a part of the plan. I did my part. I just want my money; you won't have any problem's out of me." She cried Micah's limp body lying next to hers.

****

Land of Snakes

Pamela woke up feeling a tad bit better than she did before she went to bed. She was thankful Gia had cleaned up the place, and even cooked dinner, before she left to go with her friends. Pamela stood over the stove scraping some of the smothered pork chops, yellow rice and cabbage onto her plate when she heard a knock at the door. "What do they want now," she yelled sitting her plate down on the counter. "Who is it?"

"It's Benny open up the door Pamela."

"What do you want know Benny? I don't feel like fussing with you. I don't have enough energy." Pamela said opening the door.

"I need you to come with me."

"What? I'm not going any place with you. I have to be at work in a few hours, and I am tired." Pamela said walking back into the kitchen to retrieve her plate.

"I found Micah," Benny said.

"Where is he?" She asked rushing back into the living room. She looked down the hall expecting Micah to be coming through any moment.

"I have him somewhere. Somewhere that is safe."

"Where is somewhere?" Pamela questioned with her head crooked to the side she peered at Benny. "Where is my child?"

"He is safe. I found him overly intoxicated at a gambling shack."

"And why couldn't you bring him here?"

"Because he didn't want to come with me, hell he doesn't even know I'm his father. So can you please come with me, so I can talk to Micah?" Pamela hissed going to put her plate in the microwave grabbing her pea coat, and purse she followed behind Benny.

"Where is Gia?" Benny asked as they got to the car.

"She went with some friends? Who is driving this car? I don't know these people?" Pamela questioned noticing Benny getting in the back alongside her.

"Everything is okay Pamela. He is my driver." Benny said.

Pamela didn't respond. She felt uncomfortable being so close to Benny, let alone in his presence. He had a bad vibe, and she didn't like it. She didn't like him. He was still as handsome as the day she met him years ago, but his spirit was ugly, wicked and corrupted. All that combined made him such an ugly person. *I'm doing this to see my son."* She thought to herself while saying a silent prayer, as she stared out the window. The dark concealed Pamela vision as they traveled down a long pathway. The car came to a stop, in front of a house, that sat in the middle of an open field.

"Micah's inside," Benny said noticing Pamela hesitation.

The darkness and light whispering of the wind whisking against the tress gave an ire feeling. The house was dark, not a light was on, and it appeared empty. Pamela stomach rumbled. She

Land of Snakes

didn't trust Benny. She stopped and fished in her purse, sliding the Taser into her hand. Calmly she spoke. "What kind of game are you playing Benny? Where is my son? You put one finger on me, you will die this time." Pamela said one hand on the switchblade in her pocket. She kept it in her purse with her Taser and mace.

Benny didn't respond. He just kept his stride down the hallway stopping at a door. "He is in here," Benny said opening the door.

"Why in the hell is he tied to a chair?" Pamela asked rushing into the room. Benny flicked on the light in the room, and Pamela, almost lost it. The light danced offed the silhouette of Micah's bruised face. "What did you do? What happened to my babies face?" Pamela yelled on a brick of tears as she fumbled with the ties around Micah's arms.

"He was being unruly. He attacked my man here." Benny pointed to one of the henchman that followed behind them. "He only punched him back, he will live."

Pamela stared at the man, a look on her face said she wasn't pleased shifting her look back to Benny. "You found him, now what do you want with him? I told you, he wouldn't go with you. Now look." Pamela said looking at Micah's face. Micah's was still knocked out cold from the blow.

"That's his choice. You said it yourself, he is grown. Which makes him responsible to answer for himself?"

"Well how can he do that? You let this big grizzly bear looking fool knock him out." Pamela spoke peering at Micah's face. "You," She pointed to the man. "Better hope like hell, my child is okay or I will come for you, and trust it won't be pretty at all." She warned.

"Micah is good. Why would I intentionally let someone hurt him?"

"The verdict is still out on you." Pamela turned to try and wake him. "Micah...Micah," She yelled tapping Micah on his face. Micah was out cold, he didn't bulge.

"Go get some cold water," Benny told the man who stood in the room with him. "I just wanted to talk to him. He is stubborn. He is full of that courage poured from a bottle."

"Going about it this way" Pamela pointed around. "Is not the way and isn't going to work, at all. You don't know Micah, and may never after this."

"I will deal with that once he gets up, and explain myself."

The man re-entered with a bucket of iced water.

"Pour it on him," Benny said glaring at Pamela who looked at him with a frown.

The man didn't look Pamela's way as he poured the cold water on Micah. He could feel her staring him down. Micah's body jerked from the ice cold water, but he didn't wake.

"Get some more, no ice." Benny said. The man quickly left and returned with a bucket of water.

Land of Snakes

With the second bucket of water Micah jumped, his eyes flew open and darted around the room, trying to find his surroundings. Pamela rushed over to Micah cupping his face into her hands.

"Micah, are you okay baby. It's mama. How are you son?"

"Ma?" Micah questioned looking at his mother and wondering how she got there, and where he was.

"Yes baby, it's me."

Micah looked at the men in the room. He instantly got scared. He didn't know what was going on. Who are these men? What do they want? Micah thought to himself. "What's going on Ma? Where is Gia?"

"Your sister is fine, she isn't here."

"Where are we?"

"BENNY!" Pamela yelled "Get to explaining."

Benny stepped closer to Micah. "Hey son,"

"Son?" Micah questioned looking at his mother for answers.

Pamela cleared her throat. "Micah, son this is Benny, he is your father."

"And?" Micah spat becoming angry.

"Son I understand you are into a lot of trouble here and leaving the states for a while may be good for you. I can help with that, I can get you out of the states to lay low until everything dies down, if they ever."

"So I'm just supposed to up and leave with you, based off of what you're saying? I don't know you, or shit about you. You can be a snake, like the rest of these motherfuckas' in L.A. and don't call me son, the name is Micah." Micah spat.

"You have a lot of mouth, a real reckless one just like your moves. I'm trying to help you, as your father, I don't want to see you end up like your brothers. The way you are moving, I give you a week, and you will be dead in someone's ditch. How do you think your mother will feel?" Benny voice was stern and cold.

"Don't speak for me. I can tell my child what I need on my own. I don't need your help." Pamela hissed peering at Benny.

"You don't know shit about me. Like I don't know shit about you. I will not leave out the damn country with some nigga who has never been there for me, or done shit for me. Her right here," Micah pointed to his mother. "Pamela Denise Jones has taken care of me and my siblings all of our lives, by herself so fuck you!" Benny smirked. "Pamela maybe you should fill our son in on who Bernard "Benny" Jones is, and why I wasn't a fixture in his life, along with his siblings."

"I'm grown. If you have something to say to me, Say it to me, not my mother."

"Micah I am the one at fault. It was because of me that your father wasn't in your life. So you can blame that on me, not him."

"Don't take up for this nigga ma,"

"Please. I'm not taking up for him. I don't even like him, at all. But, this isn't about me. Benny is your father, and by law still my husband, and only by law." Pamela said glaring at Benny.

Land of Snakes

Making sure he knew there was nothing there for him, and had no hope. "He came to me asking to take you to Jamaica, to save you. I said no, and my answer is still no, but, the choice is yours. I raised you to be a man, and accept the consequences of your action, and face them."

"Ma, I'm not going anywhere with him. I don't know him. He hasn't done shit for me, or been here. I am 21 years old, and don't need a father figure now. I'm already fucked up."

"Watch your mouth Micah," Pamela warmed scolding him.

"Is that your final answer?" Benny questioned. He was growing tired of Micah's rants. He was nothing like Sin, who was like him.

"Yup,"

"Cool. Your car will be repaired and dropped off at your mothers, by morning. The offer still stands son. I will be in town three more days, don't hesitate to call me, If you happen to change your mind. I just want you to think about the times you were in trouble, in over your head. How do you think you got out of most of them? Think about that then ask yourself if I was never there for you. Like how I found you tonight, and the last time you were there. Your mother knows how to reach me." Benny said walking out the room.

"I can take you home," The man who was in the room with them said following behind Benny leaving them in the room.

"You okay ma?"

281

"Yeah. Let's just get out of here. We have a lot to talk about." Pamela said helping Micah up.

Pamela and Micah walked out the house, as two men entered after walking away from Benny.

"Micah." Benny called out.

"What?"

"You should watch the people you keep company with. The girl was having you tailed, and sat up to be robbed." Benny said as he stepped into the car. Shots could be heard from inside the house. Moments later, the men who had entered the house, exited and got into the car with Benny. The car pulled into the darkness quickly vanishing.

"Let's get away from this place, it reeks evil." Pamela said climbing into the truck, followed by Micah.

Land of Snakes

TWENTY-EIGHT

Pamela couldn't sleep. So she paced the hallway and living room. She cleaned the kitchen twice, and still sleep wouldn't come. Several hours passed, since Benny's men had dropped her and Micah off. After giving Micah some aspirin to soothe the pounding in his head, he drifted off. Slowly she opened the door to the boy's room. Micah was sleep in Rich's bed. The sound of his light mummers made her want to cry. She knew come morning, he would be gone into the wind. There was so much she wanted to ask, to say to him. Pamela was always a woman of many words, for the first time, she was at a loss for words. Pamela stared at Micah, not knowing how to convoy what she wanted to say to him, or ask, because she was afraid of hearing the truth. She just wanted him close. Pamela closed the bedroom door, and peered out the large glass window that sat in the living room with the view of the street. She knew the police were more than likely watching and would keep showing up until they found Micah.

With nothing else to do, Pamela made her way back to her room, not before peeking in on Gia. She heard her creep in an hour ago. Gia was sound asleep. Pamela climbed into her bed, hoping sleep would come. The faint sound of gun shots could be heard from blocks over. "Lord when will it stop," Pamela said out loud.

Pamela flipped and flopped around her bed. She couldn't understand. For weeks she prayed for Micah to be home, to see him, and hug him. She had that, and she was still restless, even more than usual. Rays of the sun began to beam, as the sun peaked through the mountains in the distance. Pamela decided to get up, and start breakfast for Micah and Gia. She knew once Micah awoke it wouldn't be long, before he made an excuse to leave.

The strong scent of the deep fried catfish, grits and homemade biscuits and eggs awoke Gia. "Ma are you okay?" Gia asked coming down the hall to see the fest her mother was preparing.

"I'm fine. You hungry? I made fish, grits, eggs and biscuits. There's some grape jelly in the fridge."

"Yeah. But, Ma, why are you cooking all of this? It's only me and you. We can't eat all of this. Are you expecting company?"

"No," Pamela stated fixing Gia a hardy plate of food.

"It smells good in here," Micah said coming down the hall wiping the sleep out the corner of his eyes.

Gia quickly tuned to make sure she heard right. Her eyes grew wide, seeing Micah stride down the hall. "MICAH!" She yelled running and jumping into his arms. "Where have you been? I can kick your ass you know that? I called your punk ass countless of times."

"Watch your mouth. I don't know how many times I have to tell y'all." Pamela smiled watching them interact. She purposely didn't tell Gia, when she heard her sneak in, that Micah was there. Her mind drifted off to Rich and Sin and the last time they were all in her living room. This time instead of crying, she smiled. She knew there wasn't a manual, a book or even a perfect parent walking the earth. She did her very best. They had to find their own way, and making mistakes was a part of life. "Are you hungry Micah?"

"Yeah. I'm gonna' need me a nice big plate of that. You have it smelling good in here, like those meals you cooked every Sunday, before dragging his to the church house."

"That church was boring," Gia chimed.

"You meant to say it was super boring. We had to sit next to that old lady that reeked of old trash."

"Sister Hattie," Gia laughed.

"Yeah, that was her name. She use to smell like a week old hot dog water,"

"Quite it you two, that's not right. Talking about people like that. Sister Hattie was nice."

"Ma, she was nice, we know that. But, that smell wasn't. That's all we are saying." Gia and Micah burst into laughter.

"Boy come get this plate. You and your sister are just horrible," Pamela laughed. She knew her children were telling the truth. Sister Hattie was a woman at the church Pamela attended. She was a sweet old lady, but she didn't bathe on the regular or wash her clothes often. She always reeked of an unpleasant smell. Pamela made her a plate and took a seat next to her children at the dining room table. She didn't speak, just watched her children's interact. It was a sight to see, one she wanted to cherish. When they finished eating, Pamela cleared the table and cleaned the kitchen.

"Gia, can you excuse us. I need to speak with your brother."

"Oooohhhh. Micah in trouble," Gia laughed walking out of the room.

"What's good ma?" Micah asked.

"Let's go take a seat on the sofa," Pamela said grabbing herself a bottle of water. "How have you been?"

"I'm good ma. How have you been?" Micah questioned as they took a seat on the couch.

"I'm covered. But, this is about you. You look good, but, are you really okay?"

"Yeah," Micah chuckled. "Why?"

"The police have been around here looking for you, and more than once. They tore my house upside down. So I ask you again Micah, how are you son?"

Micah became nervous. He didn't want his mother to know what was really going on with him. He knew it would only make her more nervous. "What the police looking for me for?" He questioned unable to look her in the eyes. He knew she would sense a lie.

"From my understanding, it's for several reasons. In connection with your brother's murders," She paused. "Where were you that night Micah? And what business dealings did you have with that low down snake Gator?" Pamela questioned.

Micah sat and pondered the questions his mother asked him. He knew he couldn't lie. She

Land of Snakes

would see right through it. She already knew so
much. He thought hard about the words to say.
He knew she would hate him, after he told her
the truth. "I owed Gator some money,"

"You were back out there gambling heavy
weren't you? Like last night?"

"How you know that?" Micah questioned
Pamela.

"You're my child. I know more than you could
ever think, that's my duty as your mother. Like I
know your hiding something from me know. The
way you won't look me in the eye's when you
speak. I've always taught you, and your siblings
to look a person in the eyes when you are
speaking to them."

"The eyes are the windows to the soul," Micah
resisted glancing over at his mother.

"Let me ask you this. Did you and your
brother kill Kirby?"
Micah's eyes grew wide, and a bolt of anger rose
inside of him with the mention of Kirby's name
and the flashes of him on top of his mother. "Why
you ask that?"

"If I ask the question it's because I want to
know the answer. Now answer the question. Did
you and your brother Sintrell kill Kirby?"

"Yeah." Micah admitted. "Ma, why you never
said what he was having you do? I would have
handled him a long time ago. He made you
degrade yourself. He knew he could've come to
me, and told me you were falling behind. I could
have given him the money. He disrespected you.
So he got dealt with, that's how it goes. He hurt

287

mines, he had to suffer." Micah admitted becoming heated about the incident all over again.

"Not everything has to be solved with violence. When will people realize that? Taking someone's life isn't always the answer."

"Look at the world around us ma. Look where we live. People die every day, that's life. People have died for way less then what Kirby did."

"So does that also apply with your brothers? What happened that night? I know you were supposed to meet that snake at the illegal business he operated, that night. How did your brothers get there Micah? And why aren't they here with us today. And I may not be able to handle it, but I want the truth. I want to hear it from you."

"I won't lie to you ma. I've stayed away because I couldn't face you. I couldn't face the fact that I know you will hate me if I told you the truth. I never intended on Rich or Sin to be at the boogie joint that night." Micah paused glancing at the floor before he began again. "It started a little over a year ago. Things for me, and business were going wonderful. I was still getting my product from the dude Sin, had laced me with. Gator came to me, telling me he wanted in. He wanted me to pay him monthly dues of what I was making on the streets. I declined his offer. Next thing I know, the connect doesn't want to do business with me anymore. A chick I was sleeping with from time to time, that also ran

Land of Snakes

packages for me. She got caught with all of the product I had left to my name. When I was younger, and Sin was hanging around Gator, he showed him how to cook coke. So I did that, but the streets felt it was weak and didn't want it. Turk got hold of a better product, they gravitated towards him. I was angry. Angry nobody wanted to fuck with me, and wrote me off. Those who did still fuck with me only did so out of fear of Sin. A person was sending kits to Sin, saying I was in the streets taking losses and wasn't built for this life. When the streets got word of Sin appeal being approved and coming home sooner than expected, they became excited and looked over me. So I started to gamble heavy. It was something I was good at, but like everything in life, I took a lot of losses. When I did find someone to supply me with quality product, I didn't have the money. I had gambled it all away. I turned to Gator, for the money. That's were things went bad. My gambling addiction was out of control and lost it all. Since then, I've been in debt with Gator," Micah said looking up at his mother. He could tell it was a lot for her to swallow. "That night, I was supposed to meet him to pay, but didn't have all of the funds. He wanted me to force Rich into throwing the game, so that he could win 90k, on some bet. I asked Rich, despite me knowing how much the game meant to him. He declined, as I already knew he would. When Rich showed out on the field, Gator had to have had him kidnapped when I dropped him off at the bowling alley. When I got to Gator's Rich was already there and badly beaten," Micah voice cracked. He tried to hold the tears back, but couldn't. "I didn't intend on him hurting Rich, Ma I promise." He cried.

"I know," Pamela said trying to hold back her own tears.

"When I told Gator, I didn't have all the money. He had Rich brought out, by the same chick who had lost all of my product months prior. I then realized Gator had set me up the whole time. All because I wouldn't agree to pay him monthly dues. I had someone who was willing to give me the money but, she vanished with all the money, that very same night. I had to figure out a way to get some money to Gator, and him off my back. I knew with Sin, being home he would be watching my every move, every step. He rode me, like I wasn't good enough to stand on my own. On impulse, I robbed Turk's place, here on the corner. I knew he would have enough money inside to settle my debt with Gator. While robbing the place, I killed his little mans. I didn't know the place had cameras. Turk had already got at Sin. When Sin showed up to the boogie joint, he told me what happened. Once he saw Rich, he was through with my bullshit and wanted to get Rich help. He left, while I stayed and killed Gator, and the girl I found out was Gator's oldest daughter." Micah paused looking at the ground. "When I came out the boogie joint, Sin and Turk were at a stand- off with their guns drawn. One thing led to another and bullets went flying. I turned to quick, and thought Sin was shooting at me and I shot back. It wasn't until after I shot him, did I notice he was trying to protect me from someone who crept behind me. It was an accident; I didn't mean to shoot him. I didn't want to see him dead," Micah lied. "It just happened so fast. I panicked and ran. I was filled with a million emotions, and scared of going to jail. For years Sin treated me like I was beneath him, that I couldn't be on his level because he was better."

"Micah, that wasn't it. He was just being a big brother to you, he loved you." Pamela spoke trying to withhold her tears. She could hear the hurt that was inside of Micah.

"Sometimes I felt that. Sometimes I felt like, he treated me like shit on the bottom of his shoe. Everything I did wasn't good enough for him. Growing up, I wanted to be just like him. That's why I followed him and his friends around, and wanted to be around him. We didn't have a father, so I looked up to my older brother, but he didn't care, as if he didn't even see me. I wanted to be like him so much, I lost who I was and for that I started despising him for it. I slept with his girlfriend, knowing she was his. I made her ask him for money, to give to me." Micah paused before letting his next set of words come out. "A small portion of me did want him dead." Micah said low, not able to look his mother in the eyes, so he stared at the floor. "But even in his death. I'm still not good enough and I would never be good enough for Sin, or the people."

"Forget about being good enough for the people, and Sintrell. You have to be good with Micah. If you're not right with the person you are then you will always run into those issues Micah. You are good enough for whatever, it is you want. But, you have to believe that and know that. It starts with you. Do you hear me?" Pamela questioned sternly. It broke her heart to hear her child speak down on himself.

"Yeah, I hear you Ma."

"I wish it didn't take this, for you to voice yourself about your brother. I would've tried harder to help you, harder to help mend the relationship between you and your brother. Sin, maybe gone, but, you can't live with this. The guilt will only kill you."

"Some days I feel it would be better that way. My bullshit, jealous, envy and lies got my brothers killed. You may seem and say you're fine Ma, but, I know you're not. That's something I will have to deal with for the rest of my life. I have to know I am a part of the reason, you will never whole heartedl fully smile, ever again."

"The pain will never go away, losing two of my children is nowhere near easy, but I also know I have two living kids that still need me. I have already forgiven you, for your wrong doings, but you have to forgive yourself. Man up to the consequences that came along with them. I know you won't be here long. The police will be back looking for you, I'm sure of that."

"Yeah, imma.go somewhere to clear my head, Figure it all out. I know one day, judgment day, will come for me. I have to come to turns with that and live with it"

"And when that day does come around Micah you have to be right with you. Ready to face the music, of the broken tune, only you know the sound of. Not point a finger at someone else, but yourself."

"I feel you Ma, but it's time for me to get out of here. While it's still early, I don't want to be noticed and bring any more harm to your front door."

"I understand, even if I don't know why and how."

"It's because you're a woman of faith. God never lets a woman of faith down." Micah smiled.

"And you're a child of God. Be safe son. Those streets don't love anyone and bullets don't have names on them."

"I know Ma, and I will do my best." Micah stood and retreated to the room, to dress. Pamela was in the kitchen, putting away the left over's from breakfast and taking out dinner. Marvin Sapp's voice filled the room from the small radio that sat in the kitchen, as she sang along. Micah approached his mother slipping an envelope into her hands. "Please take this and get you and Gia away from here."

"No." Pamela jerked away. "I will not take that blood money. You can keep it. I don't want anything to do with that." Pamela said pushing Micah hand that still was extended with the money in it. Micah knew she would protest taking the money. Micah embraced his mother. "I love you ma. You will always be my favorite girl," Micah whispered into her ear planting a kiss upon her cheek.

"Please be safe Micah. I have an eerie feeling, but I know I have to place you in God's hands."

"I will be good Ma, just keep praying for me, and never stop."

"I never have, and I never will. But, you have to do some praying of your own."

"I don't think God ready to hear from me." Micah said, glazing in his mother's eyes.

"I just know you weren't about to leave and not say anything to me?" Gia questioned.

"What? Of course not." Micah spoke embracing his sister.

"Be careful little brother. These streets don't love anybody. They are only here to take you from those who do love you. I forgive you, Sin and Rich do too. You made a million of mistakes, turn them into lessons, and don't let their deaths go into vain, make it better." Gia said above a whisper.

"I got you sis. I love you and Kenny won't ever be a problem for you. Choose wisely next time." Micah smiled. As he slipped the envelope into Gia's hand. "Get you and Ma away from here. Don't take no for an answer." He told her.

"I got you," Gia smiled hard as she hugged her brother tightly. She found out the day before that someone had killed Kenny and his cousin. Never in a million years did she know it was Micah. She knew it would be a long time, before

Land of Snakes

she got the chance to hug her brother again. So she held on long. "I love you big head."

Micah hugged his mother one more time, before he left out the door. Pamela watched him walk out the door. She tried her hardest not to cry, but the tear just fell. Micah stopped at the top of the staircase. He wanted to turn and stay in the comfort of his mother's home, but he knew he couldn't. The police would be back, and he wasn't ready to face prison. Micah checked his surrounds for anything that looked out of place, before he exited the building. Just like he promised, Benny had his car tires repaired and parked outside. Micah popped the truck, to put his knapsack inside, when he noticed a duffle bag inside, he didn't recognize. Micah opened the bag, and was shocked at the bundles of cash inside. "Nigga looked out," Micah said with a grin on his face. He knew the money could've only come from Benny. Micah slammed the car's trunk down, and made his way to the driver side. Moving too fast, his keys slipped through his fingers. Bending down to pick them up, he didn't see the car quickly approach. When Micah stood, he could feel the barrel of a gun pressed up against his back.

"Who are you? And what do you want?" Micah asked calmly, even though his stomach was doing summer saults. With all he had done in the last few months, he didn't know who could be coming to end his life.

"The sweetest... ripest... and tightest ...pussy you ever fucked," The once sweet voice, was cold and flat causing the hairs on the nape of Micah's neck to rise, as a slight chill ran down his spine.

"What the fuck are you doing here Detective?" Micah sneered turning quickly to face Sarina, with the gun clasped between her fingers. "What you think you gone do with that gun? Oh you gone kill me now?" Micah laughed as he stepped close so that the gun could press against his chest. "Well do it. I really don't have shit to live for. I made peace with my mother. I'm just as good as dead. So shoot me Detective Sarina Lopez, with yo' snake ass," Micah spat glazing at Sarina.

"Oh don't worry your gonna' die. I just want to explain to you, just why you're gonna' die."

"You could've killed me days ago."

"It's all about timing and that wasn't the right time, I had another life to end. Like I said, I wanted you to know why."

"So why?"

"See it all started about 7 years ago, I fell in love, I fell real hard for a man. He was young, and heavy in the streets. He showered me with love, fucked me well and kept me laced. He was everything I wanted, so I thought."

"Bitch what's your point?"

"Shhhh. You have to let me finish to understand everything. Our relationship was going great, I made sure he was always two steps ahead of the police. One morning I left the apartment we shared. He was still in bed sleep, from being in the streets all night. It was the day I found out I was pregnant."

Land of Snakes

"You have a kid? Bitch you was feeding me all kinds of lies," Micah spat.

"I was so excited to get back home and tell him we were expecting our first child. When I got home to tell him, he wasn't there and didn't answer any of my calls. I thought maybe he was somewhere with a little bitch. So I rode past all of his hang outs and where he did his business. Everything was dry. Being I am the police I went and had his name ran, and found out he had been arrested. I found out Detective Ortega withheld information from me, so that he had leverage over me. He knew I was with him and had been feeding him information in order to invade the police. At the time, I had fucked Ortega a few times, nothing serious. But he hated drug dealers, and was gun hole of locking him up. I was able to get a hold of some of the evidence that he had against him, to lessen the charges. I thought it would be fine, he wouldn't get much time, when he got out we would be a family. I was wrong. Seven months into my pregnancy, he called me, and told me he didn't want anything to do with me or our son. I was devastated. The man I loved, whose child I was carrying didn't want anything to do with me, I was heartbroken. When my child was just one month old, his friends came and put me out of the condo we once shared. If that wasn't enough, my son was running a fever, I came outside to find the car he had purchased for me was gone. I later found out, his brother came and took it."

Nisha Lanae

"You were fucking my brother?" Micah questioned remembering a few years ago Sin, sent him and a few of his young friends to retrieve a car from a chick he had been messing with. Micah never saw the chicks face. The car was supposed to be given to Pamela, but she didn't want it. Micah sold it and kept the money.

"I wasn't fucking him, that's what I was doing with you, just fucking. I must admit you are a good fuck though, a coward, but your good with the dick. See I was in love with Sintrell and he made damn good love to me. I later found out Ortega paid Sin a visit, and told him how we were fucking, and that I knew they were going to raid his spot and didn't tell him, told him I wasn't nothing but a good piece of pussy. That was the reason Sin cut me off, and told me the child wasn't his and he wouldn't claim him. I was pissed, broken hearted and I wanted revenge. My son deserved to have a father. I tried to figure out a way to get back at Sin, but found no way until your name came up as his brother, and in charge of his operation. I thought what better way to get back at him, then fucking his little brother. The last time I saw you, while you were sleep, I took a mouth swap from you. I had my son tested, because you were Sin's close relative. Being Sin's DNA was in the codas, it was easy to prove he was the father. I sent the results to him and he reached back out, after years of not speaking. He told me when he would be released, and he wanted to meet his son. Now this is the real fun part, at least for me," Sarina smiled

Land of Snakes

wicked "My son never got to meet his father. That night I called you, I was down here, me and my son for him to meet Sin. When I called him, he was busy cleaning mess up for you. When I called him, he asked for a ride to the hospital for your little brother Rich. Sin forgot to hang up the phone, I heard everything. You took my son's father away from him, before he even got a chance to meet him." Sarina spoke. Her voice was cold, despite the tears forming in her eyes. "I heard you. I heard you kill the love of my life, and my child's father. It hurt me to my core, to tell my child when he asked when he will get the chance to meet his father and I have to tell him he won't get that chance. He will never meet his father, or his uncles. You're a snake Micah. A deadly slithering one, but like the old saying goes. There is always, and I do mean always a bigger, deadlier snake waiting to rip you apart and devour you whole, and destroy your existence," Sarina smiled. "And sometimes biting off the wrong mouse can be a death sentence. Micah, you have bitten off the wrong mouse," Sarina bit down on her lip as her freshly manicure nails applied pressure on the trigger. Sarina unloaded three shots, into Micah's body, just like he had done Sin. Sarina slid her shades back onto her eyes and climbed back into the awaiting town car. "Even in death, Sin still is a better man," She said flicking a piece of paper out the window as the driver pulled off.

Nisha Lanae

Pamela stood in the kitchen, the gun shots caused her heart to speed up. "Not another killing, when will it stop," Pamela said out loud.

"Fuuuuuccccckkk!" Gia cried running down the hallway.

"Girl what is wrong with you?" Pamela questioned seeing Gia in distress.

"It's Micah. It's Micah. They shot Micah," She cried.

"Wha...at?" Pamela questioned running to the window. She saw her child laying on the street, and the taillights of a black town car turning the corner. Pamela rushed outside to find Micah dead, his eyes wide open. Pamela dropped to her knees taking him into her arms. "I knew it, I could feel it." Pamela cried rocking back in forth with Micah in her arms.

"What's that stuck to his body Ma?" Gia questioned noticing something stuck to Micah's chest mixed with the blood. "It looks like a picture." Gia pushed her mother back a little to grab the picture that was stuck on Micah. Gia glanced at the picture. She didn't recognize the child on the picture. "Micah had a baby?" Gia said out loud confused why someone would leave a child's picture on top of Micah's dead body. Gia turned the picture over to see if anything was written on the back. Scribbled on the back was Sintrell Jr 2014. "Ma...you need to read this." Gia said showing her mother the writing on the back.

Land of Snakes

"Turn it around," Gia said as her heart fluttered. Pamela flipped the picture back over and everything about the child, reminded her of Sintrell when he was a young boy. "Sintrell has a baby?" Pamela said out loud confused at what was going on around her. "He never told me that."

"We have to find him," Gia said.

"But why is his picture on top of Micah's dead body? It makes no sense. What kind of messages are they trying to deliver?" Pamela questioned. She could hear the sirens coming from the distance.

"I don't know Ma, doesn't make sense to me either. Did Micah know about this child?"

"We will never know," Pamela cried. She had a grandson she may never know, because her sons were dead, along with their secrets.

****

The car came to a stop, at a light. Sarina picked up her phone. "Mommy is on her way," She spoke into the phone. She couldn't wait to cup her son's face in her hands. A knock came at the window that startled Sarina. "I'll see you in a few," Sarina hung up and rolled down the window.

"I hope you didn't think you would get away, with that shit? Yeah bitch I knew you were fucking my husband. You thought yo' ass was slick didn't you? Then have the nerve to try and smile in my face. But I do have to thank you for killing his cheating ass." Isabel smiled. "I'm gone live nice off that hefty insurance money and money from the police. Good job dirty bitch."

"Huuh?" Sarina stuttered shocked by her presence. She fished for her gun, but knocked her purse to the floor.

"Don't stutter now bitch," Isabel squeezed the trigger twice shooting Sarina in the head close range. "Snake bitch's like you don't deserve to breathe the same air as me," Isabel smiled prancing back to the car she got out of. Following her closely was the driver of the town car.

"Damn, you gangsta." He laughed hopping into the back seat. "Cuz shorty didn't even blink when she blew that bitch head off."

"That's how you do it. Let's get out of here, baby," Isabel said cupping O'Hara face into her hands and planting a passionate kiss on her lips.

"Let's go enjoy the Bahamas," O'Hara laughed as she fired up the engine and peeled off.

Land of Snakes

TWENTY-NINE

Pamela accompanied by Gia and Benny watched as they placed Micah's body alongside Sin and Rich's. There wasn't a funeral, or even a viewing of his body. With all the chaos Micah caused, everyone in the neighborhood was glad he was no longer around and applauded for whoever killed him was circling the neighborhood that had Gia constantly in an uproar. Almost everywhere she went since Micah was killed, she received dirty looks or slurs about Micah.

"You should really consider coming back home, you and Gia. What is left here for either of you?" Benny questioned as they walked away from the gravesite.

"I'm not going back to Jamaica, there isn't anything left there for me either."

"Your family is there."

"My family?" Pamela laughed. "My mother doesn't care to speak with me, unless she can control my every action and move. My brothers and my father are dead, and my sister my lovely sister. The same sister who was sleeping with my husband right in my household? Or the one whose son looks a lot like mine?" Pamela questioned.

Benny just stared at Pamela, he was at a lost for words. He didn't know she knew about that.

"You don't have anything to say now?" Pamela questioned as she made her way to the limo that Benny had rented for her and Gia to ride in.

"What is there to say?"

"Maybe for once own up to your dirt, to all the hell you put me through."

"If it would make you feel better, I apologize for putting you through a lot."

"No, it doesn't make me feel better, because it isn't genuine." Pamela slammed the door leaving Benny standing there. "Driver you can take us to where you picked us up from." Pamela rode the entire ride home silent. After nearly twenty years, those words had finally left out her mouth. Benny never knew Pamela knew he had been sleeping with her sister, when she would visit or watch the kids. It was her sister, Charlene, who couldn't wait to throw it in Pamela's face that she had slept with Benny, and just how much she loved having something Pamela had especially a man of Benny's status. Pamela hadn't spoken to her sister since that day. When she brought it to her mother, she simply told her, many women have slept with her husband. He was a man of power that many wanted. That she should try to please him more, so he wouldn't look for it in between someone else's legs. Thinking of the relationship between her and her sister made Pamela think of Micah and Sin. She wished she had the opportunity to not have let her children relationship turn out quite like the one of her and her sister.

Gia could sense her mother was going through a lot. It was the look on her face. She wanted to know more about her mother's family and why she was gun hole on not going back to Jamaica, ever in life. But, she knew if she asked now, she might send her mother over the edge.

"Thank you Sir," Gia said as she stepped out the car behind her mother.

Sitting on the stoop was an older woman with a young boy. Pamela was in another world and didn't pay them any mind.

"Are you Mrs. Jones?" The woman asked.

"Who wants to know?" Gia chimed hawking the woman.

"This is your grandson Sintrell. His mother, my granddaughter recently passed. I'm not looking to raise any more kids. I am too old for this. I found your son information and noticed he passed a few weeks ago as well. So I thought you would enjoy raising your grandson." The woman said handing Pamela a bag and then an envelope.

"There is enough in there for you and him to live comfortable for some time." The woman said rushing down the stairs jumping into a Mercedes and pulling off, not saying a word to the child. Pamela was stunned that the woman just left him, without knowing anything about her.

"Hey Sweetie, I'm Pamela, your dad was my son," Pamela spoke as she looked at him in the eyes. He was every bit of Sin's son. "Come on lets go inside, you hungry?"

"Where's my mommy?" He questioned.

"I'm not sure baby. Let's go inside so we can figure this out." Pamela led the way, and the young boy followed. As soon as they got into the house the young boy's eyes scanned the tons of pictures on the walls and tables. His eyes rested on one picture, it was a younger picture of Sin, next to a more recent picture of Sin. "That's my daddy." He pointed to Sin's picture. "My mommy always showed me his picture and told me one day I was going to meet him. Am I going to meet my daddy today?" He questioned.

Pamela was on the verge of crying. "I'm sorry baby, but your dad is in heaven with God watching over you." Pamela spoke trying her best to not confuse him.

"So you're his mommy?"

"Yes, I am his mommy."

"So that means you're my grand-mommy?"

"Yes Sweetie I am."

"Okay, can I watch cartoons now?"

"Sure baby, Gia can you turn the cartoons on for your nephew?"

Gia grabbed Sintrell Jr hand leading him over to the television where he told her his favorite shows to watch.

Pamela beamed with pride. She didn't know what God and Sintrell were up there doing, but she loved it. She would try her hardest to be a better grandmother to her grandson than she was a mother to her sons. She wanted him to be much more than his father and uncles. Pamela couldn't contain the smile on her face as she looked at the splitting image of her child. He was a true gift from God.